LIFE AFTER HURT

A Sister's Tale

INSPIRED BY A TRUE STORY

NICOLE N. SWEENEY

Life after Hurt: A Sister's Tale
Fiction Novel - Inspired by a True Story

©2020 Nicole N. Sweeney

ISBN: 978-1-7358509-0-0

Nicole N. Sweeney, LLC
26 City Hall Plaza #1064
East Orange, NJ 07018
Website: www.nicolesweeney.org

Cover Image Design: LaTanya Orr, CEO
Selah Branding & Design
Website: www.latanyaorr.com

Layout Designer: Robin E. Devonish
Maven Publishing
Website: www.robindevonish.com

Editor: CaTyra Polland, CEO
Love for Words, Polland Enterprises
Website: https://pollandllc.com/love-for-words

Photography: B. Lauren Williams, CEO
LB Designs & Consulting, LLC
Website: www.lbdesignscc.com

Website Design: Taneisha Ingram, CEO
TJ Ingram Consulting
Website: www.tjingramconsulting.com

Printed in the United States of America.

DEDICATION

This would not have been possible without the vision, provision and alignment of my Lord and Savior, Jesus Christ. Lord, I thank YOU.
You ARE my forever co-author.

To my family, I thank you for your endless support, prayers, and love.
My Father, who delivered me at birth: Dada (John Sweeney, Jr.).
My sisters: Shikeara Sweeney, Alicia Sweeney,
Jessica Sweeney, Christina Smith
My nieces & nephews: Chanel, Briana, Arianna, Braylon,
Caamara, Brielle & M. J. (Cornbread)
My grandparents: (Granddaddy) John & (Nana) Juanita Sweeney

Special thanks to the woman who birthed and nurtured me to be the woman I am today and yet to become, my dear mother Deidra Lorraine Milligan Sweeney. Your motherly love and eternal support transcend from Heaven to Earth every day. I felt your presence and prayers every step of the way. I pray you are proud. I love you dearly, Mommy.

Special thanks to my one and only brother who I've shared endless laughs with and looked up to. Markeece John Sweeney, your life wasn't in vain. We are living out your legacy.
I love you dearly, Big Bro.

To my heavenly maternal grandparents:
Sadie & Edward Milligan thank you for your
love and support.

To my ancestors whom I've never met, I stand on your shoulders.
Thank you for paving the way.

ACKNOWLEDGEMENTS

National Best-Selling Author & Writing Coach (Black-owned):

Kim Brooks

Photography LB Designs & Consulting (Black-owned):

B. Lauren Williams

Website (Black-owned): TJ Ingram Consulting - Taneisha Ingram

Hair style (Black-owned): Suite Styles Salon - Kay Sa'Rah

Manicure & Pedicure (Black-owned): Exclusive Nail Studio – LaLa P.

Make-up Artist (Black-owned): Instagram - TaNeisha Nichole

Book Cover Design (Black-owned):

Selah Branding & Design – LaTanya Orr

Layout Design: Maven Publishing – Robin Devonish

Book Editor (Black-owned): Love for Words, CEO CaTyra Polland

My Rutgers University Sisters (who know who you are)

My Forever Deb Sisters

Vanessa D.; Janice S.; Loriea K.

Kyla T. Slaughter

Principal Baruti Kafele

Michael Gowdy

Rev. Stanley D. Williams

CONTENTS

CHAPTER 1
SKATE NIGHT

Wednesday, May 13, 2009, it was a beautiful spring afternoon that day. Clear and sunny skies, birds chirping, and the touch of fresh warm wind filled the New Jersey air. I woke up that day excited to hang out with my home girl Izzie, especially after what happened the Sunday before.

It's been a year since I've graduated college from Robinson University with a Bachelor of Arts Degree in Psychology. Finally, a college degree of my own with my name on it: Journee Black. I was so happy to have my degree but hadn't secured a job in my major yet let alone any job. It's been a year since I've graduated college, so doing something fun helped me get my mind off my romantic uncertainty, being jobless, having no money, a home, and a car - ugh! Being back in my hood, hanging with family and close friends, and having a good time was the perfect thing for me to do to cope with the reality of my life.

My home girl Izzie and I talked that morning and planned to hang out. That's what home girls do; they hang. That's exactly what Izzie and I did when I returned home from college. We decided to go skating that night. Boy did Izzie love skating. That was her thing, and she was particularly good at it, too.

With her cocoa brown-skin, thick shoulder length hair, piercing hazel brown eyes and a shape that resembled the original Foxy Brown, Izzy commanded the skating rink with her beauty and skills. Izzie's beauty and skating skills were effortless.

I, on the other hand, was not a natural-born skater. I enjoyed skating but could not quite get it. I am an excellent dancer but just couldn't get that skating thing down packed. My attempt at skating didn't stop the fellas from teaching me how to learn. If anything, it attracted them even more.

I was a 5'7, magnetic lady, magnetic in my personality, beauty, intelligence, energy and aura. It was evident that God created something special about me. I had butterscotch skin with curly jet-black hair, big almond-shaped pecan-brown eyes that would light up under the sun, long black luxurious natural eye lashes, thick eyebrows, an infectious and wide smile and nose, with a dimple in my chin. My long butterscotch-brown legs and slim-thick frame always got me the unrealized attention from the guys teaching me how to skate. Quite honestly, I didn't even realize my untapped potential from within, beauty and personality wise.

While standing in the bathroom detangling my jet-black coils, I received a phone call from Izzie. I knew I had to start getting ready early; I knew that starting my typical 2-hour routine too late would make Izzie and I late for skate night at Skate 84.

I was excited to finally have something fun to do. I pick up the phone and say, "Hey, what's up, Izzie?" My typical laid-back and chill personality complimented Izzie's outgoing, funny and extrovert personality.

Izzie responded, "What's up? What's up? What's uppppp? Ready to hit up Skate 84 tonight? I have some new moves I wanna try. I've been at work thinking about it all day like bam, bam, bam!" as she's snapping her fingers and moving her feet under her desk.

I couldn't see Izzie moving, but I sure could hear her moving over the phone. I replied, "Yup! I am ready, but don't have any new moves. I'm just focusing on not falling!" Izzie and I bust out laughing.

"Okay, so I'm going to go home, change my clothes and pick you up at 8:30pm. We are going to go and have fun!" Izzie always assured Journee would have a good time with her.

I replied, "Okay cool. I'll make sure I'm ready!"

Izzie jokingly says, "Yeah start getting ready now, because you know how you are with your 2-hour routines!!"

I snapped back with my infectious smile and saying, "Girl, hush. It's only 11 in the morning. You are picking me up 8:30pm. I got time!"

Izzie busts out laughing saying, "Now you KNOWWWW!!!...."

I interrupt her and say, "Alright. Alright. I'll make sure I'm ready. Now get back to work."

Izzie responds, "Okay. Talk to you later. Love you."

While laughing on the other end, I replied, "Okay. Love you too. Bye."

I continued detangling my coils while standing in front of the bathroom mirror. Thinking about my life and next move, I became over-whelmed and anxious about my future. I just graduated college only to still be homeless, jobless, and car-less and in an uncertain relationship. I did not go to college and graduate, accumulate all this student loan debt while leaving my college friends to be homeless, jobless, and car-less. I wanted to make my family proud, but I felt stuck. Stuck in my life circumstances, relationship and stuck while looking past myself in the mirror. I asked myself, "How did I even get here to begin with?"

Just as my thought began to spiral down a negative path, I heard the water running in the bathroom. I had forgotten that I had turned on the shower to start my 2-hour routine so that I could get ready for skate night at Skate 84. I snapped out of it and began getting ready so that I could be ready and not hear Izzie's mouth about being late. So, I showered, ate, watched some television, and continued looking for jobs.

At 8:30pm Izzie was outside honking her horn and calling me. I picked up on the first ring and shouted, "Ha! I'm ready. I'll be right down."

Izzie replied, "Well, well. You've proved me wrong! I'll be downstairs waiting."

I grabbed my purse, lip gloss and jacket and went downstairs. I immediately felt the cool wind graze my butterscotch skin as the sun was just about to set. I walked down a flight of steep stairs. Izzie was blasting Single Ladies (Put a Ring on It) by Beyonce to get us hyped for the skating rink. This was the pre-party before the actual party. I opened Izzie's 2010 2-door apple red Acura coupe. Fully loaded with a sunroof, Izzie always had her music blasting letting everyone know she was coming down the street.

I bust out with a quick two-step and opened the passenger car door.

"What's up???" I excitedly shouted as I slid in the front seat of Izzie's car.

Izzie was in her own world practicing her skate moves in the driver seat. She screams over the music, "Hey Journ!!!" Izzie was always good for giving her home girls nicknames. "Are you ready to get your skate on? I've been waiting for this all day. And you know it's gonna be some cuties there!"

I chuckled and replied, "I don't know about all that, but like I said, I'm just trying not to fall!" "So, how was work today?" I said while turning down Izzie's radio.

"It was good. I had to review and underwrite some mortgage applications for several clients. It's always busy in that office, per usual," Izzie replied. Izzie was an underwriter for B&G Mortgage Company.

Izzie asked hesitantly knowing that work was a sensitive topic for me, "How about you? Have you found anything yet? I know you been looking for a while."

I gave a big sigh before answering, "Besides babysitting the little girl down the street, nothing yet. I'm still looking though. I hope to find something soon because I have to get out of here. I can't keep living like this."

Feeling the energy going south, Izzie changed the subject and said, "Look, everything will work out. You will eventually find the right job."

Izzie and I finally pulled into Skate 84's parking lot. As always, it was jumping with cuties, nice cars and good music, no matter the day of the week. The fresh crisp spring air made me excited about the summer and the longer days. Izzie and I got out of the car ready to have a good time and skate. Besides, this was exactly what I needed to get my mind off things for a little while.

Izzie made her way to the trunk to grab her Impala Black professional skates. Meanwhile, I had to rent the peanut butter skates from the rental booth inside the skating rink. Clearly, I was an amateur at the whole skating thing.

As we approached the doorway to the skating rink, we passed through a crowd of chocolatey fine men posted up against the wall. They were fine like Morris Chestnut, Mekhi Phifer and Larenz Tate. You could always count on seeing fine men at Skate 84.

Izzie was not shy speaking her mind. With excitement in her voice, she shouted, "How y'all fine men doing tonight?!"

They all replied in unison, "We are fine!"

Izzie whispered under her breath just so I could hear her, "Yes. Y'all. Are!"

The Larenz Tate-looking guy said, while fiercely gazing at me from head to toe and biting his chocolate brown bottom lip, "How you doing, beautiful?"

Coyishly, I responded, "I'm doing fine," and rushed my way pass the guys.

We finally made our way inside the rink. Izzie grabbed herself a locker while I went to the skate rental booth to rent some peanut butter skates. By the time I grabbed my skates and sat down to put them on, Izzie was on the rink skating to Buddy by Musiq Soulchild. Backwards skating, twists and turns, Izzie had it down pat! She was the skating queen and she knew it.

I joined Izzie in the rink and skated a few times around. Izzie helped me get more comfortable by skating with her. That only lasted a short while because Izzie was so excited to try the new tricks, she had been practicing at her work desk. Izzie skated by herself, everyone was admiring her skills.

Eventually, I stood off to the side while watching everyone skate. Izzie noticed something was off with me.

Izzie, with her cocoa brown-skin and body frame like the original Foxy Brown, glided over to me. "Girl, what are you over here thinking about? All these cuties up in here checking you out, andddddd the music is rocking! You should be showing off that bad body of yours on them skates!" Izzie jokingly said trying to catch her breath.

"Something isn't right. I feel Khase is up to something," I responded.

Taking a second to register what I was referring to, Izzie replied, "So what do you want to do? I'm down for whatever."

"I just need proof. I'm tired of his lies and him finessing his way out of his lies. Something is off with my relationship with Khase," I zoned out and had totally blocked out the music and where I was at in the moment. I knew once and for all I deserved the real answers that I had always felt in my gut. After all, I had nothing to lose at that point. I was homeless, jobless, and car-less. It was time for me to get some answers.

Izzie skated a few more times around the rink. She even skated with one of the fine guys that was posted up in the hallway when we came in. My mind was focused on other things, so spent most of my time on the side of the rink thinking.

I returned my peanut butter rental skates and Izzie gathered her things out of the locker. On our way out, we passed those fine brothers again. This time, the Larenz Tate-looking brother asked for my number. I respectfully declined because he had no idea the drama that he would have found himself in if he and I would have started talking. Plus, I needed answers and he didn't have them.

We got inside the car and talked before driving off. By this time, it was 1:15 Wednesday morning. Izzie reeved up her 2010 2-door apple red Acura coupe and we left Skate 84 for the night.

CHAPTER 2
RIDE OR DIE FRIEND

"Once we get to the house, you can park a few blocks down so no one sees your car. I'll go upstairs and wait by the door. I'm going to address it very calmly. Honestly, you should probably leave if you want to because I don't want you in the middle of it. Plus, I know you have to go to work in the morning," I said to Izzie.

Izzie, being the ride or die friend in that moment, said "No. I'll just stay behind in case you need me."

At 1:41am, Izzie and I pull up to the house. Izzie parked her car four houses down since I didn't want her to be noticed. Izzie parked her car and turned her car and head-lights off. I got out of the car and walked up the block. I walked up the back stairs.

The rusty brown and white three-family house was old but big. The long house sat up and away from the street. There were 15 steep, cracked, and cemented stairs leading to the back door. The sky was pitch-black with only two streetlights on the block. Dark-ness overshadowed the entire block. One of the streetlights just so happened to be near the house. It was dead quiet. Literally. On one side of the block were houses and on the other side was a cemetery.

I turned the knob, but it was locked, and the lights were off. Khase was home. I heard a car coming down the street and it eventually pulled up in front of the house. Thankfully, I had on black sneakers, a white t-shirt, and blue jeans that night.

There it was. The moment, in real time, that had me staring in the distance, in a trance. I glided down the stairs not even worried about falling. There they were, in a car like a happy family as if life was good.

Seconds later, after seeing them, I blacked out. Screaming to the top of my lungs at two o'clock in the morning, I shouted, "Are y'all fucking?! Are y'all fucking?!"

In the 4-door stone gray 2006 Ford Fusion was Khase, Gracie and baby Glorie.

I quickly approached the driver side where Khase was sitting. Khase, the self-proclaimed minister, was 6'5 in stature, light-skinned with full lips, and charismatic to a fault. He had the gift of gab and could talk himself out of anything. I mean anything. He had a very convincing personality that matched his regal, masculine look. He was a nice-looking brother.

By the time I approached Khase while he was still in the car. I went from being calm to being on 100.

"Are y'all f-ing?!" I screamed a third time while standing over Khase with his hands on the wheel looking shocked. Khase didn't answer quickly enough, so I landed a right punch on the left side of his chin, knocking off his glasses.

Now Gracie, on the passenger side of Khase's car, was a beautiful woman. She had big round, amber-colored eyes with long reddish-brown eyelashes with curly hair to match. Her smile was perfect. Baby Glorie was a splitting image of Gracie. That was her mama. Gracie stood 5'0 tall with a brick house frame.

Gracie and I are sisters and baby Gracie was my niece.

"How. Could. This. Be. 2 o'clock in the morning and the man I loved was messing around with my sister!" I had those thoughts swimming around in my mind while my hands were still flying inside the driver side of the car hitting Khase.

Trying to protect Khase from getting swung on again, Gracie got punched in the face from the crossfire. Meanwhile, Baby Glorie was confused with all the commotion that was taking place right before her little, innocent eyes.

Khase makes his way out of the car, pulling out a stack of papers from his car door. "Journee, Journee, look I have Post-Traumatic Stress Disorder! I took a test on-line and I have PTSD!"

Not even the slightest bit convinced, I could not muster up the words to respond to his fraudulent self-diagnosis. Khase threw the papers back into the car and grabbed me by my wrists.

Meanwhile, Gracie jumps out of the car and begins to scream, "Yes, Journee, yes! We are! Are you happy now?! Yes, it's true!"

When Gracie said those words to me, my entire world stopped. No yelling. No reaction. No feelings. Just numbness. This seemed to have been the only time Gracie was honest. Of all moments to be honest, this was the worst.

By this time, Izzie heard the ghetto drama that was going on she was jogging frantically down the street trying to get my attention. She screamed, "Journee! Journee!!"

Immediately, Khase realized the voice before seeing Izzie's face appear from the darkness. When Izzie was approaching me, Khase turned to Izzie, grabbed her by her shoulders and shook her aggressively while saying, "You made her do this?!?!?"

Typical Khase behavior. He never took responsibility for his own actions and always deflected and placed blame on everyone else.

Izzie pulled back from Khase's grip and firmly said, "No you did this! This is on you! If you ever put your hands on me again, I will get my cousin to whoop your...." I jumped in between them.

Khase focused on me while still trying to convince me that he had PTSD.

Gracie shouted to me, "This is not Christ-like, Journee! This is not Christ-like!"

I went numb for a second time. No yelling. No reaction. No feelings. Just numbness.

CHAPTER 3
GHETTO-HOT-
ENTANGLEMENT MESS!

There had been so much yelling and commotion that it could have woke the dead. Fortunately, it didn't wake the dead. But it did wake the downstairs neighbors.

She opened her front door and shouted from her doorstep in her Spanish accent, "I called the cops! They are on their way!"

"Great…," I said to myself, "…this was not supposed to go down like this!"

No sooner than the neighbor closing her door after yelling, three cops came on the scene and surrounded the four adults that had been arguing in the middle of the street at 2 o'clock in the morning. This was some ghetto-hot-entanglement mess!

The officer that approached had me was short and stocky, but strong. He was young in the face, but it was obvious that he took his badge serious. He seemed to be very understanding when he saw me.

He approached me in the most professional way asking, "So, what happened?"

Enraged that I had allowed myself to get that angry, I replied, "That's my sister and so-called boyfriend!"

He didn't ask any further questions. He just said, "Okay, have a seat on the curb."

I sat on the curb scared and enraged. The officer walked over to his sergeant and partner.

I was left by myself on the curb while my sister and so-called boyfriend were together concocting a story to make themselves look good while making me out to be the crazy one. This wasn't the first time doing that to me and it wouldn't be their last especially after what had happened.

Two cops and one sergeant surrounded Khase and Gracie getting their version of the story. The sergeant was tall and slim with red hair and blue eyes. He had a no nonsense demeanor. I knew based on his white sergeant collared shirt that he was the one in charge. The other cop was an African American brown-skin handsome man. He was tall, muscular, and strong. His piercing serious brown eyes could put anyone in check.

Izzie was holding Baby Glorie after she was left in the back seat of the car watching her mother and aunt argue over a man. Surely her young innocent mind couldn't possibly understand what was going. Hmph. Kids understand more than what adults give them credit for.

Because Izzie was holding Glorie near the car, Izzie had a better view than I did. Izzie heard what the officers were saying to Khase and Gracie while I remained sitting on the curb.

Khase and Gracie stood side by side in front of the cops. Gracie consoled Khase by rubbing his back as he told his "version" of the story.

Using his gift of gab in yet another moment, he frantically responded to the Sergeant saying, "Officer, I am just here trying to be a big brother to them! They are sisters and I'm trying to help them. Their..."

The Sergeant was not the least bit convinced by his answer. He cut Khase off mid-sentence and sternly saying, "Young man! There is NO way two sisters are out here arguing with each other over you, 2 o'clock in the morning, over nothing. There is something going on. Clearly, something has to be going on."

The Sergeant never got a clear answer from Khase that night. Gracie didn't say anything either. She continued to rub Khase's back to console him.

The Sergeant moved on and asked, "Whose property is this?"

Khase quickly responded, "It's mine. My name is on the lease!" Khase was finally able to tell the truth that night about something.

The same officer that told me to sit on the curb walked over to me and asked, "Is there anything in the apartment that belongs to you?

"Yes," I replied apprehensively.

The officer continued, "Alright, I'll escort you up there to get your things."

Little did the officers know, I had moved back home from college and had been living with Khase for a year now.

I stood up from sitting on the hard, cold curb. I walked up the old, cracked, and steep stairs with the officer, not even looking at Khase and Gracie. Izzie was still holding baby Glorie. Khase and Gracie stood beside each other watching me get escorted by two officers, one in front and the other behind me.

I got to the third step and Khase snarly shouted to me, "Yeah, and get your stuff out my house!"

I immediately went from 0 to 100...AGAIN. Without even thinking and forgetting I had two officers near me, I turned around to make my way towards Khase – to land another punch. The officer that walked behind me caught me in mid-air, by my arms, as I tried to leap over the officer to get to Khase.

"How could he?! Get my stuff out his house?! The very man whose idea it was for me to move in with him after I moved back home from college. The very man that wanted me in his space. How could she? She couldn't even defend me has her sister or as a woman?" I said to myself as I walked up the stairs with the officers. I couldn't help but have those thoughts while being escorted by two officers to get my stuff.

There were only but so many things I could grab that night. I had nowhere to go; nowhere to put my belongings.

I thought to myself, "Where am I going to put all my things? I can't even grab all my stuff."

The two officers and I made our way inside the house. One of the officers grabbed the keys from Khase before he made his arrogant comment.

I walked through the house grabbing what I could grab as quickly as possible. Still in disbelief with all that went down, I was angry and numb. I had to focus on getting as much as I could, as quick as I could.

I entered me and Khase's bedroom to grab some of my shoes. The same bedroom he created space for me in a year ago.

I entered the room and turned on the light so that I could see where my belongings were. The officer followed me into each room I went in as if I was the bad guy.

A few moments later, I heard Khase through the officer's radio saying, "Tell her to get out of my bedroom!"

Just when matters couldn't get any more humiliating for me, I angrily replied, "Shut-up! I'm getting my stuff!"

I shouted hoping that he could hear me. It didn't make the anger and numbness any less intense for me. Surprisingly, the two officers that escorted me didn't give me a hard time. They felt bad and couldn't even imagine the feeling I felt in my soul. When I yelled back, they didn't say anything to me.

I finally grabbed as much as I could and carried my three bags down the stairs. This would be my last time walking down those stairs. Better yet, it would my last time walking down that same road with Khase. I was done. At least, that's what I thought.

Still standing side by side, Khase and Gracie smirked in victory as they saw me walk down those steep stairs. Baby Glorie was in the car looking out the back-seat window with her big, beautiful eyes. Izzie stood away in a far distance waiting for me.

The Sergeant approached me as I struggled to carry my three heavy bags. Honestly, the weight of those bags didn't even begin to compare to the weight of anger, rage, sadness, hurt, disappointment, and betrayal that I carried.

Releasing his handcuffs from his command belt, the Sergeant began to read me my rights: "You have the right to remain silent. Anything you say, can and will be used against you in a court of law. You have the right to an attorney. If you cannot afford an attorney, one will be provided for you. You can decide at any time to exercise these rights and not answer any questions or make any statements. Do you understand the rights I have just read to you? With these rights in mind, do you wish to speak to me?"

Shocked and confused, I had to release my bags out my hand to be handcuffed. My world started flashing before my very eyes. Enraged all over again, I yelled, "Why am I being taken in?! I did nothing wrong! Sergeant, what am I being arrested for?! This is ridiculous!"

Izzie couldn't believe what was going down. One minute I was having fun, skating, and having a good time. Next minute, I was being taken away in a police car.

Izzie ran back down the street towards me, saying to the cop, "Hold the hell up! Why are you arresting her? You should be arresting their raggedy behinds!! Not Journee!"

The Sergeant replied, "Ma'am your friend is being arrested for simple assault. She's caused all this commotion and punched this young man in his face, causing physical harm."

Izzie couldn't believe it. She responded, "You're freaking kidding me!! You will hear from her lawyer, buddy!" Izzie grabbed my bags and made her way back to her car.

Khase and Gracie stood side by side with a smug look on their faces, saying nothing. Yet again, Khase was able to convince the sergeant that he was physically assaulted, in fear of his life, and wanted to press charges against me.

Handcuffed in the back seat of the smelly old police car, looking out the window, I couldn't even muster up the words to speak. Not only was I numb, but I had also become voiceless. The sergeant pulled off as Khase, Gracie and Baby Glorie walked up those old, steep, and cemented stairs as a family.

The sergeant and I arrived at the local precinct in Hopeville, NJ. He walked over to my side of the door, opened it, and reached his hand inside the car to guide my head so that I didn't hit my head on the door.

He pulled me out the car. As the sergeant and I were walking inside, there was an eerie, dead silence and guilt that filled the air. The sergeant couldn't look me in my eyes for some reason. He avoided talking and making eye contact with me.

We walked inside, and for the first time in my life, I was being booked for a crime because of some dude. They began the booking process.

The booking officer said, "Your full name."

I replied, "Journee."

The booking Policer Officer said, "Journee what?"

I answered, "Journee Black."

The booking officer replied, "Alright Ms. Black. We are going to take your mug-shot now. You will take three pictures. One facing forward, one of your left side and the last of your right side."

I complied. I didn't have the energy to resist orders or ask questions. The weight of those bags seemed to have gotten heavier, even though I had no bags in my hands.

The officer ordered me to take off my clothes in exchange for an attire that would label me for the rest of her life –an orange jail jumpsuit. After they took my fingerprints and mugshots, I was escorted in handcuffs, to a jail cell with heavy black metal bars and a tiny glass window with dirty white walls. The room was cold, scary, and exposed. Exactly how I felt that night.

I could not believe I allowed myself to get to this place in my life. Just a few hours ago, I was out having a good time skating with my home girl Izzie while trying to get my life together.

Betrayed by my sister. Betrayed by the man I loved. Betrayed by the sergeant who I thought had my back. It seemed so unreal for me, but it wasn't.

A metal bed. Closed-in walls. A grimy and smelly toilet. A small window I could barely see beyond the black metal bars. Alone. Misunderstood. Hurt. That is how I felt. My tears were the only thing that seemed to be there for me. My ENTIRE life flashed before my eyes.

I laid down on that cold, metal bed and cried myself to sleep…

CHAPTER 4
THE BLACK FAMILY

Twenty year ago...

While in a deep sleep, I went back twenty years in my life. I had come from a typical black family. Poor. Happy. And deep. Deep as in large. Six kids. Five girls, one boy. It was nothing for Joseph and Lorraine Black, my mother and father, to have a large family of six kids. They both had come from large families. Joseph Black came from a family of six, while Lorraine Black came from a family of nine.

For the most part, it was normal for African American families to create large families during the 60's, 70's and 80's. Creating a strong family unit, no matter the family size, was one of the most important goals in the African American community. Joseph and Lorraine Black used this as a pillar for building their family.

I am the third oldest in my family. Laid back, reserved with a kind heart is how I describe myself. I was thoughtful and caring in all my interactions with my family. I inherited this quality from my mother, Lorraine. I was a unique child. I was born at home on the couch and delivered by my father in our one-bedroom apartment in North Jersey. Totally unplanned, my parents would always tell the story of how I came into the world when I was ready.

It was a cold and the worst snowstorm in the 80's when I made my entrance into the world. Six feet of snow to be exact. The snow didn't stop my grandiose entrance. Butterscotch skin with curly jet-black hair, big almond-shaped, pecan-brown eyes, long black luxurious natural eye lashes, thick eyebrows, bow-shaped lips, a wide nose, and a dimpled chin, a beautiful baby girl.

My sister and brother waited patiently with excitement. Strength Black was the eldest. Her strong and no non-sense demeanor was balanced by her honey-brown glazed skin tone, soft, big light brown eyes, thick mocha brown hair, and a solid frame. Strength was tough and spoke her mind. She didn't care what others thought. She was strong in that sense. She was never a follower. A leader in her own right. Strength never thought twice about standing up for her family. She wasn't a troublemaker, but a trouble finisher. She would shut stuff down! Her name wasn't Strength for nothing.

Meaven Black, the only boy, was the second eldest. He was affectionately called Meav in the Black household. Meaven was tall, lean, and strong. He had small yet mighty brown eyes, black hair, and a GQ smile. Meaven Black resembled our father Joseph Black. He was the coolest guy to have had five sisters. Nothing fazed him because he was just that cool. A stylish and sharp dresser, Meaven was easy to remember. Being the only boy and having five sisters, Meaven was often asked, "Man, how do you do it having five sisters?" Showing off his GQ smile, he would respond "They're my sisters. I just do." Meav didn't care about having five sisters. He was too cool to care, plus he was proud to have sisters.

Eleven months after I was born, came Gracie. Gracie was a beautiful baby. She was innocent, sweet, kind, and noticeably quiet. She had big round, amber-colored eyes with long reddish-brown eyelashes with curly hair to match. Her skin resembled the beach on a sunny day: sandy brown, soft and warm. Her smile was perfect. Gracie and I were often mistaken as twins because we they were so close in age and resembled each other. Gracie enjoyed having a good time. Laughter and silliness came easy to Gracie. If anyone dared Gracie to do something silly, she would do it and nail it! Grace and I dressed alike growing up. We did everything together. From afterschool programs to prom to friends, we did it together. We even fought together. Gracie and I were the best of friends growing up.

Papa and Mama Black didn't stop there. Four years later they would have two more girls, Audacious and Joy. Audacious had similar eyes as her big brother, small and brown. They were thick as thieves. When you saw Meaven, you saw Audacious; when you saw Audacious, you saw Meaven. Audacious' s round face made her face structure unique yet fierce. She had a rose-beige skin complexion and tapered brown hair. Audacious was no stranger to laughter and having a good time. You could always count on Audacious to turn something serious into a light-hearted matter. Audacious was extremely generous and never failed to share with her family, even if it was her last. Don't be fooled by Audacious' s fun-loving personality. The fellas loved and admired her. She always had a fella trying to get to know her.

Then there was Joy Black. The baby girl of the Black family; my baby sister. Joy was the Black family's favorite. She was everyone's favorite. Joy could do no wrong.

Her sweet and easy-going demeanor made anyone fall in love with her. Genuinely special is how she was often described. She was the only sibling that had the same beautiful chocolate-golden-brown complexion like Mama Black. They were twins. I also resembled Mama Black although we were different complexions.

Baby girl Joy had innocent big brown piercing eyes, curly black hair and a smile that made the moon shine. Everybody protected baby girl Joy but she didn't need protection. Baby girl Joy was strong and tough like Strength. Although the youngest, when Joy spoke, everyone listened. Joy was responsible and completed the Black Family circle.

My mother, also known as Mama Black, was the matriarch of the Black family. Her beauty, intelligence and charm were soft, unique, alluring, and distinct. Her beautiful chocolate-golden-brown skin tone, big, brown, kind eyes and wide bright smile was what made Joseph Black fall in love with her. My dad first laid eyes on her in the 70's. He was with his boys at a club when he noticed Mama Black dancing by herself, living her best life. Mama Black didn't wait on anyone to have a good time.

Mama Black wasn't good at being a mother and wife. She was good at dancing. Whether alone, in the house or in a club, Mama Black would bust out a two-step at any given moment, especially if it was the right song. Her vintage swag and confident spirit are what drew Joseph Black to her.

Her eyes, too. Her eyes were Mama Black's secret weapon to getting Joseph Black. Mama Black was fierce woman and she knew it. After growing their love and having 5 children, Joseph and Lorraine Black married and had their last child in the 80's.

Before becoming a mother and wife, Mama Black attended dance school in her teenage years. She wanted to join the military or become a stewardess. Little did she know she would become both. Having a husband and six children, she had to keep the household in order while serving her family with grace, patience, and love. Mama Black stayed home and raised us, while Joseph Black worked two or three jobs to provide and support our family.

Now, Papa Black was a sharp man and a dresser. Papa Black was good at coordinating a nice blazer, slacks, shirt, hat, and a handkerchief. He was tall, slender, and strong. His smooth bronzed-colored brown skin, brown copper eyes and a black goatee that adorned his face gave him a firm and distinct masculine look. Having five daughters, Papa Black rarely smiled. This kept the knuckleheads away. He often referred to the guys that were interested in his daughters as knuckleheads.

Papa Black was also tough and strict but worked hard to keep our family together and around good people. When Papa Black would arrive home, my siblings and I would do a mad dash to our rooms because Papa Black ain't play. As soon as we heard his keys hit the door, we would jump off the couch, sprint to the stairs while trying to squeeze our way up the narrow staircase to our rooms. Surprisingly, we all made it to their room before Papa Black stepped foot in the house.

When Papa Black got home, he would start his evening ritual to unwind. He would play his Luther Vandross concert video, eat his chicken that Mama Black had cooked for dinner that night and drink his cold one.

Luther Vandross was a staple in the African American community. His dynamic, smooth and matchless voice was probably how a lot of the 80's babies were born. My siblings and I had become all too familiar with Luther Vandross at a young age.

Papa Black was a man of depth. Before starting his family, he was a young boxer. His Uncle Sid got him into boxing. After trying it for a short period, he became a natural and good at it. His boxing career didn't go far because soon after he started a family. So, he hung up his gloves and put his hands to use to provide for his family.

He wasn't rich and didn't have the best of jobs. He was never ashamed to provide for his family by any means. Although my parents always struggled to make ends meet, Mama Black wasn't ashamed of her family's struggle either. She supported Papa Black.

Papa Black often had low wage, tough labor jobs. Working long hours had him up and out the house before the sun rose and back when the sky was dark. He had dreams of becoming a fire fighter. He wanted to help and serve his community. But, because of a life-changing injury, he wasn't qualified to take the physical exam to become a fire fighter.

We struggled like most Black families during that time. We didn't have much. All eight of us stayed in a one-bedroom apartment when we were young. There were a lot of systemic issues we witnessed as a family. Drug deals, welfare, gang violence, discrimination, racism and disparities in the education system and the notorious crack epidemic were challenges that Mama and Papa Black fought against. They refused to become another "statistic."

A lot of memories were created in that one-bedroom apartment. We lived on the second floor of an apartment building. My siblings and I always played in the room while Papa and Mama Black watched TV or listened to Luther Vandross in the living room.

Strength and Meav, the two oldest, were like a tag team growing up. One day while we were playing in the bedroom, Meav's quarter fell out of the window. A quarter went a long way when going to the corner store in the 80's and early 90's. I could overhear Strength and Meav plotting to get his quarter. To Meaven, it was a lot of money he had lost. Fortunately, the fire escape was connected to the window in the bedroom.

Sticking his head out the window seeing how far down he had to go, Meaven said, "I'm going to go and get it. Shhh. Don't say anything." Strength agreed and watched his back saying, "Okay, I'm going to look out the window while you go down."

Now before they executed their plan, they looked at me and said, "Don't say anything, okay?!"

I quickly and nervously responded and said, "Okay, I won't say anything…"

Meav slowly lifted the old wooden window that was painted white. He stuck his leg out first to plant his feet on the fire escape. He made it out through the window and was standing on the other side of the window! He began climbing down the fire escape. Meanwhile, Strength looked out the window to watch over her little brother. Next thing you know, Strength climbs out the window, too!! Now, both Meav and Strength are outside the window, climbing down the fire escape to get that quarter. I was standing there in complete shock, and worried about what I would say if Mama or Papa Black bust through that bedroom door.

Shockingly, Strength and Meav made it down to the bottom of the fire escape where his quarter had landed. Gracie, Audacious and Joy didn't realize what was going on, but I sure did. Strength and Meav made a safe return up the fire escape and into the apartment window. Strength slid that one leg through the window, planted her foot on the floor of the bedroom and made her way back inside. Meav shortly made it back in after Strength.

Not a second later, Mama Black flung the door open to the room and said, "It's too quiet in here!! What y'all doing?" Strength and Meav looked cool, calm, and collected. Not even batting an eye, Strength innocently replied, "Nothing." Meav didn't say a word. He had a blank stare on his face.

Next thing you know, I shouted from across the room saying, "Strength and Meav just went down the fire escape to get his quarter and they came back up!" I broke the sibling code that day. I told after just agreeing not to say anything about Strength and Meav's fire escape escapade. I wasn't even sure why I said anything to begin with. I blurted it out and couldn't hold it in.

All Mama Black said was, "What?!?!?!?!?!" She gave Strength and Meav a whopping to last them for a lifetime. Mama Black wasn't usually the one that disciplined me and my siblings. It was Papa Black that gave most of the spankings. Well, that day, Mama Black wasn't having it. She went in on her two oldest kids.

After seeing how Mama Black went in, I regretted telling on my big brother and sister. It was so bad that Mama Black didn't even tell Papa Black because Strength and Meav would have had to sleep on that very same fire escape after pulling that stunt. Strength and Meav knew never to pull that stunt again. They learned their lesson.

Shortly after that escapade, my family and I moved. I was in the third grade at the time; we were excited to finally move into a house. It wasn't uncommon for poor African American families to live in apartment buildings or the projects.

The two-family house was white and green but old. There was a broken sidewalk leading up to the porch, it was big on the inside. Honestly, *anything* was bigger than a one-bedroom apartment with eight people living in it. It had four bedrooms, one bathroom, a living room and dining room. The kitchen was huge, but the floor was slanted. The bathroom was small, but way bigger than what we were used to as a family. It was right for our family.

"Man, this house is huge!" shouted Meav with his GQ smile plastered across his young face. While my sisters and I were walking around to each room, you could hear Strength shouting from her room of choice, "Don't nobody come in my room without asking first! And don't sit on my bed." Strength had a way of marking her territory when it came to *her* things. No one responded because we were all so excited about living in a house and having space to play.

Papa and Mama Black were proud standing in that house. Finally, all their hardwork, energy and sacrifice paid off. The huge space was not only filled with lots of kids, but with lots of love, happiness, and growth. My parents believed in the importance of family gatherings and having a good time. They would always host parties, inviting family and friends over to have a good time.

After moving in, Papa and Mama Black were able to furnish the house to make it our home. Gracie, Audacious, Joy and I all shared a room. Mama and Papa Black gave us bunk beds for the room. Strength and Meav had twin beds since they had their own rooms. Mama and Papa Black had their own bedroom with a queen-sized bed.

The Black Family household wasn't a home unless we had a radio. It was an absolute MUST. We always had a radio no matter where we lived. Papa Black's love for listening to music and Mama Black's gift for dancing made my parents the perfect duo.

Papa Black had the perfect radio. The radio was tall and black with various features. It had a cassette player with play, record, pause, fast forward, rewind, and stop/eject buttons. Additionally, there was the bass, tremble, tone, balance and volume button, AM or FM and the stereo and mono switch. Papa Black always had the bass up to the highest volume. To him, it added more soul to the music. At the top was a record player, and the off and on switch. Papa and Mama Black didn't have any acrylic records. They mainly played the radio or cassette tapes. The case of the radio was wooden brown with a fancy glass door to protect the radio.

That radio was a large part of our family memories. Until a horrific event took place. Papa and Mama Black were preparing for our traditional family get together. Mama Black was frying chicken, cooking macaroni and cheese and mash potatoes.

Mama Black always cooked two starches; it was cheaper and would fill our bellies. Papa Black was playing his music while cleaning the living room and creating space for family and friends to dance and have a good time.

My siblings and I were in our separate rooms preparing for a great and fun time until there was a frantic knock on our door. It was the upstairs neighbor. Not knowing what was on the other side of that door, Papa Black opened the door with his stern, straight face. The same face he was used to having because he had five daughters.

The neighbor shouted, "Get out! Get out! There's a fire!!" The neighbor ran down the stairs and out the door.

Immediately going into protection mode, Papa Black yelled to everyone while hastily walking through the house, "Get out! It's a fire! Let's go, now!" I was in the room with Gracie, Audacious and Joy playing with Barbie dolls and talking, while Strength and Meav were in their rooms.

I was nervous, scared and shaking. In that moment, all I could do was grab my little purse that was hanging on the wooden frame of the bunk bed. Gracie, Audacious, Joy and I ran out while Strength and Meav followed. Mama Black turned the stove off, dropped everything and ran out. Papa Black was last getting out of the house. He made sure that his family was out first. Eventually, he made it out the house.

Standing in the middle of the street, my family and I were surrounded by two huge red fire trucks, three police cars, concerned and nosy neighbors, and a gloomy dark sky. Red and orange fire flames and dusty gray smoke filled the clouds that were once blue.

Standing eight deep in the street, my family and I watched our very first house go up in flames along with all our belongings. I was devastated but didn't know how to put it into words at such a young age. Mama Black did on my behalf, my entire family's behalf. She let out an undignified cry. Mama Black wept in Papa Black's chest while her hands covered her chocolate golden brown face. The tears from her big brown kind eyes flowed shamelessly. My siblings and I watched her cry.

All Papa Black said in that moment was, "It's okay. It's going to be okay." He wrapped his arms around Mama Black's body and stroked her hair in comfort.

We stood there watching the fire department hose down the dangerous flames. That night, there was no radio, no fried chicken, no macaroni and cheese, no mashed potatoes, no music, no dancing, no Barbie dolls, or clothes. No creating happy memories. Nothing. There was nothing but silence between my siblings and me. Just when things seemed to be going well, life took an unexpected turn, but we still had each other.

We went back to living in a one-bedroom apartment. This time it wasn't just ours. It was a relative we stayed with that night. It went from three people to eleven people in a one-bedroom apartment.

After some time, my family and I had to move into a motel. Motels in the 90's were filled with African American families. We were living proof of that.

We lived in the hotel for two months. Papa and Mama Black had two rooms to fit everyone comfortably. On the first night we stayed at the motel, Mama Black said to Papa Black that, "One of us should stay in each of the room, having three kids in each room." Mama Black always had a plan to keep us organized and in order.

Papa Black tiredly said, "Okay."

Papa Black continued to work to provide for our family while trying to keep it together himself. They had to find a way to make it work.

While living in the motel, we rarely had home cooked meals. There were no stoves or ovens that we could use. Just water, a microwave and small refrigerator. One night Mama Black prepared dinner for us. She grabbed eight white Styrofoam cups, dumped plain oatmeal in each cup, poured hot water inside the oatmeal and began stirring with a white plastic spoon.

An unnerving silence filled that motel room while we waited for Mama Black to finish stirring the oatmeal. Baby Girl Joy interrupted the silence and innocently asked while tilting her head as worry overtook her naïve little eyes, "Mama, are we going to be here for long? I want to go home." Joy was too young to understand what was going.

Mama Black didn't even look up at baby girl Joy. She kept her focus on stirring the oatmeal so her babies could at least have a decent cup of oatmeal for dinner. Mama Black really wanted to break down and cry, like the night our house caught on fire. Mama Black held it together as much as she could that night. She responded trying to hide the doubt in her voice by saying, "We'll be going home soon, Baby girl Joy."

After eating oatmeal for dinner, I laid in the motel bed with Gracie and took in all that I was surrounded by. I noticed the motel hallways constantly smelled like Newport 100s, Colt 45 and sweat. The smells never left my memory. I went to sleep wondering when things would go back to normal.

Morning came and we continued with our daily routines. Papa and Mama Black made sure we still went to school. Hand-me down clothes, old shoes and a book bag was all my siblings and I had. Mama Black always had a way of making us look well put together with little. She always kept me, and sisters' hair braided. She was great at cornrowing our hair.

Papa and Mama Black would always drop us off to school in a long green 1976 Lincoln 4-door car. A 1976 old green Lincoln in the 90's was not a cool car to drop kids off in. Papa Black didn't care. He had no problem setting me and my siblings straight when we griped about being dropped off in front of the schoolhouse in that car.

Papa Black would intentionally embarrass us by honking his horn while pulling up to the school drawing attention to us. All the other kids that waited outside would turn and look at the car. To make matters worse, Papa Black would also honk his horn again while driving off. When Papa Black did this, my siblings and I would get out the car and act as if we didn't hear the horn.

Pick-up time was less embarrassing for me and my siblings. Mama Black would walk and pick us up without Papa Black and that green car of his.

Mama and Papa Black ensure we continued to do well in school. I was in the third grade when we experienced the fire. Somehow, I maintained good grades.

Life began to turn around for us. Mama Black's father, Grandpa Millie, was able to connect us with a church community that helped us.

Grandpa Millie was 5'11 in stature, dark brown complexion and smooth black curly hair. Grandpa Millie and Mama Black had similar skin tones. Mama Black was the better-looking version, of course. He was funny and loud. Grandpa Millie had money. He lived a simple life, but it was obvious he was financially comfortable. Grandpa Millie was a Longshoreman. He worked at the Port of New York Harbor and was responsible for the cargo that arrived on ships at ports, docking the ships, loading, and unloading cargo, checking for specific containers, and inspecting cargo for damage. Grandpa Millie was paid! He had been on that job for forty years and was due to retire soon.

Grandpa Millie helped us a lot growing up. Papa and Mama Black were grateful for his help and support. One day Grandpa Millie introduced Papa and Mama Black to one of his good friends, Elder Bluestone. Grandpa Millie and Elder Bluestone had been friends for over 25 years.

Elder Bluestone was 6'8, caramel brown complexion with small black eyes and a flat top. Elder Bluestone had a powerful yet gentle presence. He was a devout Christian and was extremely involved in the church community. He had a beautiful and kind wife with four children, two boys and two girls. Elder Bluestone had been the Superintendent for the White Falls School District for over 15 years and was well-known and well-connected in his community.

When introduced, Papa and Mama Black met up with Grandpa Millie and Elder Bluestone at a small local diner while my siblings and I were in school. They went during Papa Black's lunch break because he couldn't afford to miss any hours of work. At the meeting, Elder Bluestone invited Papa and Mama Black to his church that Sunday.

Grace and Mercy Baptist Church was the name of the church. It was in Hopeville, New Jersey. Papa and Mama Black accepted the offer. They accepted all the help they could get. After all, living in a motel with their six kids was taking a toll on them. They needed the extra support and encouragement to get through this rough season.

Grandpa Millie was glad the introduction went well. Papa and Mama Black were glad, too. Papa Black headed back to work while Grandpa Millie took Mama Black to pick up the kids from school that day. Grandpa Millie loved seeing us and we loved seeing him.

Grandpa Millie would always give us a dollar. That seemed like a lot of money as a kid. We would always buy snacks from the corner store. My favorite snacks to were Nutty Bars, Funyuns Chips, a green quarter juice and peanut chews. I made that dollar go a long way.

After Grandpa took us to the store, Grandpa Millie dropped us off at the hotel. It was a hopeful day for us. It gave Mama Black something new looking forward to.

As soon as we got in the motel, Mama Black began preparing dinner. That night we had peanut butter and jelly sandwiches. Papa Black arrived later that night. We had completed our homework, eaten, and bathed by then.

CHAPTER 5
AFTER THE FIRE

Papa and Mama Black talked about going back to the old house to see if any of their things were salvageable. It was too emotional for Mama Black to even begin processing anything about that night. Mama Black decided not to go.

That Saturday, Papa Black took off from work so that he and his good friend could go the house and see what they could find. Our house that was full of furniture, the smell of fried chicken and short-lived memories was now empty besides the ashes.

Papa Black had been best friends with Wess for over 20 years. Wess was a cool and smooth brother. His smooth milk-chocolate brown skin matched his smooth walk and the tone of his voice. He was always there whenever Papa Black needed him. He was like an uncle to us and a brother to Mama Black. He was always there for our family during good and bad times.

Standing in front of the house for a second before going in, Papa Black began to feel the same emotions Mama Black felt that night. Tired and discouraged. This time, he didn't have to be strong for the family. Wess was there to be strong for him. Wess patted Papa Black on his back and said, "It's alright, brother. I got you. It's okay. WE will get through this." Papa Black was too overcome with emotions to respond. He just shook his head in agreement with Wess.

Papa Black and Wess walked up the stairs and opened the door. As expected, everything was burned by the fire. The couch, television, beds, cooking utensils, clothes, coats, toys, even the radio was burned and unusable. Complete devastation. Nothing was able to be salvaged. Besides, if it did, the smell of the smoke would have been too strong to keep it anyway.

Papa Black and Wess walked through the house quiet and observant. Papa Black thought about some of the pictures that could have been lost in the fire. Thankfully, those were untouched. Papa Black was grateful he walked out the house with those family pictures. Pictures from Mama and Papa Black's wedding, my siblings and I when they were babies, and even pictures of Mama and Black.

Papa Black loved pictures. Mama Black did, too, but Papa Black held them sacred.

They were important to him, a keepsake for future generations. Papa Black and Wess left the house after an hour of looking through things. Wess gave Papa Black the brother dap and a hug before they went their separate ways.

Papa Black returned to the motel. When he walked in the door, Mama Black had Audacious in her lap braiding her hair, while the rest of us were watching *The Simpsons* on television. My siblings and I loved watching that cartoon. It was how we spent most of our time with each other.

Still braiding Audacious' s hair, Mama Black turned to Papa Black with a concerned look on her face, "So, how did it go with you and Wess? Anything we can keep?" Mama Black could tell by the look on Papa Black's face that it wasn't good news, so she had prepared herself for the worst.

Papa Black couldn't hide his emotions any longer. Tears welled up in his eyes. "Lorraine, everything is gone. Me and Wess walked through the house and there was absolutely nothing worth keeping. It's all gone."

Mama Black stopped braiding Audacious' s hair for a moment. She got up and went over to where Papa Black was standing. The motel wasn't big, so Mama Black didn't have to walk far. As she walked over towards him, Papa Black pulled out the stack of pictures from his pocket. "These were untouched and the only thing that didn't get burned," Papa Black said full of emotion.

Mama Black took the photos and looked through the album. "Wow. Of all things, these didn't get burned." This gave Mama Black exactly what she needed to keep going. Papa and Mama Black hugged.

Mama Black finished braiding Audacious' s hair. Soon after, she prepared us for bed. Mama Black would often read us bedtime stories, but no longer did since our books were destroyed in the fire. Mama Black tucked us in and gave us a kiss on our cheeks.

Elder Bluestone invited Papa and Mama Black to Grace and Mercy Baptist Church earlier that week. The morning of, Mama Black decided we would stay at the motel with Papa Black and he would just drop off her off at the church.

Morning service started at 11am. Papa and Mama Black got us up that morning and made us get ready. Although we weren't attending church with Mama Black, Papa and Mama Black didn't play around with leaving us by ourselves, especially in that motel. They always arranged their schedules to make sure one of them stayed with us. Mama Black was usually with us since Papa Black worked so much.

After Mama Black finished getting dressed, they piled up in that long green 1976 Lincoln 4-door car. The Lincoln was large and spacious. Papa Black would drive, Mama

Black was the passenger and Baby Girl Joy would sit in between them, since she was the baby. The rest us would lap it up in the back.

Audacious would sit on someone's lap while Strength, Meaven, Gracie and I had a seat. We named that car *The Pickle* because it was long, green, and loud!

Papa Black pulled up to the church. Mama Black got out that the car and closed the door with all her strength. That car door was heavy!

I was a back-seat window rider. I enjoyed chilling in the back seat and looking at the scenery. When Mama Black got out the car, I watched her walk elegantly up the church stairs while holding on to the church banister. You couldn't even tell Mama Black had dropped six babies. She was snatched!

That day, Mama Black wore a short sleeve red chiffon knee-length dress and black shoes. She carried a black sweater in case it got cold, along with her black pocketbook. Mama Black often wore her thick, black shoulder length hair in a ponytail towards the back. Being a Mama of six meant creating a routine that was as low maintenance as possible.

Mama Black had adorned herself with iridescent gold clip-on earrings, red lipstick, and blush. She often used her lipstick as her blush. Anything on Mama Black's chocolate golden brown skin was radiant. Her skin created the look.

Mama Black finally got to the top of the stairs, turned around, waved, and smiled at us – her family. Papa Black honked the horn three times to acknowledge Mama Black's wave. My siblings and I excitedly waved back at Mama Black. She opened the church doors and went inside. Papa Black drove off with all six of us. Papa Black didn't have to worry about not having Mama Black around. He didn't play when it came to us. He could raise his voice one time and we would straighten up. We knew not to mess with Papa Black.

On the ride back to the motel I couldn't help but admire the beauty of the church from the outside. The church was huge. The steps that Mama Black had just walked up were white cemented stairs with black mosaic tiles throughout, adorned with beautiful black iron stair railings. The church house was made of red bricks with a large gold steeple that seemed like it was touching Heaven. It was beautiful.

CHAPTER 6
AN UNEXPECTED BLESSING!

Our weekend was different since we were at the motel. During a normal weekend, my siblings and I would watch Thank God It's Friday (TGIF) on Fridays. The 90's show line up consisted of: Family Matters, Step by Step, Boy Meets World and Dinosaurs.

Saturday's cartoon line ups were: Duck Tails, Gargoyles, Tiny Toons, Ninja Turtles, Thundercats, Tales Spin and Tom and Jerry. Saturday afternoon, Mama Black, myself, and my siblings would watch Soul Train. I would often imitate the dancers on Soul Train by dancing in front of Strength. Shaking and gyrating like the Soul Train dancers, Strength would sit there and crack up in laughter at my dancing. It was nothing for me to imitate those dancers because I loved dancing.

Sunday at 1o'clock in the morning, Mama Black and I watched Show Time at the Apollo. This was me and Mama Black's bonding time. I enjoyed it and would stay awake the entire time.

Sunday morning, we spent time playing Nintendo, lounging around and sometimes finishing up homework. Our routine had changed drastically since staying at the motel. Instead, we were just trying to make it through each day living there.

When we returned from dropping Mama Black off at the church, we all stayed in the same room with Papa Black until Mama Black returned home from church.

A few hours had passed before Mama Black returned. My siblings and I were used to being around Mama Black. When she returned, our family felt complete. Mama Black was the glue that held the Black family together.

Mama Black had been dropped off by one of the sisters from the church. The sister lived in the area and offered to drop Mama Black off at the motel so that Papa Black didn't have to load all of us back into the car to pick her up.

When Mama Black walked into the motel room, there was something noticeably different about her. Different in a good way. Mama Black turned to Papa Black in that small, dark motel room and said, nearly screaming, "The church took up an offering for us and gave us $1000!!! I was not expecting it. They heard about our situation with the fire and the Pastor did an offering and gave us $1,000." Mama Black was so excited that she didn't even care if the motel neighbors heard her.

Papa Black was just as excited. In his own serious and masculine way, he replied, "What?!?! Aw, man. Wow! I'm so grateful!"

My siblings and I were too young to understand what was going on. All we knew was that Mama Black returned from church happy and excited. We hadn't seen her like that since before the fire. This was the beginning of Mama Black's trust in God. Mama Black always had a good moral compass but her experience at church helped her begin her walk with God.

Papa and Mama Black knew this was an opportunity for a fresh and new start for our family. They decided to use the money as a deposit to get an apartment. Papa and Mama Black were so excited.

Mama Black called her parents. Mama Black spoke to Nana Eve and Grandpa Millie separately. Her parents were just as excited and happy. Grandpa Millie was especially happy since he had introduced Mama Black and Papa Black to Elder Bluestone which led Mama Black to the Grace and Mercy Baptist Church. Mama Black was so thankful, and everyone could tell. Things were looking up for our family – the Black family.

Papa and Mama Black began their apartment search shortly after receiving the church offering. They wanted to get us out of that motel as soon as possible. It was time for a better life.

After an exhausting and long search, Papa and Mama Black found a three-bedroom apartment that was a great fit for our family. The apartment was in the same building as our old one-bedroom apartment – where I had been born. Papa and Mama Black liked the apartment because it was within walking distance to our schools.

The three-bedroom apartment was on the fourth floor, the very first door at the top of the staircase. When entering the apartment, there was a long hallway that led directly into the living room. Before the living room, there was a room on the right-hand side, that was Meaven's room. Like usual, he had his own room. On the left-hand side was the bathroom. Across from the bathroom was Papa and Mama Black's bedroom. Next to the bathroom was the kitchen. It was small but doable. Walking further down the hallway was a huge living room with five large windows that wrapped around the apartment. The windows added a lot of natural sunlight.

The last room, off the living room, was large and had double doors. That room was for all the girls. Five growing girls in one room. Strength wasn't too excited about sharing a room with her younger sisters. None of the bedrooms had a fire escape so Strength and Meav couldn't get too far in that apartment.

We moved in a few weeks after we received the church donation. We got settled into our apartment and began creating new memories as a family.

CHAPTER 7
A SURPRISE GIFT

We settled in nicely thanks to the Elder Bluestone and the Grace and Mercy Baptist Church for giving us a new start at a better life. Papa Black continued to work while Mama Black stayed home with us.

Mama Black had her routine with us down to a science. She ran a tight ship. Every morning, Mama Black would see Papa Black off to work and would begin her adventure of waking up six kids who had to be at school by 8am.

One day in elementary school, Gracie, Audacious, Joy and I didn't get on the bus after school. I know – what were we thinking?! Somehow, we missed the bus and decided to walk home with a group of our friends. I knew better, but I did it anyway. I felt wrong walking with my younger siblings and friends without letting Mama Black know.

Mama Black called that school and they told her that the bus picked us up and dropped us off at our designated stop. Mama Black's mother instincts kicked in and she went on a hunt! Trying to be cool by walking home with our friends laughing and joking, Mama Black pulled up on us.

When I saw Mama Black, I immediately stopped laughing. She saw us walking up the block towards her. When Mama Black got closer to us, she had the *"Black Mother Look"* on her face.

Mama Black invented the look. The *"Black Mother Look"* was used anywhere, at any given moment to let her child or anybody's child know that they ran the risk of getting a beating, spanking or grabbed up. The look was also meant to remind a child of the power their mother had to take you out and bring you back and realize that you may have lost your ever-loving-mind! All this came from a look – that was Mama Black's look.

Well, that day that's the look Mama Black gave me. Looking at me while hollering, Mama Black said, "Journee, you know you are not supposed to be walking home from school without me. You know better! You should have waited for me or called me from school. I thought something happened to y 'all! Don't you ever do that again!"

I had no rebuttal. I was wrong and too scared to respond. I knew Mama Black was right. The walk home seemed like forever. Mama Black wasn't happy. I learned my lesson that day.

We all made it home safe and sound. Surprisingly, I wasn't on punishment. When we got in the house, Mama Black continued with daily routine. She had all the kids do homework together at the table while she prepared dinner. Mama Black would answer homework questions in between cooking dinner.

Oftentimes, Gracie and I did our homework together since we were in the same grade. We shared the same teachers, friends, and clothes. We were like twins growing up. When in public, people would often ask if we were twins. We would always say yes, although we weren't. It was fun for us to pretend to be twins. We were only 11 months apart so we could pull it off.

Gracie was fun, cool, and silly growing up. She was quiet and shy until she warmed up to you. She always helped with chores around the house. Mama Black would often say to us, "Gracie always washes the dishes without me having to asking her!"

In the Black family household, there was always a sink full of dishes. With two adults and six kids that constantly ate, there was always a dish or two that needed to be washed. Gracie washed them faithfully.

Mama Black would tell Grandpa Millie that Gracie would always wash the dishes. This earned Gracie a couple of extra dollars from Grandpa Millie when he would come around. Gracie was already special to Grandpa Millie. They shared a birthday. Grandpa Millie threw Gracie birthday parties at school to celebrate their birthday. He bought her entire class cake, ice cream and candy.

Since Gracie and I were in the same grade, I would go to Gracie's classroom to enjoy the celebration. Gracie always loved the celebration and looked forward to it every year. Grandpa Millie stopped the school celebrations once she started middle school. When Gracie got too old for the classroom celebrations, Grandpa Millie would give her extra money. Gracie made out well either way!

Mama Black made a big deal for each of us on our birthdays. Mama Black had a special way of making us feel like we were the only child on our birthday.

One year, I wanted a pair of black and white FILA sneakers for school. A few months prior, Mama Black, my siblings and I were in downtown Hopeville shopping for a few things for the house. We stopped in a sneaker store called Sneaker Stadium. I fell in love with these black and white FILAs. I wanted them so bad, but Papa and Mama

Black couldn't afford them. Most of the kids in my class wore name brand sneakers and clothes. Not us. We wore whatever Papa and Mama Black could afford. Pumpkin Seeds sneakers were all Papa and Mama Black could afford. We had them in almost every color.

Mama Black would often remind us of what was more important. She said to me while in the sneaker store, "Your friends' parents don't have six kids to take care of like me and your father." I walked out the store that day without the FILA sneakers.

One day when my siblings and I came home from school on my birthday, Mama Black had a surprise waiting for me. I dropped my book bag and coat in the living room and went to the bathroom. I was in there for a while. When I came out, Mama Black, Strength, Meav, Gracie, Audacious and Joy were all huddled up in that long hallway near our brown wooden china cabinet, a staple in every African American household.

Mama Black said, "Journee, we have a special birthday gift for you. Here it is!" I had no clue what was going on or what the gift could be. Next thing you know, Strength and Mama Black pull a bag from behind them, handing it to me. I immediately knew what the gift was when I saw the FILA bag.

I screamed while jumping up and down, "Ahhhhh! The sneakers!! Thank you, Mommy! You got them! Thank you!" Almost knocking Mama Black down with a hug, I dropped to the floor right in that long hallway after hugging Mama Black. I could not have opened that bag fast enough. I put those FILA sneakers on and instantly felt *da bomb*!

The next day, I wore my birthday sneakers to school and received a lot of compliments from classmates and teachers. I felt so good! And it was because of Mama Black.

CHAPTER 8
PAPA BLACK'S INJURY

Papa Black worked at the Samson Chemical Plant. He enjoyed working there because the people treated him well and genuinely cared about our family. They always did nice things for Papa and Mama Black. Later that week, Papa Black came home in pain.

While on the job, Papa Black was doing his normal routine of making his rounds at the chemical factory plant to ensure no one was left in the building. Someone left one of the gauges open and the chemical fumes leaked and filled the air. The chemical substance was so strong it filtered through his eye protectors and burned his eyes. He rinsed his eyes hoping that would take care of it, but it didn't. The burning had only gotten worse for Papa Black.

Miraculously, Papa Black made it home while driving with chemically burned eyes. Papa Black arrived home in pain and said to Mama Black, "My eyes were burned on the job. And I had on my eye protectors."

Mama Black replied extremely concerned and yelling from shock, "What?! What happened?!"

Papa Black said, "Someone left the gauge open and there was a slow leak that I did not realize until it was too late." Papa Black was fighting to keep his eyes open. They were red and hurting.

Mama Black said, "You should go to the hospital. That is a serious accident!"

My siblings and I knew something was wrong with Papa Black but didn't want to ask too many questions since they looked concerned and worried.

Papa Black tried to tough it. He replied, "I'll be okay. I'll just go to sleep and see how it is in the morning." Papa Black was more concerned about providing financially for his family than his own physical well-being. Overnight, it got worse. Papa Black went back to work the next day although his eyes didn't get better.

Mama Black was concerned and able to persuade Papa Black to go to the hospital to get his eyes checked out. Papa Black finally gave in. He knew this was no ordinary injury. The pain made it extremely difficult to see and drive. Mama Black didn't drive. Papa Black was the only driver in the household.

As the breadwinner and head of the household, Papa Black often put his family before himself. Family meant everything to Papa Black, and he tried his best to show that through working hard.

My siblings and I saw Papa Black as an invincible superhero, not ever getting hurt. It was different for us to see Papa Black vulnerable, hurt, and injured. We were scared for Papa Black. Mama Black explained to us that Papa Black would be okay.

Papa Black finally arrived safely to the hospital and was seen by the emergency room doctor. Barely able to see his way through the doors, Papa Black approached the front desk. Papa Black was a fighter. He wasn't a boxer for nothing.

He reached the receptionist desk and with every ounce of strength left in him, Papa Black said, "My eyes were injured while at work. I can barely keep them open. I feel stinging and a burning sensation. My eyes are red, and my vision is blurry. My eyes feel extremely weak."

The receptionist nurse said, "Hi my name is Nurse Mary Eliza Mahoney. I'm sorry you are feeling this way. Sir, what is your full name?"

Nurse Mary had beautiful features. With an oval face and smooth warm perfect brown skin, Nurse Mary had a full nose and lips, and defined cheekbones. Her eyes reminded you of someone that genuinely cared; they were medium-sized and brown. Her hair was naturally curly and black.

Papa Black said, "Joseph Black."

Nurse Mary said, "How did this injury occur?"

Papa Black said, "While at work, someone left the gauge open and there was a slow leak that I did not realize until it was too late. The chemical substance somehow filtered through my eye protectors and burned my eyes."

Nurse Mary said, "Mr. Black, I am so sorry this happened to you. I know you must be in pain. Is there anyone here with you that can complete your paperwork for you since you can't see?"

Papa Black said, "No. My wife and family are home. It's just me. I didn't want to bring to my wife and all six of my children here."

Nurse Mary replied astonished, "Wow six kids?! You don't even look like you have six children. No problem, Mr. Black. Let's hurry and get you taken care of so that you can get back home to your wife and family. I will help you complete the paperwork. We will get you seen right away!"

Papa Black said while laughing at her comment about having six kids, "Thank you! They keep me going!"

Nurse Mary escorted Papa Black to a hospital bed and had him lie down and rest while waiting to be seen by the ER doctor.

No sooner than Papa Black had laid down, the ER doctor entered the room. Dr. Rebecca Davis Lee Crumpler was a young African American female doctor. Dr. Crumpler really cared for her patients. It was evident in her bedside manner. She took her time, asked the right questions, and repeated things to make sure her patients understood her.

Dr. Crumpler was a beautiful woman. With dark mahogany brown skin, Dr. Crumpler had a powerful presence. She stood 5'9 and had a thick frame. Her hair was short, thick, and natural. She had full lips, a small nose, and wide story-telling eyes.

Dr. Crumpler introduced herself, "Hi Mr. Black. My name is Dr. Rebecca Davis Lee Crumpler. But you can call me Dr. Crump. I understand that your eyes hurt. Can you explain to me what happened?"

Papa Black said, "My eyes were injured while at work. I can barely keep my eyes open. I feel stinging and a burning sensation. My eyes are red, and my vision is blurry. My eyes feel extremely weak."

Dr. Crump replied, "Wow. I'm sorry to hear. I know you are in pain, but let's get you checked out so we can get you home to your wife and six kids. Nurse Mary told me you have six little ones at home! Wow. God Bless you and your wife. They must keep you busy, huh?"

Dr. Crump approached Papa Black with her small black ophthalmoscope.

Papa Black laughed, while still in pain, "Yes. They do keep me busy. With five girls and one boy, there's always an adventure. What can I say?!"

Dr. Crump smiled while looking in Papa Black's burning red eyes. Dr. Crump replied, "I am sure it is always an adventure. Mr. Black, you have suffered some injuries in both your eyes. Based on my assessment and your symptoms, it looks like you've suffered from corneal perforation. What that means is that because the chemical got into your eyes, there is full thickness damage to your cornea. Therefore, you are experiencing these symptoms."

Dr. Crump continued, "I am going to give you some pain-relieving medication, topical antibiotics to reduce the risk of infection, eye drop lubricants to apply to the eye surface to prevent your eyelids from sticking to the cornea as it heals, and anti-inflammatory medication. Since it is bright and sunny outside, we are also going to give you eye patches to wear until your eyes recover."

Taking it all in, Papa Black replied with deep concern in his voice, "Will I lose my eyesight? I have to provide for my family, Dr. Crump."

Dr. Crump paused before answering with a straight face. Dr. Crump changed her facial expression and said with a smile, "Mr. Black, I am happy to say that you will be okay. Your eyes will heal in two weeks and you will be able to see your babies grow up."

Papa Black was happy, relieved, and grateful in that moment. He replied, "Thank you Dr. Crump and Nurse Mary. You both have been helpful and it's great to know that there are doctors that still care, and look like me. Thank you."

Dr. Crump smiled and said, "Okay, Mr. Black! You are all set. Nurse Mary will give you the prescription. I am also going to refer you to an ophthalmologist. Make an appointment in a week to make sure you didn't have any other injuries. If there are other instructions, please follow them. In the meantime, you will need to get someone to drive you home. I don't suggest you take the risk driving. You can leave your car parked here or have someone pick you up and another person to drive your car. Be well, Mr. Black."

"Thank you, Dr. Crump. I appreciate your help," Papa Black replied.

Papa Black was able to make it to Nurse Mary's desk from the hospital bed. He asked if he could use her phone to call his friend to pick him up. Nurse Mary complied and Papa Black called his best friend Wess. Nurse Mary helped him dial the numbers.

An hour later, Wess arrived with another one of Papa Black's best friend, Raul. Raul was cool, laidback, and chill. He also was married and had 3 children. He was 6'1, mocha brown, and had round black eyes with a distinct mustache and pearly white teeth.

Wess and Raul were Papa Black's best friends for over 20 years. He often hung out with them. They had a strong brotherhood. They helped and supported each other when needed, especially when their families were in need.

Wess and Raul entered the Emergency waiting room and saw Papa Black sitting there with both of his eyes covered with patches. Although Papa Black was still in pain, he felt better.

Wess and Raul walked towards Papa Black. While walking towards him, Wess announced himself in an attempt not to scare him. Wess said, "Joe, it's Wess and Raul here to come and pick you up, man. How ya' feeling, man?" They called him Joe for short.

Raul interjected and said, "Yeah, man. We here for you. Ready to go?"

Papa Black replied, "Hey man! You here too, Raul?! Ah, man. I can't thank y'all enough. I really appreciate y'all, man. This means a lot."

Wess said, "Man, this is what we do. Us Black brothers must stick together. If we don't do it, nobody else will be there for us." Raul just smiled in agreement.

Raul said, "Joe, I'll drive your car back to the house and Wess is going to drive you home in his car. I'll follow y'all to the house." Papa Black handed Raul his car keys.

Papa Black replied, "Okay. I appreciate y'all. Thanks, man."

Wess and Raul helped Papa Black out the chair and began walking him out the door. Before Papa Black left the waiting room area, he yelled to Nurse Mary, "Thank you, Nurse Mary! Thank you for your help today. You take care."

Nurse Mary replied with a smile, "You're welcome, Mr. Black. You be well!"

Papa Black had his arms hanging around Wess and Raul's necks as they walked him to the car. Thankfully, Papa Black, Wess and Raul were all around the same height. It made getting Papa Black to the car easy.

Papa Black got into the car with Wess and Raul drove Papa Black's car. The hospital wasn't too far from the house. It only took them 15 minutes. Before dropping Papa Black off at home, they picked up his prescription. Papa Black had everything he needed before going home.

When they arrived, Raul pulled Papa Black's car in his parking spot located behind the building. Wess parked in front of the building and waited for Raul. Raul arrived and they helped Papa Black out the car. They walked him inside the building and up four flights of stairs. The building didn't have an elevator, just stairs.

When they finally arrived at the apartment door Mama Black was waiting for him. Mama Black wasn't sure what her husband would look like, so she made sure she remained calm while waiting. Wess and Raul walked Papa Black inside the apartment, in his room and put him on the bed.

Before leaving, Mama Black said, "I thank you both so much. Joseph is blessed to have you as friends. We couldn't have done this without the two of you. Thank you."

Raul replied, "No problem. That's what we are here for."

Wess co-signed saying, "Lor, we are family, and this is our brother. We got each other. I know he would do the same for us. Let us know if you need anything."

Mama Black tried to hold back the tears, but they came streaming down her chocolate golden brown face. Wess hugged Mama Black assuring her that everything was going to be okay. Wess and Raul said their good-byes to Papa Black and left.

I was very worried about Papa Black. We had never seen Papa Black like that before. He had on eye patches and needed help from Mama Black. Although Dr. Crumpler said that he would be fine, Mama Black knew that there was a possibility that things could get worse.

When Papa Black got settled in, he laid down and slept. Mama Black cooked him some fried chicken, rice, and peas the night. Chicken was Papa Black's favorite thing to eat. Papa Black ate in the room while my siblings and I ate at the kitchen table. It felt different not having Papa Black at the dinner table.

It was a somber night. We were on our best behavior. If we did argue and fight with each other, we did it quietly so that Papa and Mama Black didn't hear us. We didn't quite understand all that was going on, but we knew we didn't want to stress our parents out.

The next day, Papa Black felt some relief. While this was a good thing, Papa couldn't go back to work for a while. This meant no income. This was added pressure for Papa and Mama Black.

The following week, Papa Black was seeing and feeling a little bit better. He drove himself to the ophthalmologist. Thankfully, the doctor's office was only five minutes away from the house, so he didn't have far to go.

Papa Black finally arrived and was immediately seen by Dr. Luther. Dr. Luther was a Caucasian middle-aged man with blue eyes, red freckles, and brunette hair. His 6'9 height made one think he could be a basketball player and not a doctor. He was intelligent, professional and knew his stuff.

"Mr. Black, what brings you in today?" Dr. Luther said enthusiastically.

Papa Black said, "Well, my eyes were burned while on the job. I had on my eye protectors. Someone left the gauge open and it was a slow leak that I did not realize until it was too late. The chemical substance somehow filtered through my eye protectors and burned my eyes. I went to the emergency room last week and she recommended I come see you in a week to make sure there weren't any additional injuries. So, here I am."

"Wow, did you come here by yourself today?" Dr. Luther replied.

"Yes. It's just me. My wife had to stay home with our six kids. Plus, the drive was only five minutes away," Papa Black replied.

"Wowzers! Did you say six kids?! You guys are like the Brady Bunch, huh!?! I thought I had my hands full. My wife and I only have two kids: a boy and girl. I take my hat off to you, Mr. Black!"

Papa Black was never fazed by the comments people would make after he told them he had six kids. Papa Black was proud to say he and Mama Black had six children. Mainly because no one would ever think he and Mama Black had six little ones. It was fun for Papa Black to see people's reactions.

Papa Black chuckled before answering, "Thank you, sir. I guess we are the Black version of the Brady Bunch – the Black Bunch!"

They both laughed.

Dr. Luther returned to the matter at hand. He said, "Mr. Black, I'm going to check your eyes using two devices to make sure there aren't any further damages beyond the surface of your cornea. We are going to have you sit on this chair, rest your chin and forehead on this bar and look at the phoropter. After this exam, we are going to perform a corneal topography – which is a computerized diagnostic test. We are administering these tests to see if there are any curvatures in your cornea and to observe its current shape."

Papa Black replied, "Okay, Doc. I don't understand what you are saying, but okay."

Dr. Luther replied, "In other words, the cornea – the front window of your eye – is responsible for about 70 percent of the eye's focusing power. An eye with normal vision has an evenly rounded cornea. If the cornea is too flat, too steep, or unevenly curved, less than perfect vision results."

"Understood. That makes sense. Thank you," Papa Black replied.

Dr. Luther examined Papa Black's eyes in silence. With his eyes were still slightly burning, Papa Black wondered what was going on behind those machines and in Dr. Luther's head. Dr. Luther was able to capture some adequate images and give Papa Black his results. Dr. Luther stepped out the room and returned 10 minutes later.

Returning to the room, Dr. Luther said with relief while sitting on a gray stool with wheels, "Mr. Black, you are one lucky man. Fortunately, you will not lose your vision. Your cornea was slightly flattened by eight percent. Your body has the capacity to heal itself. The cornea can recover from minor injuries on its own. Your healthy cells will eventually slide over and patch the injury before it causes infection or affects your vision. That's why your eyes have been getting better. Had you not had your eye protectors on, it could have been worse. The deeper the injury to the cornea, the longer it will take to heal. God was on your side."

Papa Black replied, "Thank you for the thorough explanation. I'm not a lucky man.

I'm a blessed one. If I can't see, I can't work. If I can't work, then I can't provide for my family. I am thankful."

"Yes, you are, Mr. Black. You, your wife, and children are blessed. Listen, I am going to write you a note so that you can rest and stay home for another week, and completely heal before going back to work" said Dr. Luther.

"Thank you, Dr. Luther. I thank you," Papa Black replied.

They shook hands and Papa Black grabbed his note and left.

Papa Black returned home safe and sound and told Mama Black the great news. Papa Black's spirit was lifted hearing that he would return to work soon.

Papa Black called his job and informed them when he would return to work. They were very understanding and were glad to hear that Papa Black was doing well.

This was the most time Papa Black spent at home. It was different but good for us to be around Papa Black.

CHAPTER 9
RESILIENCE

Papa Black made a full recovery from his injury and finally returned to work. Unfortunately, Papa and Mama Black fell behind on the household bills. He didn't want to file a lawsuit because he felt that wasn't the right thing to do. He was loyal to the company. So, Mama Black had to find work to make ends meet.

Since Mama Black dropped us off and picked us up from school every day, the entire school knew who Mama Black was. She was the only Mama that had six children that were all close in age. Mama Black would faithfully stand outside the school ten minutes before dismissal, waiting for us to get out of school.

After a while, the school administration team grew to know Mama Black very well. They liked Mama Black's spirit, personality, and character. She volunteered as a lunch aid at the Harriet Tubman Elementary School. Gracie Audacious, Joy and I attended that school. Strength and Meaven attended different schools since they were older.

Mama Black worked with other Black women in the cafeteria preparing breakfast and lunch for the kids. Mama Black wasn't above helping. Serving was a part of her moral compass. She knew so many people helped her and her family in their time of need, so it was natural for Mama Black to help. She was a true servant.

Volunteering for six months, Mama Black had developed a beautiful, genuine relationship with two lunch aides that worked at the Harriet Tubman Elementary School.

Ms. Greenbridge and Ms. Cherriblossom were brown like Mama Black, but shorter than her. Ms. Greenbridge had ebony colored skin with soft round eyes and long lashes. She was short and petite but strong in her presence and cared for those around her. Her hair was jet black and her smile was contagious.

Ms. Cherriblossom was sassy, and fun, but didn't play. She knew how to make Mama Black laugh. Her sensual brown complexion reminded you of Lupita Nyong-o's soft earth tone skin. Ms. Cherriblossom also was petite with a curvy frame.

Ms. Greenbridge, Ms. Cherriblossom and Mama Black all became the best of friends. Ms. Greenbridge and Ms. Cherriblossom also had kids who attended the same school as Strength, Meaven, Gracie, Audacious, Joy and I. Over time, Strength and

Meav had become friends with Ms. Greenbridge's daughters while Gracie and I became friends with Ms. Cherriybloom's daughter.

There was an opening for a lunch aide position at the school. Ms. Greenbridge gave Mama Black all the tips she needed to know for the interview. Ms. Greenbridge and Ms. Cherriblossom wanted to see Mama Black and her family succeed. Mama Black appreciated her friendship with them.

Interview day came and Mama Black remembered all that Ms. Greenbridge had shared with her. Mama Black walked into Principal Stanley's office with confidence, charisma, and boldness. Mama Black knew that God was on her side and couldn't fail her or her family.

Mama walked in Principal Stanley's office a volunteer. An hour later, Mama Black walked out a lunch aide at the Harriet Tubman Elementary School! Mama couldn't wait to thank the ladies and share the good news with them.

With a neutral face, Mama Black walked into the cafeteria where Ms. Greenbridge and Ms. Cherriblossom were. Ms. Greenbridge couldn't wait to hear the news! She was more excited than Mama Black was.

"So, so how did it go?!" Ms. Greenbridge proclaimed. Ms. Cherriblossom stood quiet in the background waiting to hear Mama Black's response.

With a poker face, Mama Black said, "Well, y'all this will be my last day here…"

Mama paused. Ms. Greenbridge said, "Ohhhh, no! They should have given you that position. I'm going to say something to them!"

Mama immediately interjected, "…as a volunteer! I'm officially a lunch aide! They hired me!"

Ms. Greenbridge couldn't help but bust out in laughter, "Mrs. Black, you know what…I'm going to get you. Come here and give me a hug! Congratulations! I am so happy you are officially a part of our team."

Ms. Cherriblossom wasn't as easily fooled. She said, "I knew she was lying when she walked in her talking about her last day here. We knew you would get it. Congratulations!"

Mama Black was so excited. She knew this would help Papa Black and her family.

Later that afternoon, Mama Black picked up the kids from school as usual. She had a different stride in her walk. She felt happy and thankful that she could contribute to her family in a different way.

I felt a different type of energy coming from Mama Black that afternoon. I knew it was good energy, but Mama Black didn't tell us that she had gotten the job yet.

Papa Black arrived home that evening from work right before Mama Black served dinner. We sat at the dinner table while Mama Black made everyone's plate, including Papa Black's. Dinner time for my siblings and I was fun and silly. We used this opportunity to secretly make fun of and laugh at one another.

Without fail, Papa and Mama Black would always have to tell us, "Don't talk with food in your mouth."

When this happened, we would giggle underneath our breath so that Papa and Mama Black couldn't hear us. When we just couldn't hold it in, we would bust out in laughter.

Dinner time was fun, intimate, and tight for the Black family, my family. Typically, kitchen and dining room tables were made for a family of six. Very rarely were there tables made for a family of eight. If it were made, Papa and Mama Black couldn't afford it. So, we made do with what they had. Papa and Mama Black somehow always made it work with the six of us.

When everyone received their plates, Mama Black said, "I have an announcement for everyone tonight." Immediately everyone stopped playing with each other to tune into what Mama Black had to say.

Before getting her announcement out, Audacious said, "I hope it's not another baby! It's already too many of us!"

Typical Audacious turned something funny during a moment of seriousness. Everyone couldn't help but burst into laughter. Even Papa Black laughed. But after realizing what it would mean to go from having six kids to seven, Papa Black immediately stopped laughing.

Papa Black said with a straight face, fork in hand and peaked ears, "You're not pregnant, are you, Lor?!"

Mama Black paused for a moment and crossed her arms. We all looked at Mama Black with intensity.

Mama Black sarcastically replied, "No, silly. I'm not pregnant. I got the position as a lunch aide at Harriet Tubman Elementary School!"

Journee and her siblings wiped their foreheads in relief while Papa Black sat back in his chair and dropped his fork on his plate saying, "Now that's good news! Congratulations, Lorraine! You've earned it."

My siblings and I responded saying, "Congratulations, Mama! We are happy for you."

Gracie asked, "Is that why you were so happy when you picked us up from school today?"

Mama Black replied in a sweet and loving voice, "Yes, baby. That is why. Mr. Stanley gave me the job on the spot, and I start tomorrow. God worked it out!"

Mama Black was so happy and so was our family. This would be a great benefit for us as a family, considering that we were practically starting over due to the fire almost a year ago.

CHAPTER 10
PAPA AND MAMA
BLACK'S ANNIVERSARY

Mama Black's position as a lunch aide worked out perfectly because she was able to work decent hours without it interfering with her pick-up and drop-off time. It was the perfect opportunity for Mama Black.

The school year was wrapping up and the summer months were near. We loved the summertime because it meant no homework, more play time outside with our neighbors and friends, swimming pools, ice cream and sleeping in.

Black loved all kinds of music but during the summertime in the 90's, he repeatedly played Summertime by Will Smith. This song always reminded me that school was out, and the summer months were approaching. Papa

My family and I lived right next to a park before it was turned into a football stadium. Papa and Mama Black would let us play in the park for several hours during the summer.

Papa and Mama Black had strict rules for us when we were at the park. We had to stay inside the park where Mama Black could see us from the window. We also had to stick together and not leave one another. That meant if one of us had to go to bathroom, we all had to do go even if we didn't have to use the bathroom. No one could go to the corner store without Papa or Mama Black. Lastly, once the streetlights came on, it was time to come in the house. This was how Papa and Mama Black Family kept their family safe.

This summer was a little different for my family. It was Papa and Mama Black's 9th wedding anniversary, and my siblings and I wanted to help them celebrate it. It wasn't often Papa and Mama Black went out on dates. They couldn't afford it. It was extremely hard trying to find someone to babysit six kids that were silly, comical, and energetic.

So, Papa and Mama Black celebrated with their six kids. We tried to create a romantic dinner date for Papa and Mama Black's anniversary. We each had a role in the celebration.

Strength and Meaven helped with cooking and cleaning the dishes (Mama really did the cooking, but they helped), Gracie and I were the waitresses, Audacious and Joy were in charge of setting up the silverware and cups, and selecting and playing the music. Luther Vandross and The Whispers were Papa and Mama Black's favorite singers, so that's what we played.

Gracie, Audacious, Joy and I made the decorations, too. Using orange construction paper, we created a big sign that was hung on the wall near the table Papa and Mama Black would have dinner at. The sign said, "Happy 9th Anniversary Papa and Mama. We love you: Strength, Meaven, Journee, Gracie, Audacious and Joy." It was fun putting it together.

Papa and Mama Black loved seafood. They celebrated with lobster, shrimp, broccoli, corn, and Sprite. Mama Black loved Sprite; it was her favorite. When Mama finished cooking dinner, she finally let us take over and host their dinner.

Papa and Mama Black sat at the table in the living room and waited to be served by their six children. Strength made Mama Black's plate while Meaven made Papa Black's plate. Gracie and I didn't have aprons but used one of Mama Black's kitchen towels to rest over our forearms while bringing out their dinner plates. We really tried giving them the exquisite restaurant atmosphere. We also came back to pour their Sprite in a fancy glass.

Papa and Mama Black were so patient. We were so excited to serve them. Every 10 minutes Gracie and I would approach Papa and Mama Black asking if they needed anything. The answer was always, "No, we are just fine."

They didn't even make us go to our rooms. We all enjoyed celebrating Papa and Mama Black's 9th anniversary that evening.

Summer was ending and the school year was about to begin. Mama Black continued her job as a lunch aide while Papa Black continued working at the Samson Chemical Plant. Papa Black made a full recovery. My siblings and I went back to school.

CHAPTER 11
GOD, CHURCH & FAMILY

Mama Black had gotten more involved at Grace and Mercy Baptist Church - the same church as Elder Bluestone and his family. Mama Black would attend Christian Growth Class on Mondays, Bible Study on Wednesdays, and regular church service on Sunday mornings. Rev. Thomas Watkins was the Pastor of the church and led the classes.

Grace and Mercy Baptist Church had a membership of 350 intergenerational members. Members ranged from newborn to 90 years old. It was an intimate and close-knit church. The more Mama Black attended, the more she began to grow in the word of God. She desired to learn and teach her family the ways of God.

Papa Black couldn't attend that often. He was either working late or tired from a long work week. So, my siblings and I often accompanied Mama Black to church service every Sunday and sometimes Christian Growth Class or Bible Study.

Mama Black loved attending Grace and Mercy Baptist Church. She felt a sense of connection with the ministry and some of the women there. When Mama Black talked to Grandpa Millie, she shared her experiences at Grace and Mercy Baptist Church. Grandpa Millie was elated to hear that things were going well with the church and Elder Bluestone.

Overtime, Mama Black had developed a sisterly friendship with Elder Bluestone's wife, Deaconess Bluestone and Rev. Watkins's wife, First Lady Watkins.

Deaconess Bluestone stood 5'11, had luxurious honey-brown long straight hair, fawn-brown skin complexion, small hazel brown eyes, and full lips. Her personality was gentle and tender. She was a strong woman. She and Elder Bluestone had four kids together, so Deaconess Bluestone understood what it was like to raise a big family. She and Mama Black had that in common.

Elder and Deaconess Bluestone were a great couple. They genuinely loved each other and shared similar passions. They treated people with the love of Christ and helped those in need. Their care and support for Papa and Mama was genuine.

Elder and Deaconess Bluestone had four teenage kids, two boys and two girls. All their names began with a K: Kaison, Khase, Kaydence and Kimber Bluestone. They were an athletic family; they loved sports and excelled in sports. They were also musically inclined. It was obvious that Deaconess Bluestone was blessed with the gift of music. She was a talented organist and would get Mama Black going every Sunday.

Every time Deaconess Bluestone touched the organ keys, Mama Black would jump out of her seat and cut the church rug. Literally. Mama Black would dance, dance. Mama Black didn't play when it came to her church songs. Most church folk would catch the Holy Spirit and shout. Not Mama Black. She would just dance how David danced in the Bible. Some would even argue that Mama Black danced better than David. It was obvious that Mama Black loved dancing. Wherever there was music, space, and a rug, she danced.

Mama Black had also become close with First Lady Watkins. They were like sister-friends. Now, First Lady Watkins was a woman of distinction. Her fragrance, swag, confidence, and personality were captivating. She had rich cacao-brown soft skin, small light brown almond-shaped eyes, and thick silky coils. She often wore her hair in twists that would hang between her shoulder blades and bounce as she walked up the aisle to her seat. Every Sunday, I couldn't wait to see what she wore because First Lady Watkins was an elegant and chic dresser. Her afro-centric style and wisdom was intriguing and made any young girl want to mimic her style and effortless grace. First Lady Watkins was down to earth and accepted everyone. She was all that a church congregation could ask for in a First Lady.

Mama Black admired both Deaconess Bluestone and First Lady Watkins. Those were her girls and they loved and respected Mama Black, too. While Mama Black was new to her walk with Christ, Deaconess Bluestone and First Lady Watkins embraced her and my family. We all had become one big family.

Since Mama Black didn't drive and Papa Black couldn't always drop us off at church, we were often picked up by the church van or by Elder Bluestone. After a while, all of the neighbors knew that when they saw that 15-passenger tan van that had *Grace and Mercy Baptist Church – Rev. Watkins, Senior Pastor* plastered on the side, it was there to pick up the Black Family. We took up most of the seats in the van. There were so many of us!

Every Sunday before getting on the van, Mama Black would have her "mama talk" with us. She would often say while only moving her lips, "Y'all better be on your best behavior. Don't ask me for anything. No, you cannot go to the corner store. After Sunday school is over, come right upstairs to the sanctuary. No arguing with each other and you will sit your behinds quiet and still while Pastor Watkins is preaching. Y'all will not embarrass me. Do y'all understand?!"

We all answered in unison, "Yes, Mama."

Mama Black didn't play. She had no problem pinching our little legs if we started acting up. In fact, we knew when Mama Black was upset with us because she would give us a look while folding her lips together. We straightened up when Mama made that face. She found a way to keep us in order when Papa Black wasn't around.

It was routine for us to go to church with Mama Black. We had to get up extra early to make it to Sunday school. Yup, Mama Black had all six of us in Sunday school. Waking up six little human beings for school, let alone for church was a struggle. Mama Black didn't care how much of a struggle it was getting us up every morning. She was committed to attending church every Sunday.

My siblings and I enjoyed going to church but didn't like staying in church for hours. Like most Black churches, attending church was like a 9-5 job. Once you were there, expect to be there for a longggg time! Eventually, going to church had become fun for us. There were other youth our age that we were close to. It really was a close-knit church.

Overtime, my siblings and I had become more involved in various ministries at Grace and Mercy Baptist Church. Well, mainly, me, Gracie, Audacious and Joy. Strength and Meaven weren't involved but did attend church every Sunday. They weren't really into that. Mama Black didn't force them to participate in activities. But, Gracie, Audacious, Joy and I all joined the youth choir.

Deaconess Bluestone would often play for the youth and young adult choir. Although they were older than us, Elder and Deaconess Bluestone's children were a part of the choir as well. Kimber, the youngest of the Bluestone family, would direct the choir.

Every fourth Sunday was Youth Sunday. The church loved to hear the youth choir sing. Two of Mama Black's favorite songs to hear by the Youth Choir were *Genesis* and *He Reigns*. Mama Black would really cut a church rug when she heard those two songs. It gave her hope, strength and joy for her and her family.

Like Mama Black, I especially enjoyed going to church and singing in the choir. It had become a safe, fun space for us at such a young age. That's where I gained a strong understanding of church and God, and the foundation that was being set in my life.

One Sunday, I heard the lesson differently than I normally did. This time, I felt God in her heart. Sister Johnson, who taught Sunday school for the younger kids, was a gentle and sweet woman. It was obvious that her walk with Christ was strong and unshakeable. She took joy in her ministry and sharing God's promises with the youth of the next generation. That's what she did for me that Sunday morning.

Sister Johnson had honey-brown skin and small gray eyes. She was a thick and attractive woman but often dressed ultra-conservatively. She was known for her Jheri curl – that was a popular hairstyle often worn in the black community in the 80's and early 90's. Every Sunday, Sister Johnson would wear a satin-polyester long shirt, with a navy blue polyester pleated skirt, tan stockings, and black shoes with a kitten heel. Her nails were always nicely filed and polished. She wore a gold ring on her pinkie finger and a gold-plated watch on her wrist. Sister Johnson loved to wear her pink Sophia Loren Zyloware Vintage eyeglass frames. When Sister Johnson would walk across the classroom floor, you would hear her stockings rubbing together. When Sunday school was over, she would always give me a peppermint.

The lesson Sister Johnson gave was always filled with love and strong conviction. I had always wondered if she met Jesus personally because of how she spoke of Him. Sister Johnson didn't just know of Jesus, she *knew* Him. Even at a young age, I wanted that for myself.

Sister Johnson always started her lesson with a prayer and would begin teaching from the children's biblical workbook. Salvation was the topic that Sunday morning. Sister Johnson would often stop her lessons to ask questions to make sure we understood the message.

Sister Johnson said, "Salvation is to be saved by God from the consequences of sins or the wrong that we do."

A student in the class raised their hand and asked, "What does salvation mean, Sister Johnson?"

Excited to see the students engaged in her lesson, Sister Johnson smiled and answered, "Salvation means deliverance, to rescue or save."

The student that asked the question seemed to have better understood Sister Johnson's statement.

I asked, "Sister Johnson, so what are we being saved from? I am not in any danger or harm so how can I be saved if I'm already safe?" I was a very witty and smart little girl.

Sister Johnson wasn't expecting that question, so she answered the best that she could.

She replied, "Well Journee, that is a very good question. Technically, no, we are not in danger in this moment because we all are safe and well in this building. But this is a different type of danger. This is the kind of danger that can keep us *from* God's family or keep us *within* God's family. Similarly, if we make wrong decisions and get in trouble with the law that can keep us away from our mommy, daddy, and family. But, when we make the right decisions, we stay within our homes and with our families."

Another student blurted out, "Oh, I ain't going to no jail so I'm gonna listen to my mommy and daddy." Sister Johnson couldn't contain her laughter, so she let out a good chuckle before responding.

Then she replied, "No we don't want any of you in jail." But Jesus is the only one that can save us so we need Him in our hearts; we need a relationship with Him so we can stay within his family."

Then I asked, "Well how can we get Jesus to save us?"

"Great question, Journee!" Sister Johnson continued, "Well, John 3:16 – 18 tell us that: *For God so loved the world that he gave his one and only son, that whoever believes in him shall not perish but have eternal life. For God did not send his Son into the world to condemn the world, but to save the world through him (NIV). '"*

The students in the class seemed to have understood the message Sister Johnson shared that morning. Sister Johnson was so excited. She continued the lesson saying, "Giving your heart to Jesus Christ is important, boys and girls. If you desire to accept Jesus in your heart and you desire to be in God's family, raise your hand."

I was the only one that raised my hand. Class was just about over. Sister Johnson prayed the class out and kept me after class for a few extra minutes.

Sister Johnson uttered in her sweet and calming voice, "Journee, I saw that you raised your hand to accept Jesus Christ in your heart during class. Do you want to accept Christ in your heart today?"

I innocently replied, "Yes."

Sister Johnson said, "Wonderful. I am going to say a prayer and I want you to repeat after me, okay?"

I replied, "Okay." She grabbed my hand; we bowed our heads and closed our eyes.

Sister Johnson said and I repeated after her: "Dear God, I thank you for my life, my family and your Son Jesus Christ for dying on the cross for my sins. Jesus, I acknowledge you as my personal Lord and Savior. Come into my heart and live within me. I believe that you've heard my prayer and have accepted my salvation. In Jesus' Name, Amen."

Sister Johnson hugged me so tightly that I couldn't breathe for a moment. Some of Sister Johnson's Jheri Curl juice got on my cheek, too. It was okay because I knew Sister Johnson was a nice teacher.

A few minutes later, Sister Johnson pulled Mama Black to the side in the vestibule right before Sunday morning church service started. Sister Johnson explained to Mama Black that I had accepted Jesus Christ as my and Savior, and that we had prayed together. Mama Black was surprised yet excited. She wasn't sure how bringing her babies to Grace and Mercy Baptist Church would influence but, it was going in the right direction. At least that's what Mama Black had thought, hoped, and prayed.

Mama Black turned to me and hugged me tightly. She gave the best hugs. She was the best hugger in church and in our family. I loved Mama Black's hugs. Mama Black was so proud.

Later that evening, my family and I had Sunday dinner together, like usual. That night she made spaghetti; it was quick, easy, tasty and a filling meal. Sometimes Mama Black added sugar to her spaghetti. When Mama Black did cook, it was hard keeping leftovers with six kids and two adults. Mama Black preferred cooking for multiple days so she didn't have to cook every day. Eating leftovers was always an option in the Black Family household.

During dinner, my siblings and I continued with our normal routine, jokes and laughter. When the joking and laughing got out of hand, Papa Black would almost always shut it down by saying, "Don't talk with food in your mouth. Be quiet and eat your food."

We would giggle quietly while looking at each other and trying not to get caught by Papa Black.

After cooking over a hot stove, Mama Black didn't have the energy to tell us to be quiet or stop playing around. So, most of the time she just tried to eat in peace and enjoy her meal.

Moments passed by and Audacious finished her drink. Audacious asked Mama Black, "Can I have some more to drink?"

Before answering, Mama Black looked over at Audacious's plate to determine whether she would allow her to get something more to drink. Mama Black had a rule: eat your food first and then you can have a drink. Mama Black was pleased with the small amount of food Audacious had left to eat.

Mama Black cautiously replied, "Yes, go ahead."

So Audacious got up from her chair, grabbed her cup and headed to the refrigerator. She pulled out the clear pitcher that had the cherry Kool-Aid in it that Mama Black had made while preparing dinner.

Audacious sat her cup on the counter and poured her cherry Kool-Aid. She took a quick sip before putting the pitcher back inside of the refrigerator. Audacious walked back to the table very carefully, giggling for no reason. She was silly and always ready to have fun. She took another sip while walking back to the table and accidently hit her toe on Papa Black's chair while passing him to get to her seat. Audacious immediately dropped the cup and screamed. When she dropped the cup, her cup of cherry Kool-Aid flung all over Papa Black's face, ear, shirt, and shoulder.

Papa Black looked upset. Audacious frantically runs out the kitchen because she knew Papa Black was going to get her. Mama Black, me and my siblings knew he wouldn't. We just looked at Papa Black.

Shortly after, Papa Black busted out in laughter saying, "Hahaha! That was funny!"

When Papa Black said that, he gave permission to go ahead and laugh. Whew! Everyone started cracking up. When Audacious heard everyone laughing, she peaked her head in the kitchen and saw everyone laughing, even Papa Black!

Mama Black said while laughing, "Girl, get your behind in here and finish your food. Your father is fine." Papa Black was wiping his face and still laughing. Everyone continued to laugh while Audacious ate the rest of her spaghetti.

After dinner, Gracie washed the dishes and Mama Black helped dry them. Everyone went to bed and prepared for a new week ahead.

CHAPTER 12
EVICTION NOTICE

Papa and Mama Black were always the first ones to get up in the morning. That morning, Mama Black saw something on the floor near the front door when she looked down the hallway. She said to herself, "I tell these kids all the time to pick up after themselves. They don't listen!" Mama Black walked towards the front door and picked up what was on the floor.

She opened the white envelope and it was an eviction notice. Papa and Mama Black were behind on rent and the apartment complex served them with eviction papers. Mama Black's heart sunk to her stomach. She immediately walked back into the bedroom where Papa Black was.

"Joe, look at what I've found. They must have slipped it under the door last night or early this morning," Mama Black said while closing the door behind her and whispering so that we couldn't hear her.

Papa Black replied, "I thought they were going to give us an extension. I'll stop by the leasing office before work and talk to them."

Mama Black had a look of worry and fear in her eyes. Her mind went back to those motel rooms that we stayed in just two years prior. Mama Black simply said, "Okay."

Papa Black left for work and Mama Black continued with her morning routine. She woke us up for school. It was like pulling teeth trying to wake up six kids. Mama would wake us up two at a time. There was only one bathroom so only two could fit at a time. Mama Black got everyone out the house and off to school.

After dropping us off at school, Mama Black arrived to work but not like her normal self. She was worried for her family and didn't know what would happen if she and Papa Black didn't come up with $780 dollars in back pay for rent. They had 30 days to come up with the balance. That was a lot for Papa and Mama Black. Papa Black was out of work for a couple of weeks and was unable to receive worker's compensation. They just didn't have it.

Mama Black was having all these thoughts while at work. Papa Black was too. The end of the day came, and Mama Black completed her work shift and picked us up from school. We arrived home and immediately started our homework while Mama Black prepared dinner. That night it was hot dogs and French fries. Mama Black didn't feel like cooking a big meal with all that was going on.

Papa Black arrived just in time for dinner. When we sat together for dinner that night, it was a somber evening. Papa and Mama Black were quieter than usual. My siblings and I felt something going on but didn't know what exactly. So, we didn't have our usual sibling banter because they felt the heaviness.

Dinner was done, but we had a few minutes before Mama Black would tell us to go to bed. So, Strength, Meaven, Gracie, Audacious, Joy and I went to Meaven's room after dinner. When something was going on, we would always come together to talk. We called it a *Sibling Meeting*. The *Sibling Meeting* could happen at any point of the day, anyone could call the meeting for whatever reason and everyone had an opportunity to speak. Everyone's voice was heard. And the ultimate rule was: *No Parents Allowed* and no one could share with Papa and Mama Black.

Our *Siblings Meetings* gave us the chance to build our siblingship while talking about things that were important to us. Strength was the eldest, so she started the meeting off. "So, what do y'all think is going on with Papa and Mama?" said Strength.

Often quiet but observant, Joy said, "Maybe Papa lost his job." Everyone looked at Joy and nodded in agreement.

"That maybe it, Joy. That was good guess," replied Meaven.

Audacious said, "Well if Papa losses his job, what does that mean? Will we have to live in that smelly motel again? I don't like being there. It smelled like rotten baby diapers in those hallways." Of course, everyone bust out laughing, including Audacious.

Gracie chimed in and said while laughing, "Yeah, Audacious. I don't want to go back there either!"

Journee replied, "I don't know what it is, but Papa and Mama seemed a bit stressed about whatever it is."

Strength and Meaven agree, "Yeah. They did look stressed."

A second later, Mama Black interjected. She yelled, "Strength, Meaven, Journee, Gracie, Audacious and Joy, let's gooo! It's time to go to bed."

Everyone matched Mama Black's voice volume replying, "Okay, Mama!"

The *Sibling Meeting* was adjourned, and the girls went to their room.

Little did we know, Papa and Mama Black had meetings of their own. Papa and Mama Black talked. "So, what did they say at the leasing office? Are they going to give us an extension?" Mama Black asked while closing their bedroom door.

Papa Black sat on the bed and let out a deep sigh, "Lorraine, they said we have 30 days to come with the outstanding balance on top of next month's rent or else we will have to leave."

There was a long and silent pause between Papa and Mama Black. They didn't know what to say to each other. There was fear, frustration, and loss of hope. With six kids to feed and clothe, a combined salary of $21,500 dollars, car insurance and other household amenities, Papa and Mama Black were poor. They just didn't have it.

Having fears of being homeless again, Mama Black said, "Well, what are we going to do, Joseph?! I don't want to us to have to live in a motel again! We just can't do it!"

"I know, Lorraine. I don't want that for us, either. We will figure this out." Papa Black replied.

Mama Black sat on the bed and put her head on Papa Black's shoulder. They sat there in silence. They eventually went to bed.

It was finally the weekend, and no one had to think about getting up early. It was a stressful week for Papa and Mama Black. My siblings and I didn't know what was going on but we felt something wasn't right. Everyone felt stressed, but this didn't stop us from our normal Saturday routines. Mama Black didn't bother waking us up on Saturday mornings. She allowed us to sleep in sometimes because of the long week. Plus, it meant that Mama Black had a little more peace and quiet to herself without six kids fussing, asking her for something or just being up under her. Mama Black loved and adored her kids, but she enjoyed having her peaceful moments as well.

Even though Papa Black stayed home some Saturdays, my siblings and I would always go to Mama Black if we wanted or needed something.

Mama Black would often say, "Why are you asking me?! Ask your father! He is here too!"

We knew Papa Black would probably say no, so asking Mama Black was easier. Plus, we spent most of our time with Mama Black, so we were used to asking her.

Papa Black was a tough shell to crack. He would say no first and then maybe give a "yes" later. So, we knew they had a better shot at asking Mama Black for what we wanted and needed.

One thing that Papa Black always said yes to was us doing household chores. Papa and Mama Black didn't play when it came to household chores. We washed dishes and windows, swept, vacuumed, cleaned the toilet, tub, stove, and oven, dusted the mini blinds, polished the television, tables, and even the china cabinet. Because there were six of us Saturday cleanings didn't take long. One kid per room was Mama Black's system. Afterwards, we watched television or played video games.

Sunday morning came and Mama Black went back to her routine of waking us up for Sunday school. The church van was outside at 8:30am sharp and Mama Black did not like having the church van waiting for us. When everyone wasn't ready at the same time, Mama Black would send Gracie and Meaven downstairs because they were usually the first ones ready. Meaven would tell the church van driver that Mama Black and the rest of us are right behind them. The church van driver was always nice and patient. He would often reply with a smile, "Okay, no problem!"

When Mama Black and the rest of us finished getting ready, we would fly down four flights of ceramic stairs. When Mama Black got in the van, she was very apologetic to the driver and the two elder women for having them wait. One of the church women was very understanding and was often happy to see us. The other church mother didn't want to hear it. She barely acknowledged us. Mama Black noticed it but didn't say anything about it.

My siblings and I would make our way to the back of the church van while Mama Black sat in the middle row. When Mama Black finished saying her apologies, she would look over her shoulder barely turning all the way around just to give us her usual *Mama Talk*. Mama Black was already frustrated for being late, so she really wasn't playing with us that Sunday morning. We remained quiet the entire ride to church.

The driver had to make two more pick-ups. When we finally made it to the church, Mama Black gave us the second *Mama Talk*.

She said, "When we get out this van, y'all better go straight to your Sunday School class and not to the bathroom trying to fix your hair and clothes. Had y'all gotten up early, you would have had time for that. Go straight to your Sunday school class," Mama said while clenching her teeth together and just moving her lips. When Mama Black talked like that, she always meant business!

We just replied, "Yes, Mama."

We all got out of the van, quietly and went straight to our classes. After Sunday school was over, everyone congregated in the Sanctuary to give their Sunday school report. This part was fun for me because I enjoyed giving the report to the congregation on behalf of my class.

Sister Johnson gave me the class envelope to read. When they called the Great and Mercy Baptist Church Youth Sunday School Class up, I excitedly and nervously walked up to the front of the church facing the burgundy cushioned pews and the intergenerational crowd of congregants.

With a small manila envelope in hand with money and writing on the front, I recited, "Good Morning. GMBC Youth Sunday School scripture reading for today is 1 John 1:9. It is Sunday, June 8, 1997. Total students, 10. Total Offering, $6.80. Sunday School Teacher, Sister Johnson."

I handed the envelope to the class secretary and sat with the rest of my class in those burgundy soft cushioned pews. Once everyone reported out and the Superintendent of Sunday School gave a summary of the lesson then prayed us out before service at 11am.

Before church service started, everyone greeted each other with hugs and kisses. Grace and Mercy Baptist Church was a friendly and loving church. That's why Mama Black loved it so much.

This Sunday was different for Mama Black. She was quieter than her usual. Thinking about all that was going on personally, Mama Black's faith and trust grew stronger in the Lord. She didn't know how God would make a way for her and her family, but she knew that He would.

Preaching from Mark 5:36, Rev. Watkins entitled his sermon: *You are Never Without Hope.* He preached with such strong conviction, "In Mark 5, a man named Jairus pleaded with Jesus to bring his daughter back from the dead. Rev. Watkins reminded the congregation that: 1. There is no limit to what God can do. The same thing He's done for others, He will do for you; 2. God will honor your trust in Him; 3. God said it one time and spoke life into a dead situation; 4. You have power when you really believe. 5. There's always HOPE and there's nothing too hard for God!"

Those words really resonated with Mama Black. She believed in God and believed that God would make things better for her and her family. As Rev. Watkins finished his sermon, he extended an invitation to join the church and/or become saved and a candidate for baptism. Mama Black felt a stirring in her soul. When Rev. Watkins made invitation, Mama Black stood up from the pew she sat in and walked towards the front of the church as a demonstration of her new journey of trust and faith in Jesus Christ.

My siblings and I sat in the pews and watched Mama Black go to the front. We didn't fully understand what was going on, but we were excited to see Mama Black in front of the church. We didn't talk amongst ourselves during service that Sunday. We just sat and watched.

Curious to know what was going to happen next, Audacious leaned over to Meaven and said, "Do you think Mama is going to announce she's pregnant to the whole church?!"

Meaven just looked at her with a straight face and turned his head forward to watch Mama Black. He didn't even respond because he had no idea where Audacious was getting this from. Strength over-heard Audacious talking but couldn't quite make out what was being said. She just leaned forward to make eye contact with Audacious and just shook her head to remind her to stop talking. Strength almost had Mama Black's *Mama-No-Nonsense-Face* down packed, too. Audacious immediately closed her mouth and looked straight ahead at Mama Black.

The church clerk, Sister Brookings, had soft light skin colored like the Kalahari Sand and silver colored hair. Her eyes were nutmeg brown, and her lips were thin. She spoke with Mama Black and hugged her after they finished talking. Rev. Watkins walked out of the pulpit, closer to the front pew.

That Sunday, Rev. Watkins had on an all-black ankle length robe with gold trimmings, bell sleeves, velvet sleeve panels and 2 gold embroidered crosses that would lie on his chest.

Rev. Watkins handed Sister Brookings the microphone and said, "Here we have Sister Lorraine Black who has come as a candidate for baptism and she's come to join the Grace and Mercy Baptist Church as a member!"

The entire church clapped in excitement and happiness. Rev. Watkins took the microphone and said, "Sister Black, we welcome you with open arms. We are excited to have you as a member of the Grace and Mercy Baptist Church. We accept you and all your beautiful children and know that there's always hope. To God be the glory."

Mama Black wiped the tears from her eyes and hugged Sis Brookings and Rev. Watkins. First Lady Watkins left her pew to give Mama Black a hug of love, welcoming her to the body of Christ.

We also clapped for Mama Black in excitement. We didn't know exactly what happened, but we were happy for Mama Black. Once church was over, we all walked to the church van to go home.

It was quiet on the ride back home. Mama Black spent most of her time staring out the window that Sunday. She didn't quite understand the decision she made, but she knew it was the right thing to do. She felt it in her spirit.

Finally, the van driver pulled up to the 4-story brick apartment building that had a corner store and laundry mat on the left and an old park on the right. The driver said while pulling up, "And we've arrived at the Black's humble abode!"

Mama Black replied in a calming voice, "Thank you for getting us here safely. Take care."

The driver replied, "You're welcome. And welcome to the family, Sister Black." Mama waved, smiled, and closed the door.

Everyone except for Joy ran to the front door. Joy waited for Mama Black while she closed the van door. Joy grabbed Mama Black's hand and looked up at her. Mama Black looked back at Joy and said, "Joy, God is going to bring us some joy as long as we keep walking with Him."

Joy was young at the time and didn't understand what she meant. So, Joy just smiled with her innocent young eyes as her and Mama Black walked to the front door, holding hands.

By the time we got upstairs we were excited and couldn't wait to tell Papa Black what happened. Papa Black was in the living room watching television and relaxing.

Interrupting his Luther Vandross at-home concert playing on the VHS and the floor model television, Gracie jumped with excitement, she ran up to Papa Black and says, "Papa! Papa! Mama joined the church today!"

Papa Black focused his attention on Gracie and asked, "She did what?!"

Mama Black had made it to the living room by the time Gracie told Papa Black what had happened.

Mama Black overheard the conversation and chimed in, "I joined the Grace and Mercy Baptist Church today and I gave my life over to Christ."

Papa Black replied, "Wow. I didn't know you were going to do that today."

Mama Black quickly replied, "I didn't know either until I was in church today. I was moved by Rev. Watkins' sermon today and I felt it was the right thing to do for me, you, and the kids."

Papa Black said, "Congratulations. I know this was something you must have wanted to do so I'm happy for you."

Mama Black smiled and walked to their bedroom to change her clothes and prepare dinner for the evening and the next couple of days. Papa and Mama Black's relationship was under a lot of stress and pressure. Bills piled up while their money stayed the same. They really were struggling.

CHAPTER 13
MY 1ˢᵀ CAMPING TRIP

In fourteen days, Papa and Mama Black had to come up with $780 in back-pay for rent and $780 for the current month's rent. They had no idea where they would come up with $1,560. School was over so that meant Mama Black wasn't bringing in income for the summer. It was extremely hard for Papa and Mama Black to save. How could they save when they had rent, car insurance, eight mouths to feed, a phone and light bill, school clothes, supplies, gas, doctor visits and more?

Sometimes there were months Papa and Mama Black had to decide which bill wouldn't get paid for that month just so they could put food on the table. We couldn't even afford to go on family vacations. Our vacations were going to the park, visiting family that lived in the area, and attending afterschool program activities and events.

That summer, I went on vacation. It was more like a camping trip, my first one. A sister from the church offered to pay my way to attend a camping trip to Camp Lenoloc in Bear Mountain, New York. She had two daughters and her eldest daughter was attending the camp as well. She wanted to bless another little girl, and this time it was me.

Mama Black was so excited and appreciative of this kind gesture. She knew she couldn't afford to take her kids on vacation, so Mama Black appreciated it that much more when others gave her children opportunities that she and Papa Black couldn't.

It was a cool summer, a late Friday afternoon and Mama Black helped me pack and get my things together for the camping trip. I was the kind of kid that didn't mind going to unfamiliar places without my parents or siblings. I was always open to new experiences.

The sister from the church picked up Mama Black and I. Joy came along, too. She picked us up from the house and took me the bus that would take me to Bear Mountain, New York. Papa Black stayed home with the rest of my siblings.

We arrived at Camp Lenoloc. I grabbed at duffle bag from the trunk while Mama Black helped Joy out the car so that they could walk me to the bus.

Mama Black held Joy's hand while talking to me, "I want you to have a good time and enjoy yourself. I know you will have fun. Oh, and make sure you say, 'thank you' to the Sister from the church, okay?"

"Yes, Mama. I will. Thank you," I answered.

Mama Black whispered so the other girls getting on the bus couldn't hear, "Oh Journee don't forget about the little snacks in your bag. And I didn't give you anything to drink because I didn't want you to have to go to the bathroom." Mama Black was very thoughtful when it came to her family.

"Okay, Mama. Thank you," I responded with a little bit of nervousness in my voice. This was my first time being away from family and around strangers, by myself, for an extended amount of time. But I was up for the new adventure.

"Okay. We will see you later. Love you, dearly." Mama Black planted a sweet kiss on my left cheek. It was the sweetest kiss ever.

"Love you, Mama. Bye, Joy. See you later," Joy smiled, waved good-bye and I got on the bus.

Mama Black and Joy made their way back to the car and waited until the bus pulled off.

I sat quietly the entire bus ride because I didn't know anyone. The sister from the church daughter arrived at camp the night before so I didn't know anyone on the bus. By the time we arrived, it was dark and time for bed. The camp counselor greeted us and showed us to our cabin.

I stepped off the bus and looked at the camping grounds in amazement as I had never seen anything like it before. I was so excited to be there. The camp counselor escorted us to the cabin to drop off our bags so we could grab a bite to eat before going to bed.

That night, I had chicken fingers and fries with Hawaiian punch juice. I enjoyed my meal and was excited to see what the next day would bring.

The camp counselor escorted me and the other little girls back to our cabin and told us that we had to be up by 8am for breakfast and the first set of activities. I went to the bathroom, changed into my night clothes, and fell fast asleep. I was a little cold overnight but had a good night's rest.

I got up that morning and headed to breakfast. On the way to the cafeteria, the camp counselor walked towards me and stopped me before getting breakfast.

"Journee, your mom just called a few minutes ago. She wanted to make sure you got here safely," the camp counselor told me.

Journee replied, "Okay. Did she want me to call her back?"

The camp counselor responded, "No. She just wanted to make sure you arrived here safely that's all."

I smiled and said, "Okay. Thank you." I kept walking to the cafeteria to get something to eat. Breakfast options were cereal, oatmeal, and fruit. I had Corn Flakes and a banana for breakfast. That's usually what I would eat at home.

While at camp, I learned how to swim, participated in a dance routine with the other little girls, hiked a trail and even made a couple of new friends.

A few days passed by and the same camp counselor came to me with a white envelope in her hand and said, "Here you go, Journee!"

With a hug smile on my face, I replied excitedly, "What's this?!"

The camp counselor replied, "It looks like a letter from your mom! She's sweet to write this for you. Not many girls that come to camp get a letter from their mommy."

With a huge grin plastered on my face, I said, "Thank you! I can't wait to read it!"

I waited until it was bedtime to read the letter so that I could read it without any interruptions. Evening came, I read the letter:

"Dear Journee, I know you are having a good time. What did you do since you have been at camp? How was your swimming? Did you make new friends? I know you did. Did you see anything special when you went hiking ☺? What kind of food do you have, is it good? I already know you are on your best behavior and obeying the adults if they are telling you the right things. Are you swimming every day? I want y'all to have all the fun you can. See you soon. ☺ Love you, MOM."

I couldn't help but smile after reading that letter from Mama Black. I also received a smiley face sticker from my baby girl Joy. The sticker was on the back of the letter. Mama Black had such a unique way of making us feel like they we were her only child. That's how much love she had and showed to each of each of us.

I immediately got her pencil and paper to write back to Mama Black. I replied,

"Dear Mommy. I miss you a lot. I'm having a lot of fun. Tuesday, I went swimming. It was a lot of fun. I went hiking, dancing, and to nature class. This is bad news; I was cold so cold at night that blanket wasn't warm enough. Mommy guess what you forgot my pillow and wash cloths, but that's okay. From your daughter, Journee. To: the best Mommy. I Love You."

Camp had finally ended, and it was time for me to return home. I packed my bags and got on the bus. After an hour-long ride and to my surprise, Papa, Mama Black, and all my siblings were in the car when the bus pulled up. They were all there to pick me up!

I ran off the bus towards Mama Black and hugged her like I hadn't seen her in years. Mama Black had her arms wide open. Although they didn't say they missed me, I knew my siblings missed me by the million and one questions they asked me when I got in the car.

"So, Journee, how was camp?" Gracie asked in excitement wondering how her big sister enjoyed camp.

I replied to Gracie, "It was so much fun! I went swimming, hiking, and they had a talent show where I did a dance routine. I was cold at night, though. But it was fun!"

"Did you see bears?!" Gracie continued to ask me more questions while everyone else listened.

I exclaimed, "No! Thank God! But if I did, I would have run back to my cabin and hid under my bed!" Everyone laughed.

Papa Black pulled up to the house and parked in the parking lot. Everyone got out the car and started making their way walking up the stairs. When Papa and Mama Black were with the kids, Mama Black would walk in the front, Papa Black and Meaven walked in the back, and my sisters and I walked in the middle. We had our very own way of operating as a family unit.

After walking up four flights of stairs, Mama Black looked down in her purse to grab her keys to open the door. When she looked back up, there was a pink notice stuck to the door that read: *"YOU ARE BEING ASKED TO LEAVE THE PREMISES IN 7 DAYS IF YOUR OUT-STANDING BALANCE IS NOT RECONCILED. IF YOU DO NOT LEAVE, AN EVICTION ACTION MAY BE INITIATED AGAINST YOU. THANK YOU, MANAGEMENT."*

Mama Black snatched the letter off the door fast so that we didn't see it! But Strength saw the letter. She asked Mama Black, "What was that Mama?"

"Oh, it was nothing. Some sticker on the door," Mama said trying to avoid having that conversation with her oldest daughter.

But Strength was the eldest and had been with Papa and Mama Black the longest. Very often Strength knew when things were off. Strength didn't respond but she knew something wasn't right.

Mama Black finally opened the door and turned the lights on. It was almost bedtime, so Mama Black told everyone to start getting ready for bed. My sisters and I went to our room and Meaven went to his.

Mama Black pulled Papa Black in their bedroom and closed the door behind her. Mama Black went into her purse and pulled out the bright pink notice.

"I found this on the door when we came in. Look." Mama Black showed Papa Black the notice she found on the door. Mama Black's eyes began to well-up with tears as she knew where this could possibly end. Papa Black held the letter with both his hands while reading it.

This time Papa Black read it out loud:

"YOU ARE BEING ASKED TO LEAVE THE PREMISES IN 7 DAYS IF YOUR OUTSTANDING BALANCE IS NOT RECONCILED. IF YOU DO NOT LEAVE, AN EVICTION ACTION MAY BE INITIATED AGAINST YOU. THANK YOU, MANAGEMENT."

After hearing it out loud, Mama Black began to weep and sob, as quietly as she could. She didn't want us to hear her. She was tired, scared, and afraid. Yet again, Papa Black hugged Mama Black, trying to console her. It seemed like it was happening all over again. Homeless, this time it wasn't because of a fire.

Papa Black quietly said, "I'll ask my job if we can borrow the money and we can pay them back. When I go in tomorrow, I'll ask them first thing in the morning."

That gave Mama Black some relief. She knew Papa Black had built a good relationship with his boss and it was likely that they would give it to him.

Wiping the tears that flooded her chocolate golden brown cheeks, all Mama Black could say was, "Okay."

Mama Black got herself together before leaving the bedroom. She didn't want to us to see her crying. She opened the door and shouted, "Are y'all ready for bed?"

We knew Mama Black was coming to make her rounds to our rooms. Everyone shouted, "Yes, Mama!" Mama Black walked to our rooms to say her good-nights and to cut the lights off. She did this every night.

CHAPTER 14
OUTSTANDING BALANCE

Papa Black got up that morning feeling nervous but determined to do what he needed to do for his family. Papa Black rehearsed in his head what he would say and how he would ask his boss for $1,560.

Papa Black pulled into the parking lot and sat there for 5 minutes. He got out the car and headed into work. Papa Black said his usual good mornings to his colleagues and eventually made his way to the breakroom. He grabbed a cup of water to cool himself down since he didn't know which way the conversation would go.

Papa Black walked to his boss, Mr. Ritz's office. Mr. Ritz was a very wealthy Caucasian man and the Chief Executive Officer of the Samson Chemical Plant. Mr. Ritz was a tall, red-haired, brown eyed gentleman. He really liked Papa Black and his work ethic. He knew Papa Black had a large family that he worked hard to provide for.

Papa Black stood in the doorway of Mr. Ritz's office trying to get his attention. Mr. Ritz looked up and said, "Good Morning, Joseph! Good to see ya this morning. How ya doing?"

Mr. Ritz was always nice to Papa Black. Mr. Ritz put his hand out to shake Papa Black's hand. Papa Black reached out and shook his hand.

Papa Black replied nervously saying, "Good Morning Mr. Ritz. I'm doing fine. Listen. I want to ask you something and I hope I am not outside of my boundary for asking you this. But my family and I are in a tight bind and could use some financial help."

Looking puzzled and concerned, Mr. Ritz said, "Sorry to hear that Joseph. But, what's the bind?"

"Well, Mr. Ritz. My wife and I fell behind on our bills and we're about to be evicted. We have nowhere else to go. I was wondering if you could help us with the outstanding balance for our rent." Papa Black took his cap off when he entered Mr. Ritz's office and began to squeeze the brim while asking for money. Papa Black was nervous.

Mr. Ritz asked, "Well, how much is the outstanding balance?"

Papa Black responded, "It's $1,560."

Mr. Ritz answered, "Joseph, you're a good man. Let me see what I can do. I'll let you know by the end of your work shift."

Papa Black put his hand out to shake Mr. Ritz's hand out of respect and said, "Thank you, Mr. Ritz. My wife and I really appreciate it. Thank you so much."

Mr. Ritz replied, "You're welcome. I'll get back to you."

Papa Black walked out the office and began his work shift. He went to his security post to ensure no one entered the building without being checked in. A few hours passed and it was break time. Papa Black called Mama Black while on his lunch.

"Hello?" Mama Black picked up the phone sounding like she just had been running.

"Hey, Lorraine. It's me, Joseph," Papa Black replied.

"Hey. How's work going?" Mama Black said.

"It's going well. This morning, I asked Mr. Ritz about helping us out with the balance. And he said he will see what he can do. He's gonna let me know before my shift ends today," Papa Black said with hope in his voice.

"Wow. That's great news. But do you really think he's going to give us the full balance? I mean, $1,560 is a lot of money – if y'all don't be quiet while I'm on this phone!" Mama Black was having two conversations. She was responding to Papa Black while trying to get us to be quiet.

Mama Black continued, "Sorry. These kids...So yeah, do you really think he's gonna do that?"

Papa Black replied, "I don't know, but I'm hopeful."

Mama Black responded trying to have an ounce of hope as well, "Okay. Well, let me know."

"I will. My break is over, so I'll see you and the kids later." Papa Black hung up.

Papa Black went back to his post and soon his work shift was coming to an end for the day. He didn't know what Mr. Ritz would say or give to him. After all, Mr. Ritz was not obligated to give Papa Black anything on top of his regular paycheck.

Papa Black's shift was over in 5 minutes. He heard a resounding voice over the loudspeaker saying, "Joseph, please report to Mr. Ritz office. Joseph, please report to Mr. Ritz office at this time."

Papa Black left his post immediately and walked into Mr. Ritz's office. Mr. Ritz was sitting down behind his Cherry Oak Wood desk filled with pictures of him and his family. Papa Black entered and Mr. Ritz said, "Joseph, please have a seat." Papa Black sat down.

Mr. Ritz said, "Joseph, as I said earlier, you're a good man and I admire your work ethic. We were able to help you out in the amount of $560. That was all we could do at this time."

Papa Black remained humbled and thankful on the outside but crushed on the inside. "Mr. Ritz, I appreciate what you have done for me and my family. You didn't have to do this, so I thank you."

"You're welcome, Joseph. Best of luck to you and your family. I hope everything works out for you. I'll see you tomorrow."

Papa Black grabbed the enveloped of cash, shook Mr. Ritz's hand and walked to his car. While he was thankful for Mr. Ritz's kind gesture, there was disappointment and frustration Papa Black was feeling. He couldn't understand how he worked so hard trying to make a decent living, yet his family was struggling to make ends meet. Deciding between paying household bills or keeping food in his children's bellies frustrated Papa Black.

He felt the pressure of being an African American man. He didn't plan to live his life like this. He had dreams of becoming a fire fighter one day, but it was cut short after being stabbed as a teenager and nearly dying. Papa Black was tired but determined to keep fighting for himself, his wife, and his family.

Papa Black arrived home after dinner. My siblings and I were preparing for bed, Mama Black was in the kitchen. She was sweeping under-neath the kitchen table when Papa Black entered the kitchen. Realizing Papa Black was there, Mama Black stopped sweeping but still held the broom in her right hand.

Mama Black asked, "Hey. So, what happened?! How did it go?!" Mama Black was very eager to find out how it went at Papa Black's job.

"Well, it went okay. Mr. Ritz was only able to give us $560," Papa Black replied.

Mama Black felt deflated. She only had the strength to say, "Oh."

Papa Black continued, "I went down to the leasing office and told them all we had was $560. I asked if they could give us an extension."

At this point Mama leaned the broom against the refrigerator and took a seat. She did not know what else Papa Black was going to say so she sat down to brace herself.

Mama Black replied, "Joseph, what did they say? Will they give us an extension?"

There was a long pause before Papa Black answered. When he finally answered, Papa Black sadly replied, "They wouldn't take the $560. They want the full balance. They said we have to leave by next week."

Mama Black threw her head on her forearms while still sitting at the kitchen table. Mama Black didn't know what else to do or say. Tears came rolling down her face as she continued resting her head on her forearms. All she could think about was being homeless with 6 kids. Again.

Papa Black was just as disappointed. He sat down next to Mama Black and didn't have many words to say in that moment. Papa and Mama Black just sat there quiet. Gracie and I walked into the kitchen not realizing what was going on. We wanted to ask Mama Black where our matching shirts were. We often dressed alike and wanted to wear their shirts outside tomorrow so we could be twins.

We walked in the kitchen laughing with each other. Gracie said, "Mama, have you seen our purple shirts with the flowers on it? Me and Journee want to wear them tomorrow when we go to the park."

I realized Mama Black's head was down on the table resting on her forearms. I tapped Gracie's shoulder to let her know we should leave the kitchen. With sadness in his voice, Papa Black just said, "Y'all go back in the room."

I grabbed Gracie's hand and we left the kitchen.

Mama Black lifted her head up and tears continued to stream down her face. She said, "Homeless, again? How could this be?"

Mama Black got up, swept up the pile, threw it in the trash and put the broom between the wall and the refrigerator. Mama Black walked into their bed and closed the door behind her. Papa Black just sat there. He didn't have any answers and felt helpless knowing that his family was going to be homeless. Again.

Papa Black got up from the kitchen table and went to the girls' room. He knocked on the door before entering their room. When he knocked, we all yelled in unison, "Come in!"

Papa Black entered our room. He said, "Y'all finish getting ready for bed, cut this light out and get in the bed."

We all replied in unison, "Okay, Papa." Papa Black closed the door behind him.

We whispered amongst each other trying to figure out what was going on. Papa Black walked to Meaven's room. Papa Black knocked again and Meaven said, "Come in."

Papa Black replied, "Finish getting ready for bed, cut this the light out and get in the bed."

Meaven replied, "Okay."

Papa Black returned to his and Mama Black's bedroom. Mama Black was lying down in the bed and had still been crying. Papa Black didn't have any words, so he didn't speak. He got in the bed and laid there with Mama Black.

CHAPTER 15
HOMELESS, AGAIN

The next morning, Papa Black got up like usual and went to work. Although he had extra cash from what Mr. Ritz had given him, he still needed his minimum wage paying job. Papa Black left the house while Mama Black woke us up. She wasn't sure where we are going, but she knew she had to prepare the kids to begin packing their things.

"Girls! Girls! It's time to wake up," Mama Black shouted while busting the door wide open. Mama Black didn't knock on the door like Papa Black did. She truly was the Queen of her castle.

"It is time to wake up. Go brush your teeth, wash your face, and get some cereal. Once you finish that, come back to your room, and start packing your stuff up," Mama said nonchalantly.

We all sat up in our beds, barely awake with our hair standing on our heads. Since there were five girls on one bedroom, we had to share beds except Strength. She had her own twin sized bed. Gracie and I shared a bed, and Audacious and Joy shared a bed. Gracie and I slept on the top bunk bed and Audacious and Joy slept on the bottom. It was fun for them as it was all they knew.

The girls had to share the bathroom with each other so that everyone could use the bathroom in a timely fashion. While we were getting ready in the bathroom, Mama Black went to Meaven's room to wake him up.

Mama Black knocked on Meaven's door. She entered his room and told Meaven the same thing she just told us. Mama Black left out while Meaven laid there for a little while until we finished using the bathroom. He eventually got up and went into the bathroom. Meaven always had the bathroom all to himself.

Mama Black began packing up her stuff even though she had no idea where they would end up next. We wanted to ask what was going on but knew it wasn't time to ask questions. Instead, it was time to do what Mama Black told us to do.

The afternoon rolled around, and Papa Black called the house during his lunch break.

"Hello?" Mama Black picked up of the phone.

"Hey, Lorraine. It's me, Joseph," Papa Black responded.

"Hey," Mama Black replied feeling stressed.

Papa Black said, "So I spoke to my mother and she said we could stay with her until we find something."

"She said yes to 8 additional people staying in her one-bedroom apartment?! That's a lot, Joe. I don't feel comfortable putting that burden on your mother. I appreciate it, but that's a lot," Mama Black replied sounding even more concerned.

Papa Black answered, "I know. I don't want to put that burden on her either, but it is our only option until we find something else."

"So, what are we going to do with all of our furniture and belongings?" Mama Black asked.

"We can put them in storage until we find a place. There's a place downtown that charges $20 per month. I called and they have a unit big enough to fit our stuff in. We just have to pack everything in as tight as possible," Papa Black had said.

He continued, "Listen, we can talk more about it when I get home, but we'll stay at my mother's house until we find something."

Sounding unconvinced, Mama Black replied, "Okay, Joseph. I'll see you when you get home."

Papa Black said, "Okay. See you later." They both hung up.

Papa Black got home that evening and Mama Black was stilling packing. Because of Mama Black, we were able to pack most of our belongings. Mama Black also packed some of Papa Black's things too. They had three more days to have everything packed and out the apartment. We had only been there 2 and ½ years but we were moving again.

Papa and Mama Black didn't like shuffling us from place to place, but life's circumstances didn't allow us to have the luxury of stability. They were extremely stressed, but they did the best they could with what they had.

Papa Black called his best friends, Wess and Raul to help him move our belongings to the storage unit. With eight people in the household, we accumulated a lot of furniture during the time we lived there.

Wess and Raul walked in the apartment ready to help.

Wess said, "What do you want me to take in my truck?"

Papa Black replied, "Can you fit beds in your truck?"

Wess replied, "Sure. Where are the beds?"

Papa Black said, "They are leaned up against the wall by the door." Wess grabbed the beds, one by one, and loaded them in his truck. Raul helped with the television and bed frames.

With the help of Wess and Raul, Papa Black was able to get most of our things in the storage unit. Wess and Raul were strong and young, so they were able to move things quickly.

Since the beds were in storage, we had to sleep on the floor for the next three days. We didn't mind. It was fun for us. My siblings and I didn't realize how much they were struggling. We had each other and spent most of our childhood cracking jokes on each other and having fun.

The third day had finally come, and it was time to leave the apartment. With the help of Papa Black and his friends, Wess and Raul, we were able to get everything in storage just in time. Mama Black managed to hold it together without breaking down and crying like she did earlier.

Little did we know, we would stay in three places before finding a place to call home. But Papa and Mama Black made sure we were always together, moving as one family unit no matter what.

CHAPTER 16
NANA JOSEPHINE'S HOUSE

It was a Saturday morning when we arrived on Nana Josephine's doorstep with several bags and some Barbie Dolls. Meaven just had clothes and his Hess toy truck. His video games were in storage.

Nana Josephine opened her door with a big smile on her face welcoming her family into her home. Now, Nana Josephine was not your average lady. She was a very classy woman. Her skin tone was warm and brown like the earth glistening in the sunlight. Her eyes were radiant and brown, while her cheekbones were defined and structured.

Nana Josephine always had long, groomed fingernails that she would paint many different colors. She always adorned her right pinkie with a gold-plated ring with a black emerald-cut diamond. Not only that, but Nana Josephine also had a walk that matched no other. She turned heads with her walk and graceful stride. Her sweet voice and kind spirit always preceded her and brought her entire look together.

"Come on in! I'm so happy to see you all," Nana Josephine said while holding her arm out hugging everyone as we walked in.

"How are you doing, Ms. Josephine? Thank you for allowing us to stay with you. I know it's not easy taking in a family of our size. But I really do thank you." Mama Black wanted to make sure Nana Josephine knew she was appreciative of her sacrifice.

Nana Josephine grabbed Mama Black's hands while looking in her big brown eyes. She said, "We are family. That's what we are supposed to do." Nana Josephine and Mama Black hugged.

Everyone finally got in the house and settled in. Nana Josephine lived in a one bed-room, one-bathroom apartment that was only big enough for her. So, having eight more people made it very crowded and tight. While staying there, we all slept in the living room.

Inside the living room was a long silver-blue couch with a plastic cover, a television, a small coffee and dining table, and Nana Josephine's infamous black and gold wall unit, it was huge.

Nana Josephine's infamous wall unit was like a family tree. There were pictures of her mother, great-grandmother, brother, grandmother, aunts, children, grandchildren, and her dogs in that wall unit. Nana Josephine's wall unit was history for the Black family.

One of the most intriguing items in Nana Josephine's wall unit was an article about her great-grandmother being an ex-slave. Nana Josephine was big on keeping items and pictures that would tell the Black family story. She was the Queen of the Black family memorabilia. Everyone knew not to touch Nana Josephine's wall unit or anything inside of it. But Nana Josephine shared the history and pictures with us at a young age.

When it was time for bed, Nana Josephine would go to her bedroom while we slept in the living room. Mama Black and Joy slept on the couch while the rest of us slept on the floor. Thankfully, the floor was carpeted so sleeping on the floor wasn't that bad. Plus, we were used to it. This wasn't our first time going through something like this.

Papa Black made sure we had plenty of blankets to cushion the floor. It wasn't the best situation, but it wasn't the worse either. I often thought that to myself. Plus, having five other siblings to go through life like this made it a little easier. But it wasn't easy for Papa and Mama Black.

Papa Black continued going to work while Mama Black and Nana Josephine stayed at home with us. The summer days seemed long but would go by fast. Mama Black made sure she kept us in line, making sure we didn't act up at Grandma Josephine's house. Usually Mama Black was lenient at home, but not when it came to someone else's home, even if it was a relative. So, every morning before Nana Josephine would come into the living room, Mama Black would wake up us to give us the *Mama Talk*.

With Mama Black's serious, no-non-sense look, she would say in a calm but stern voice every morning, "I don't want y'all acting up in your grandmother's house. Do not go in the refrigerator without asking first. Y'all will go in the bathroom two at a time to shower and wash up, except Meaven. Journee, no 20-minute showers. Do not ask for anything that we don't have. Y'all will clean up after yourselves. And no fighting and arguing. If y'all don't listen, you are going to get it from me and your father."

We were really scared to act up this time. Mama Black laid out the rules every morning. This time, Mama Black wasn't playing so we made sure we listened to her.

There was a daily routine for us. Everyone got up from either the floor or the couch, folded our sheets and blankets, and put them in Nana Josephine's closet. Then, we showered, ate breakfast, and watched television. Mama Black always braided our hair, so she didn't have to do it every day. It was one less thing Mama Black had to worry about, having five girls.

Sometimes Mama Black would let us play outside. This gave Nana Josephine a little break from having so many people in the house while giving us something fun to do.

Mama Black took a break from going to church because she felt embarrassed that she and her family were homeless again. Mama Black knew she would go back because she really loved it there but, she felt she needed a break. Plus, Papa and Mama Black were going through a lot and needed to figure out our next move as a family.

CHAPTER 17
NANA EVE'S HOUSE

Since they didn't have any major bills, Papa and Mama Black saved their money for our next apartment. Papa Black took on extra hours at his job to help save more. Between Papa Black's checks and the $560 dollars given to us from Mr. Ritz, Papa and Mama Black were certain they would get a home soon for their family.

It didn't happen quick enough for the Black family. Their two-month long routine with Nana Josephine turned into one-month routine with Nana Eve. A week earlier, Mama Black spoke to Nana Eve asking if we could stay with her for a few weeks or until they found another apartment. Nana Eve agreed. That Saturday evening, we were yet again, on another relative's doorstep. After packing our bags and toys, we said our good-byes to Nana Josephine. While on the car ride to Nana Eve's house, Mama Black gave her *Mama Talk* again.

Nana Eve was Mama Black's mother. They had the sweetest mother-daughter relationship. Mama Black had such high regards for her mother and always showed Nana Eve so much love.

They would talk on the phone for hours, laughing and sharing secrets with each other. Mama Black made us build a relationship with her too.

Nana Eve was also a unique woman. She was firm yet kind, strong yet gentle, and wise yet humble. Nana Eve's personality was one that reminded you of the kind of woman that was a part of the Black Panther Movement: fearless and powerful.

Nana Eve was a radiant looking woman. Her flawless and smooth skin tone was a warm cinnamon-brown complexion. Her eyes were vivid chestnut brown that told a compelling story, and she had a smile that was gentle and sincere. Nana Eve was a thick woman, only 5'2. Her hands and arms made your think twice about what you would say because she could very well lay you out. Her hands and arms carried so much strength. Nana Eve also liked pranking people just to get a good laugh. She had a brown wooden derby cane that she would bang against the wall to get everyone's attention. When she did get everyone's attention, she would just chuckle and smile. Nana Eve was a funny lady but didn't take mess from anyone.

Nana Eve lived in a large two-bedroom apartment. There was a flight of stairs that led to her living room. Nana Eve's living room was spacious. She had a huge cobalt blue velvet sectional sofa, a dark oak wood vintage Zenith floor model television, large windows with old drapes and a mahogany brown grandfather clock that was next to the television.

We were so excited to be at Nana Eve's house. Her large sectional sofa meant more of us could sleep on the couch. I was happy about that!

Next to the living room was the kitchen, dining room and the bathroom. Down the hallway, were two bedrooms. Of course, Nana Eve had the bigger bedroom. She had a chair in her bedroom where Mama Black would sit when they talked for hours every day. We would play outside of Nana Eve's apartment complex while they talked.

Papa Black continued working while Mama Black stayed with us. Papa and Mama Black were tired, but they kept it pushing. Since they didn't have major bills, Papa Black was able to save every paycheck. This would help with putting down a deposit on our next home.

After staying with Nana Eve for four weeks, it was time for us to move. My siblings and I had fun staying at Nana Eve's house. Papa and Mama Black were thankful to Nana Eve for letting us stay with her.

CHAPTER 18
GRANDPA JOSEPH, SR.'S HOUSE

Next stop was Grandpa Joseph Sr.'s house. Grandpa Joseph Sr. was Papa Black's father. Grandpa Joseph Sr. was fun-loving and full of life! His look and rambunctious personality resembled George Jefferson from *The Jeffersons*. Grandpa Joseph Sr. had caramel brown skin. He had hair on the sides of his head but none of the top. He was often mistaken for George Jefferson. He would get a kick out of it when people would walk up to him and ask if he was George Jefferson. Grandpa Joseph Sr. would often say that he was, but eventually people caught on and realized he was too tall to be George Jefferson, he was 5'9.

Grandpa Joseph Sr. was full of life; he always enjoyed having a good time. He was silly and outgoing.

Before we arrived at Grandpa Joseph Sr.'s house, Mama Black had the *mama talk* again. Mama Black knew taking in eight additional people in a household wasn't easy, so she wanted to ensure we were on our best behavior. When we arrived, we had our same bag of clothes and toys that we had brought with us to Nana Josephine and Nana Eve's house. This was the third place we stayed in a span of two months.

We arrived on the doorstep and Papa Black rang the doorbell. Grandpa Joseph Sr. was expecting us, so he automatically buzzed the door open to let us in. We entered the one-bedroom apartment that had a short hallway. The bedroom and bathroom were a few steps from the main entrance. A few steps past the bedroom and bathroom were the living room and kitchen. The living room and kitchen were combined. Grandpa Joseph Sr.'s apartment was intimate and quaint.

As we entered the living room, there was Great-Grandma J and Aunty V. Great-Grandma J was Papa Black's grandmother and Aunty V was his aunt. They also lived with Grandpa Joseph Sr. in that intimate and quaint apartment.

The household grew from three to eleven overnight. Although we were staying there temporarily until we found something, it was tight and crowded. But Grandpa Joseph Sr. was happy to be with his grandkids. Papa and Mama Black were blessed because they had family that was supportive and helpful.

When we settled in, Papa Black and Meaven put the bags and toys in the bedroom where we would sleep and get dressed. As usual, there was always more than one to a bed if there was a bed. However, we were used to it and didn't think much of it. We just piled in the bed with each other and slept head to toe. Sharing a bed with each other was better and more comfortable than sleeping on a hard floor.

While Papa Black and Meaven were in the room putting our bags away, Mama Black made sure me, and my sisters hugged and kissed Great-Grandma J and Aunty V. Great-Grandma J was the sweetest great-grandmother. She loved and adored her family. Although she was bound to a wheelchair, she was a woman of beauty and elegance.

Her sweet and tender voice matched her soft and feminine look. Her smooth bronze skin tone was rich with wrinkles that represented all the good years God had given to Great-Grandma J. Her defined and high cheekbones made her look younger than what she was. She was petite in size, her silver hair was full, healthy, and bouncy. Great-Grandma J was like an antique doll: priceless and rare.

She was the matriarch of the Black family. Her beloved husband and our great-grandfather, The Bull, was two times her size. He was 6'4, dark-skinned, tall, and hand-some. He also had huge hard-working hands. She often told stories about him and how he got his nickname. Like a bull, he was strong and tough. Everyone loved and respected him, too.

Great Grandpa died when Papa Black was a teenager. My siblings and I didn't get a chance to meet him, but Papa Black always told stories about him, so we grew up know-ing about him.

Now, Aunty V was the only girl. She and Grandpa Joseph Sr. were close siblings. Aunty V's glowing java brown skin tone and small black eyes made her desirable to any man that encountered her. Her smile was bright and endearing. Her thick hourglass shape really made guys fall at her feet but her humble spirit and intelligence always overshadowed her beauty.

I was the first to get up and hug Great-Grandma J and Aunty V. When I got up the entire room got quiet. I had a feeling what it was but was too embarrassed to ask in that moment. Immediately after hugging Great-Grandma J and Aunty V, I walked to the bath-room. Shortly after closing the door behind her, Mama Black knocked on the door.

Knock. Knock. "Journee, it's me, Mama. Open the door," Mama Black said.

I opened the door knowing what Mama Black was going to tell me. With tears in my eyes, I cried, "Mama, I need pads. I'm bleeding."

I had on gray sweatpants that day, so it was obvious that my menstrual cycle started. The blood leaked through my clothes. I was so embarrassed.

Mama Black said, "It's okay, Journee. I'll bring you some clean clothes and underwear. Take a shower. I don't have any pads and the stores are closed. So, you are going to have to use tissue until your father goes to the store tomorrow morning."

I was even more disappointed and embarrassed that I had to use tissue instead of a pad. Tissue! Papa and Mama Black had been really struggling and often couldn't afford most necessities. And the little money they did have, they wanted to make sure they kept for our next apartment.

I finally took a shower while Mama Black went into the living room to clean the stain on the couch. Mama Black cleaned that spot as if it were never there. Mama Black was magical in every way.

Mama Black always showed up when we needed it the most. Then, she went into the bedroom to get me extra clothes and underwear. I washed and changed but hesitantly made my way back to the living room. I was so embarrassed.

As soon as I entered the living room, there was an awkward silence, but not for long. Grandpa Joseph Sr. yelled, "Welp, granddaughter, it's okay! You have nothing to be embarrassed about! You're a growing up to be a fine young lady!"

Everyone bust out laughing while Papa Black said, "Pops, that is not what you were supposed to say. You were supposed to just be quiet."

Grandpa Joseph Sr. replied, "Oops. I was just trying to give my granddaughter some encouragement!"

I finally bust out laughing like everyone else. I felt better afterwards. It was very natural for Grandpa Joseph Sr. to blurt out exactly what he wasn't supposed to. Grandpa Joseph Sr. was funny and fun to be around.

Mama Black responded while giggling, "Well I think that's our cue to call it a night. Let's go y'all. Time for bed." We said our good-nights and headed to the bedroom to get some sleep. Papa Black hung out with Great-Grandma J, Grandpa Joseph Sr., and Aunty V before he made his way to bed.

By 6:30am Papa Black had already left for the day. Papa Black went to the store to pick up some pads for me and gave them to Mama Black.

That morning Grandpa Joseph Sr. made some home fries with peppers and onions. You could smell it all the way in the back room. Grandpa Joseph Sr. loved being around his family and cooking was how he expressed his love towards his family.

At 7:30am, Mama Black started waking us up. As usual, Mama Black yanked the covers off us while tapping and shaking us. If we were being too sluggish, Mama Black would pour a small cup of water on us. Boy did that wake us up!

Mama Black didn't have to do it that time because we woke up when Mama Black told us to. Mama Black woke me up first so that I could put on a pad.

"Journee. Journee. Wake up, baby. Papa got you some pads," Mama Black whispered so that no one else heard her.

I answered Mama Black while still half sleep. "Yes, Mama?" I responded.

Mama Black replied, "Journee, wake up baby. Papa got you some pads. Go put one on."

Now I really woke up because I heard pads. "Papa got me some pads? Okay. I'm getting up."

I grabbed the pads Mama Black had handed to me and went straight to the bathroom. When I walked outside the bathroom, I got a better smell of Grandpa Joseph Sr.'s delicious home fries. I couldn't wait to get some.

While I was in the bathroom, Mama Black continued waking up my siblings. There were three beds in that small room: a day bed and a queen-sized bed. It was tight, but Papa and Mama Black made it work.

By the time I returned to the bedroom, everyone was up, cracking jokes and laughing at each other. Mama Black let us have our moment.

Audacious was sitting on the edge of the bed with her hair standing on top of her head. Her stocking cap fell off while she was sleep.

Meaven began teasing her, "Dang, Audacious! Did you get into a fight in your sleep or WHAT because you look like somebody beat the breaks off you?!"

Everyone busted out in laughter. Although Meaven was the only boy, he held no punches when it came to teasing his sisters. Audacious just laughed and looked for her stocking cap.

Mama Black made all the girls wear stocking caps to keep their hair neat overnight so that she didn't have to do it every day. They couldn't afford regular head scarves, so we used Mama Black's old stockings to put on our heads when it was bedtime.

Finally, everyone was up and ready to start the day. So, Meaven made his way to the bathroom first. Then, Strength and Joy went next, then Gracie and Audacious, Mama

Black was last. Once everyone was dressed and ready, we made our way to the living with Grandpa Joseph Sr., Great-Grandma J and Aunty V.

"Heyyyy grandkids and Lorraine! Good morning. How ya doing this morning?" Grandpa Joseph Sr. shouted each morning. He was always full of energy and excitement. It didn't take much to get Grandpa Joseph Sr. excited.

We replied in unison, "Good Morning Grandpa, Joseph. We're fine."

Mama Black also replied, "Good Morning Mr. Black, Great-Grandma J and Aunty V. How did y'all sleep?"

They all responded, "We slept just fine."

Grandpa Joseph Sr. replied, "Very good. Very good. Listen, I made you guys some home fries. Please have some. Eat as much as you want. We ate already so you can have the rest of it."

"Thank you so much, Mr. Black. We really appreciate it. And thank for allowing us to stay with you guys until we get back on our feet," Mama Black said while grabbing plates and handing them to me and Strength.

Grandpa Joseph Sr. replied, "Oh, no problem daughter-in-law. We are family and we look out for each other." Mama Black looked at Grandpa Joseph Sr. and smiled graciously.

We all sat at the small kitchen table and ate our delicious home fries. Grandpa Joseph Sr. looked upon us with joy and happiness because he was able to serve his family.

After breakfast, everyone made their way to the couch to sit and watch television. Grandpa Joseph Sr. asked Mama Black if we wanted to watch cartoons. Mama Black didn't want to impose so she automatically said no and that we were fine. We really wished Mama Black would have had said yes because we would rather watch cartoons than the news or soap operas like *The Young and the Restless, All My Children or Bold and Beautiful.*

We were tired of watching soap operas. Mama Black watched them all the time and often talked to the television while she watched them. Mama Black really liked *All My Children*. But her favorite was *The Young and the Restless* because of Shemar Moore. She loved her some Shemar Moore. He was her celebrity crush, but Papa Black didn't know it.

Eventually, Grandpa Joseph Sr. turned to cartoons. We watched Looney Tunes that until early afternoon. When it was time for lunch, Grandpa Joseph Sr. told Mama Black that we could make peanut butter and jelly sandwiches. We enjoyed a good PB&J sandwich. There was also juice in the refrigerator that he said we could have.

Mama Black went to the kitchen area and began making sandwiches for all of us including herself. As Mama Black made the sandwiches, Papa Black called the house phone to check in to see how things were going. Grandpa Joseph Sr. answered.

"Hello?" Grandpa Joseph, Sr. answered.

"Hey Pops! It's Joseph. How ya doing?" Papa Black said.

"Oh! We're doing well over here. How you doing, son?" Grandpa Joseph Sr. replied.

"I'm doing well. Just calling to check-in. Is Lorraine near you? Can I speak to her?" Papa Black responded.

"Oh, yes. She's right here. I'll give the phone to her." Grandpa Joseph Sr. handed the phone over to Mama Black while saying, "Lorraine, it's your husband. He wants to speak to you."

Mama Black stopped making the sandwiches and walked over to the phone. Strength automatically took over to finish making the sandwiches.

"Hey, Joe. How's it going?" Mama Black said immediately after she put the ear to the phone.

"It's going well. Listen, I think I found an apartment for us. It's a two-family house in the same neighborhood that's not too far from the kids' school. I think we should go look at it soon," Papa Black said with so much hope in his voice while speaking to Mama Black about this potential apartment.

"Really?! What street is it on?" Mama Black asked excitedly.

"It's on Freedom Lane off of Main Street," Papa Black responded.

"Okay. How much is the deposit? How much are they asking for?" Mama Black responded.

"Well, they are asking for $1,000 for the deposit. By the end of this week, I will have it. Between what Mr. Ritz gave us and the checks I was able to save, we'll have the full deposit." Papa Black said.

"How much is the rent?" Mama Black responded.

"It's $700 a month," said Papa Black.

"Wow. That would be a blessing. Okay. Let's check it out and see. When should we go?" Mama Black said.

"I get paid on Friday. We can look at the place on Saturday and decide from there," Papa Black responded.

"Yes! Okay. This is great news," Mama Black responded with a big smile on her face.

"Alright. I'll see y'all later," Papa Black said.

"Okay, see you later," Mama Black replied.

Mama Black hung up the phone like she had received the best news in the world. Grandpa Joseph Sr. couldn't help but ask, "Everything alright, daughter-in-law?"

"Yes, Mr. Black. Joe was just telling me about a potential place that we are going to look at on Saturday," Mama Black said.

Grandpa Joseph Sr. said, "Oh, that's wonderful news. Glad to hear!"

By the time Mama Black hung up the phone, Strength had finished making everyone's P&J sandwiches including Mama Black's. My siblings and I overheard the conversation but didn't ask Mama Black about it because we knew if we asked, Mama Black would say, *stay out of grown folks' business.* So, we just waited until Papa and Mama Black discussed things with us.

Around 5:30pm, Papa Black returned home with excitement, hopefulness and promise in his eyes. By the time he arrived, we were eating dinner. Mama Black helped Grandpa Joseph fry chicken and bake macaroni and cheese. Papa Black came just in time to eat and spend time with his family before bedtime. After dinner was finished, Mama Black told us to say our good-nights and prepare for bed. Papa Black sat with Grandpa Joseph Sr., Great-Grandma J and Aunty V. They talked for a little bit before heading to bed.

When Mama Black walked us to the bedroom, Papa Black was so excited to tell his family the promising good news.

"So, Pops – Lorraine and I may have found a potential place. We are going to look at it on Saturday with the kids and see how it goes," Papa Black said ecstatically.

Grandpa Joseph Sr. said, "Son, that's great to hear. I hope everything works out for you and my daughter-in-law."

"Thanks, Pops!" Papa Black replied.

Great-Grandma J was happy when she heard the news as well. In her sweet and gentle voice, she said, "Lil Joseph, I'm proud of you. God Bless you. Everything is going to work out for you!"

Papa Black held Great-Grandma J in such high regard. He really respected his grandparents and always thought highly of them.

Papa Black got up from the couch and walked towards Great-Grandma J as she sat in her wheelchair. She had a warm smile on her face. Papa Black kneeled down and gave her a warm hug saying, "Thank you. I love you."

Great-Grandma J replied, "You're welcome, grandson. I love you, too."

Papa Black ate dinner before going to bed. By the time he went into the bedroom, we all had fallen fast asleep except for Mama Black. Mama Black was up folding some clothes. They began talking.

"Hey. How's it going?" Papa Black whispered to Mama Black as she continued folding clothes. They didn't want to wake us up, so they continued to whisper to each other.

"Hey. It's going well. How are you feeling?" Mama Black responded.

"Lor, I'm feeling good about this apartment. It's been months since we've been able to eat, sleep and live comfortably. I have a really good feeling about this," said Papa Black.

"Yes. It has been a while. The kids are growing so beautifully. I just want them to enjoy their childhood and have fun," Mama Black whispered.

"Yes. I know. We will do just that. Let's see how everything goes on Saturday and we will take it from there," Papa Black said while taking off his black, old, rugged work boots.

"Okay," Mama Black replied.

Mama Black finished the last pile of clothes and then she put them away. Papa and Mama Black eventually went to bed.

The rest of the week was full of hope and promise for us. Papa and Mama Black were excited about the possibility of finally getting our own space. Everything felt like it was finally falling into place.

CHAPTER 19
STARTING FROM SCRATCH

That Saturday morning, the sun was shining, the sky was clear and blue, and Mama Black didn't have to make several attempts to wake us up that morning. We knew it was going to be a good day!

Papa Black called the landlord that morning to confirm the appointment. The landlord confirmed that we were able to take a tour at 11am to see the house and decide.

Everyone had eaten, was dressed and ready to go. Papa Black told Grandpa Joseph Sr., Great Grandma J and Aunty V that we would return in a few hours because we were going to look at house. We piled in the car and made our way to 108 Freedom Lane in Hopeville, New Jersey.

Hopeville was about fifteen minutes from where Grandpa Joseph Sr. lived. When Papa Black pulled up in front of the house, all of us looked out the car window in amazement. Everyone was happy and had a smile on their face when Papa Black pulled up in front of the house. The house was big and white with large windows that wrapped around the house. The stairs looked like you were entering a mansion. We had never seen a house so beautiful, clean, and huge. We were so excited and couldn't wait to see the rest of the house.

Mama Black sat on the passenger side of the car, with the window down slightly leaning her head out of the window. The beautiful smile on her face while looking at the house gave us all hope.

Gracie blurted out in excitement, "Wow! This house is huge!"

Papa Black replied, "Yes, it is, Gracie. Yes, it is."

Papa Black was excited and proud in that moment. He was finally able to find a home that was fitting for the size of his family and a home that we all were excited about. Moving into such a beautiful home would be a fresh start for our family.

The landlord had already arrived and was standing on the porch to greet us. Papa Black parked and everyone immediately got out the car with huge smiles on our faces.

It was a one-family house with a backyard. We never had a backyard that we could play in. The previous house we lived in had a backyard, but we couldn't play in it. It was filled with junk and overgrown weeds. So, having a home with a clean and open backyard was exciting for all of us.

The landlord stood on the porch smiling back at Papa and Mama Black as he could see the happiness all over their faces. They couldn't wait to take a tour of their soon to be new home.

Before entering the house, the view from the outside was jaw-dropping. The house sat on a hill which made the house look that much bigger. While walking up the twelve stairs, you couldn't help but notice the lawn was freshly manicured; the grass was short and neatly cut. The stairs were made of gray, white, and black cobblestones with black banisters.

There were six white columns that complimented the long and wide porch. The front door had a white screen door and a black door with a small peep hole. The house had a very antique and traditional look to it.

We finally made it to the porch after admiring every little detail that they had seen on the outside of the house. We continued to beam with excitement and happiness. The landlord greeted Papa Black with an extended hand. "Mr. Black?! I'm Jafari. It is a pleasure to finally meet you!"

Mr. Jafari was no taller than 5'6. His deep brown earth tone skin was captivating and mesmerizing. His pearly white teeth had a way of making his skin and smile glow. Mr. Jafari also wore bifocals which were noticeable like his bright smile.

Papa Black extended his hand and said, "Yes. I'm Mr. Black. Nice to meet you, Mr. Jafari. This is my wife, Mrs. Black and our children." Mama Black also shook Mr. Jafari's hand.

"Hello kiddos!" Mr. Jafari said after shaking Mama Black's hand.

We all answered in unison, "Hello, Mr. Jafari."

Mr. Jafari replied in astonishment, "Wow! Your kids are so well behaved and respectful."

Mama Black replied with a cunning smile while looking at us, "Well, thank you."

Little did Mr. Jafari know Mama Black had given us that *Mama Talk* again so we knew better than to act up! We understood when Papa and Mama Black were trying to take care of business we had to be on our best behavior.

Mr. Jafari continued, "Well, shall we go in to take you on a tour?"

Papa Black replied, "Yes. We should. Let's do that." Papa Black had a stern look on his face. He was very rigid and serious in public places with his wife and children. He instantly went into protective mode.

Mama Black entered the house first while Papa Black entered last, making sure that that everyone made it in the house before him. Once all of us entered the house, we were so excited.

Mr. Jafari began his tour. He stated, "This is the atrium area and to right is the family room. The family room is spacious, as you can see. It has wrap-around windows with a small fireplace, newly wooded floors, and a sufficient heating system. The space is big enough to fit your family in here comfortably."

Papa Black just nodded while Mama Black said, "This is a very nice space."

We continued the tour and made our way into the dining room. It was also very spacious and nice. It had large windows. Attached to the dining room was the kitchen. The kitchen had a huge refrigerator, an island, several cabinets, a microwave, and a dishwasher.

When Gracie saw the dishwasher, she was incredibly happy. That meant she didn't have to do the dishes anymore since she was the main one, out of all of us, to wash the dishes.

Mama Black turned to Gracie and said, "Look Gracie! They have a dishwasher. You don't have to do the dishes anymore."

Gracie responded with a bright smile on her face, "Yes, Mama! Now I really love this house!" Everyone started laughing; even Papa Black cracked a smiled.

The next area we viewed was the backyard.

"This is the backyard. It has a lot of green space for the kids to play outside. Unfortunately, we can't go out there now because they are still fixing it up. But this is the backyard," Mr. Jafari replied.

We all looked through the screen window at the backyard. Mama Black was impressed and happy there was a space for her kids to play while keeping a close eye on them. Papa Black was also impressed but he didn't show any emotion. We continued touring the house. Next, it was time to see the bedrooms.

Sensing they liked the house, Mr. Jafari smiled and said, "Next we will take a look at the bedrooms and bathroom, upstairs!"

Trying to contain our excitement, my siblings and I responded in unison saying, "Yes!" Everyone busted into laughter. Papa Black also laughed in that moment.

As we made our way back towards the atrium, we walked up the staircase that lead us to the bedrooms and bathroom. The staircase had white spindles with a black banister. The staircase curved into the upstairs area which added an elegant look to the space.

As Mama Black walked up the staircase while gliding her chocolate brown hand up the black banister, she said to Mr. Jabari, "This is a nice staircase and banister. I really like how the staircase curves into the hallway upstairs."

Just like Mama Black paid attention to the details with her family, she also paid attention to the details in the things she would buy.

"Thank you. This design has been here for years. We just did a new paint job to give it an extra appeal," said Mr. Jafari.

Mama replied, "Very nice job."

We finally reached the upstairs hallway. The first room we viewed was the largest bedroom. Papa and Mama Black would automatically get the largest bedroom. The large window let the sunlight in, the natural lighting was nice. The room also had a tiny nook near the window. Mama Black loved this feature. She had never seen one before, but she could see herself sitting there in her quiet time when we were asleep. With every room we visited; we grew more attached to the house.

The next three bedrooms we visited weren't as big as Papa and Mama Black's potential room, but it was bigger than the previous apartment we lived in. This meant all the girls didn't have to share one room. Strength and I would share a room while Gracie, Audacious and Joy would share another room. Meaven always had his own room. It was the perfect place for our family size.

The last room to visit was the bathroom. Like the bedrooms, the bathroom was also big. However, the walls were covered with floral vintage wallpaper. Fortunately, that was the only area in the house that had wallpaper. It complimented the ceramic yellow bathroom tub and sink, and white tiled floors.

The bathroom was the least appealing of all the rooms, but it felt like home to us. Mama Black loved the flow of the space and its open floor concept. Based on Mama Black's face during the entire tour, she was already sold on the house the moment she stepped foot on the property. Mama Black couldn't contain her smile, but Papa Black kept his poker face.

The tour was over, and Mr. Jafari asked, "So, what did you guys think about the house?"

Joy, in her innocent and sweet voice, blurted out, "I love it!" Everyone couldn't help but look at Joy and smile.

Mr. Jafari quickly answered, "Well, the little lady has spoken!"

Papa Black also felt like it was home for him and his family but didn't give any indication that he liked it as much as Mama Black.

Papa Black began to ask questions. He said, "So, does the rental include heat and hot water? How is parking? Is the lease month to month or yearly? How much is the deposit and rent per month?" Papa Black kept all his questions until the end.

Mr. Jafari replied, "Great questions, Mr. Black. Since you are renting, it will include heat and hot water. There is no overnight parking on the street, but you can park in the driveway. It is a yearly lease. Lastly, the deposit is $1,000 and $700 per month. Mr. Jafari continued, "Any further questions, Mr. Black?"

Papa Black paused for a moment before responding. He thought to himself that there were really no issues with the place. He really liked it for his family. Papa Black could see himself and Mama Black raising us here. He had a great feeling about saying yes but wanted to get Mama Black's input before making the final decision.

After Papa Black's deep thought, he responded to Mr. Jafari saying, "Mr. Jafari, thank you for giving us the tour. I'd like to talk to my wife for a moment. Could you give us a moment to discuss?"

"Sure. Absolutely. I'll step outside for a bit. Come grab me when you're ready. Please, take your time," Mr. Jafari said.

Papa Black replied, "Thank you."

Papa and Mama Black walked from the atrium back into the kitchen. They wanted their privacy and didn't want Mr. Jafari to hear what they were discussing. My siblings and I stayed in the atrium area while Papa and Mama handled business. Meaven and Audacious were being silly, cracking jokes while Strength and Joy laughed hysterically. Gracie and I were playing a hand game called *Slide*. We loved playing that game together. We would play extremely fast and would laugh when one of us messed up.

Papa and Mama Black finally made their way into the kitchen. Facing each other, Mama Black said, "So, what are your thoughts?"

Papa Black paused for a slight moment and replied, "Well, I think it's a really nice place. The kids seem to really like it. It's big and comfortable enough for all eight of us." Papa Black continued, "Not only that, the rent is affordable."

"Yes. The rent is affordable. It is also not too far from work for us or school for the kids," Mama added to the conversation.

"That is also true," Papa Black responded in agreement with Mama Black. They both paused for a moment in silence before saying anything else.

After a while, Papa Black said, "I have the deposit on me. Let's do it." Mama Black looked at Papa Black surprised and shocked.

Mama Black replied with her eyes widened, "You have the deposit?! That is great news! I didn't know we had the full amount." Mama Black was so happy she beamed with joy. Mama Black felt that she and her family were that much closer to having their own home. It was finally happening.

Papa Black responded, "Yes. I have the full amount. We could let him know we want to put the deposit down today if we wanted to."

Mama Black barely let Papa Black finish his sentence, "I think we should."

Papa Black agreed and replied, "Okay. I'll let him know we will take it."

Papa Black walked past us as we played and told jokes in the atrium. Mama Black left the kitchen and made her way to check on us. We all stayed inside until Papa Black returned.

Mr. Jafari stood on the wrap around porch with his hands in his pockets. He paced the porch back and forth hoping Papa and Mama Black liked the house and would take the offer. Papa Black opened the door and stepped out on the porch and walked towards Mr. Jafari.

"Mr. Jafari. Listen, my wife and I have decided we want to take it. What are the next steps?" Papa Black kept a straight face while talking.

Mr. Jafari replied with a smile on his face saying, "That's great news, Mr. Black. If you are interested in moving forward, we will need a deposit of $1,000 today and we will have you sign the lease agreement."

Papa Black replied, "Okay. Where's the lease?"

Mr. Jafari saw that Papa Black was serious. "Mr. Black, it's in my car. I'll go grab it and bring it right back," he replied.

Papa Black replied, "Okay."

Mr. Jafari went to his car, grabbed his folder, pen, the lease agreement and a receipt book. He walked back up the cobble-stoned stairs prepared to do business with Papa Black. He handed the lease over to Papa Black to read. Papa Black took a few minutes to look it over. He even called Mama Black to the porch so that she could also read over the lease. Mama Black made her way outside and looked at the lease agreement. She nodded to Papa Black as to say that the lease agreement was legit.

Papa and Mama Black felt good about their decision. It was like it was meant to be for us. Papa Black did another glance over before he and Mama Black would sign it. They finally signed it and gave Mr. Jafari $1,000 in cash. Mr. Jafari wrote out a receipt for them as proof that they had given him a deposit. Now, the house was officially there's to move in. Mama Black was so overjoyed! Papa Black was too, but he just didn't show it.

"Mr. and Mrs. Black, congratulations! I will go to the office to process the rest of your paperwork. You can come by tomorrow at noon to pick up your house keys," Mr. Jafari confirmed.

Mr. Jafari began putting his paperwork back into his folder. Then, he stuffed the $1,000 in cash in a manila envelope and stuck it inside of his folder. Before locking up the house, Mr. Jafari added, "You have my number. If there's anything that comes up, please don't hesitant to call me. I'll see you tomorrow at noon." Mr. Jafari put his hand out to shake Papa Black's hand first, and then he shook Mama Black's hand.

"Thank you, Mr. Jafari. I'll see you tomorrow at noon," Papa Black replied while looking Mr. Jafari straight in his eyes.

Papa and Mama Black had finished their business and now it was time to go back to Grandpa Joseph Sr.'s house. Mama Black called to get our attention. We were still inside playing. Mama Black would always call Strength first since she was the oldest.

Mama Black shouted, "Strength, Meaven, Journee, Gracie, Audacious and Joy! Time to go!" Audacious was the first one out the house. She busted out the front door, running. Then it was Strength and Joy. Strength was holding Joy's hand. Gracie and I walked out together laughing and giggling with each other while Meaven was last. He made sure all his sisters got out first, like Papa Black taught him.

Mama Black stood on the porch with a beaming smile on her chocolate golden brown face. Papa Black still had his poker face on. My siblings and I didn't know what was going on, but we felt it may be good news. Papa and Mama Black didn't say anything while on the porch. They began walking down the cobble-stone steps towards the car. Mr. Jafari stayed behind to lock up the soon-to-be Black family's place of residence.

As soon as everyone piled into the car, Mama Black couldn't wait to share the good news. Papa Black started the engine and began driving. Mama Black looked in the back seat to see the excitement on her babies' face once she told us the great news. Mama Black was good at playing tricks on us. Before she told us the real news, Mama Black had a sad look on her face. She said, "Well, y'all. I know you guys like the house, but we won't be moving there."

Audacious replied while slapping her hand against her forehead, "Aw, man!

Strength said, "Oh well. We will find something else."

Meaven, Gracie, Joy and I didn't respond because we didn't have anything to say.

Mama Black stayed quiet for a moment while Papa Black had a smirk on his face. No one could really see it because he was driving and facing forward. A few moments passed by and Mama Black shouted, "Sike! Just joking! We got the house! Now you guys have a backyard to play in!"

Gracie shouted with an innocent smile on her face saying, "Mama! You got us again." We all started laughing. But we were all so excited and happy!

I added, "Yes! Now, we have our own space."

Mama Black replied, "Yes, baby. We sure will."

The car ride back to Grandpa Joseph Sr.'s house was a happy and exciting one. It's been a while since we've had our own place. Papa and Mama Black felt things were finally coming together again for our family.

They pulled up to Grandpa Joseph Sr.'s house full of energy. Even Papa and Mama Black were full of energy. Papa Black couldn't wait to share the news with Grandpa Joseph Sr. Once they got inside the house, Papa Black shared the good news with Grandpa Joseph Sr., Great-Grandma J and Aunty V. They were just as happy as Papa Black.

CHAPTER 20
NO ANSWER

It was the next day and Papa Black called Mr. Jafari at 11:30am to give him a heads up that he was on his way to pick the keys. Mama Black had decided to stay behind with us at Grandpa Joseph Sr.'s house. When Papa Black called Mr. Jafari, he couldn't reach him. Papa Black called him once more. Still no answer.

After Papa Black called the second time, Mama Black said to Papa Black, "Maybe he's busy or didn't hear the phone ring. Just stop by there. He knows you are meeting him there by noon. Just go there."

Papa Black replied, "Okay, you're right. I'll leave now. I'll be back soon."

Mama Black responded, "Okay. See you later."

Papa Black left his father's house to meet up with Mr. Jafari. He pulled up to the house five minutes before noon. Papa Black couldn't tell if someone was in the house from his car, so he got out and walked up those cobble-stoned steps. The doors were locked, so Papa Black knocked on the door several times. He even looked through the large window where you could see the family and dining room. Still, no one was in sight. Mr. Jafari wasn't inside the house. Papa Black then decided to go to the backyard to see if he was there. He wasn't there. He was nowhere to be found.

Papa Black went to his car and sat there for a while. "Maybe he's running late," Papa Black thought to himself.

A half hour passed. Then, an hour passed. By this time, Papa Black had been waiting for a long, stressful hour. Papa Black grew more and more frustrated the longer he waited on Mr. Jafari in his car. He decided to go the nearest pay phone to call Mr. Jafari. After all, Mr. Jafari made it clear that Papa and Mama Black could call him at any time for anything.

So, he drove around the corner. He pulled up the nearest bodega that had a pay phone on the corner. Papa Black had the option of putting $.5 cents, $.10 cents, or $.25 cents in the pay phone to call Mr. Jafari. Papa Black always had change on him, so he inserted $.25 cents because he knew he was going to give Mr. Jafari an ear full for his lateness.

The phone rung, no one picked up. He called Mr. Jafari again. No answer, again. For the third and last time, Papa Black inserted his $.25 cents into the pay phone, still no answer. Papa Black was infuriated.

He went back around to the house and sat there for another hour. It was 2:30pm. Mr. Jafari never showed up. He stole Papa and Mama Black's hard-earned money and never had any intentions on renting the house to them.

After waiting for hours, Papa Black went back to the house with his family. When he arrived, we were in the bedroom playing. Mama Black was in the living room with Grandpa Joseph Sr., Great-Grandma J and Aunty V. The television was on, but stillness and disappointment filled the room.

Papa Black walked into the living room like he had the entire world on his shoulders. He was disappointed and discouraged. As soon as Mama Black laid her eyes on him, she asked in a confused and frustrated tone, "What happened?!"

Papa Black dropped his body in the chair as if he didn't know what to say. So many things went through his mind. Papa Black gathered all the energy he had left in him in that moment. Papa Black replied, "I sat there for two and a half hours waiting for Mr. Jafari. He never showed up. I called him from the payphone several times. He never picked up. I left a message on his voicemail. I stood by the phone booth for a while to see if he would call it back. Nothing. I went back around to the house to wait for him for another two hours. Still nothing."

Without hesitation, Mama Black replied, "That no-good-son-of-a-gun! How dare he?! We gave him our last! How could he do this to a struggling family?! Now we have to start from scratch! $1,000 gone! Just gone! I can't believe this!"

Mama Black was just as angry and appalled as Papa Black, except Mama Black was expressing by yelling.

Grandpa Joseph Sr. interjected Mama Black's yelling. He responded, "Daughter-in-law, I know you're upset. It will be okay. You guys can stay here as long as you need to."

Those were the only words that Grandpa Joseph Sr. could say to ease the stress and hopelessness Papa and Mama Black felt in that moment. Great Grandma J and Aunt V didn't even have the words to say. They remained quiet. They knew how hard Papa and Mama Black worked to save that money for their family. Then, to have it just disappear while still not having a home to show for it made it that much more difficult and hurtful.

Grandpa Joseph Sr. continued saying, "Well, can you guys take him to court and get your money back?"

Papa Black replied, "Pops, by the time we take him to court and pay court fees, it wouldn't be worth the time or money. Plus, I can't take off work."

Grandpa Joseph Sr. replied, "Okay, son. I understand. Everything will work out for y'all."

Papa Black replied, "Thanks, Pops. I appreciate it."

Mama Black was still fired up. She responded, "We were all so excited and happy to move into that place. The kids are going to be disappointed when we tell them. I just can't believe he did this! He's a con artist. That's what he is!" Mama Black just couldn't understand how someone seemed so professional yet was a scam artist. Papa and Mama Black didn't see that coming, but they learned a lot that day.

Great-Grandma J finally spoke in her sweet, gentle voice. She said, "I know you both are disappointed, but trust God. Everything happens for a reason. He will make a way for you and the family."

After hearing that, Papa and Mama Black just sat there in silence. There was something reassuring when Great-Grandma J spoke. When she spoke, things would happen. Not right away, but eventually. That was what Papa and Mama Black needed to hear in that moment.

Papa and Mama Black eventually went into the bedroom to share the news with us. When they walked in, Gracie and I were playing dolls together while, Strength, Meaven, Audacious were playing a card game. Joy just sat there and watched while she held a brown teddy bear. When Papa and Mama Black walked in, it was obvious they had to share something serious with us.

Walking into the bedroom first, Mama Black opened the door and said, "Hey y'all. What are y'all up to?

Strength responded while still looking at the cards in her hands, "Nothing, Mama. We are just playing cards."

Papa Black had entered right behind Mama Black. He stood there and said, "Me and your mother have to talk to y'all about something." Because of Papa Black's serious tone, we immediately stopped what we were doing and gave Papa and Mama Black our undivided attention. Papa and Mama Black had come inside the room, closed the door, and sat on the bed.

Mama Black started the conversation off. She asked, "Do y'all remember the house we went to go look at yesterday?"

All of us replied in unison saying, "Yes, Mama."

Strength added, "What happened? Are we still able to move in?"

Papa and Mama Black paused for a moment before responding. Papa Black chimed in and said, "No, Strength. That's what we came in here to talk to y'all about."

Then Meaven said, "So we aren't moving there anymore?"

Papa Black responded by saying, "No. We aren't moving there anymore. I went to pick up the keys from Mr. Jafari and he never showed up."

Joy replied innocently saying, "So, is he coming tomorrow since he didn't show up today?"

Mama Black said, "Well, Joy. We are not sure. Your father and I think that if he didn't show up today, then he probably won't show up tomorrow."

Joy said, "So that means we can't move in that nice house and we aren't going to have a backyard anymore?"

Tears began to well up in Mama Black's eyes. She couldn't respond immediately because she felt the frustration and hurt all over again. Mama Black felt so violated, disrespected and helpless.

Papa Black took over the conversation. He answered, "No, baby girl. We won't be able to move there and that won't be our backyard."

We just sat there quiet and sad. Although we didn't understand all that was going on, we were just as disappointed as Papa and Mama Black. We looked forward to living in a house that was spacious with stairs and a backyard. It was our dream.

Papa Black continued, "For the time being, we will stay here with Grandpa Joseph Sr., Great-Grandma J and Aunty V. Mama and I are going to keep looking for the right house for us as a family."

It was quiet for a moment. Mama Black allowed the tears to touch and caress her chocolate golden brown cheeks. Mama Black's tears represented not only the disappointment for herself, but for her family. There was nothing that Mama Black desired more than to provide a better life for her six children. That was important to Mama Black, and Papa Black, too. When things didn't go as planned, she felt she was failing her family. But it would never stop Papa and Mama Black from trying. They would keep fighting for a better life for our family.

Mama Black finally responded after wiping the tears from her beautiful face. She said, "Everything will work out for us as a family. We will keep God first, pray and trust that we will get a house that's just for us. We just have to stick together."

"Okay, Mama. It will be okay," I responded. I got up and walked over to Mama Black and gave her the biggest hug I could. As Mama Black hugged me back, more tears came streaming down her face.

Papa Black said, "Yes. It will be okay. We will stick together as a family."

CHAPTER 21
EVERYTHING HAPPENS
FOR A REASON

The next day, Papa Black went back to work while Mama Black stayed at the house with us. While everyone else was still asleep, I woke up and wanted to check in on Mama Black.

I whispered to Mama Black, "Mama?"

Mama Black responded while not even turning around to see who it was. She knew all our voices. She replied sweetly, "Yes, Journee."

I replied, "Are you okay?

Mama Black stated, "Yes, I'm okay, baby. Are you okay?"

I replied, "Yes. I'm okay."

Mama Black replied, "Good."

A few moments later, the rest of my siblings woke up. We knew Mama Black was still a little sad from the day before, so we made sure we behaved. We didn't want to add any extra stress on Mama Black.

By the time everyone got up and dressed, Grandpa had finished making his infamous home fries with peppers and onions. Afterwards, we rushed into the living room. It was routine for us to get up and dressed, and then eat Grandpa Joseph Sr.'s delicious home fries. We went to the living room, sat down, and ate breakfast.

Grandpa Joseph Sr. said, "Good Morning, family! How you doing today?"

We all responded saying, "Good Morning. We're fine Grandpa!"

Mama Black replied, "Good Morning Mr. Black. We are doing fine, thank you. How are you guys doing? Thank you again for all that you've done for us."

Grandpa Joseph Sr. responded in lighthearted-manner, "Oh, you're welcome daughter-in-law. That's what we are here for."

Mama Black graciously replied, "Thank you."

We continued eating breakfast, while Grandpa Joseph Sr., Mama Black, Great-Grandma J, and Aunty V watched the news. The news coverage that day was the tragic story and death of Princess Diana. For some reason, Mama Black had liked Princess Diana and felt sorry for her sons. Mama Black watched that news coverage the entire day. It took her mind off things for a moment. She needed that.

After finishing breakfast, Mama Black told us to either go in the bedroom and play or stay in the living room and be quiet. We all went to the bedroom to play. We immediately went back into the bedroom while Mama Black stayed in the living room Grandpa Joseph Sr., Great-Grandma J and Aunty V. Mama Black needed something to get her mind off what happened yesterday.

A few hours passed by, and the phone rang. It was Papa Black. He called just to check-in and see how things were going with us and Mama Black.

Grandpa Joseph Sr. picked up the phone after the third ring. He answered, "Hello?"

Papa Black replied, "Hey, Pops. This is Joe. How y'all making out over there?"

"We are doing fine. We had breakfast not too long ago. The kids are in the room and Lorraine is sitting here watching the news coverage about Princess Diana," Grandpa Joseph Sr. said.

"That's cool. Can I speak to Lorraine for a second," Papa Black asked.

"Sure, son. I'll pass the phone over to her right now," Grandpa Joseph Sr. replied.

While unraveling the telephone cord, Grandpa Joseph Sr. said, "Here you go, Lorraine. It's your husband on the phone."

Mama Black didn't realize the phone had rung and that Grandpa Joseph Sr. was talking to Papa Black. She was so engaged in the news coverage about Princess Diana. Mama Black got up from the couch and walked over to where Grandpa Joseph Sr. had been talking to Papa Black.

"Hello?" Mama Black said.

"Hey. How's it going?" Papa Black responded.

"It's going okay. The kids are just in the room playing and I'm in the living room just watching the news. How is it going for you?" Mama Black replied.

"It's going okay. Just working," Papa Black answered.

"Oh ok. Did you hear from Mr. Jafari?" Mama Black asked hoping that the reality of their situation would have changed since they've last spoke.

"No, Lorraine. I didn't hear from him," Papa Black replied in a hopeless tone.

Papa and Mama Black were silent on the phone for a moment.

"I just can't believe he did that. He took all our hard-earned money and left a family hanging. What a sad man to steal from a family! He doesn't know our living situation. We could be living in a shelter or on the street for all that he knows. And for him to take that money from us and our kids and here we are still homeless! May karma find him when he least expects it!" Mama Black snapped. She went from hurt to mad.

Papa Black didn't blame her disappointment and frustration. He felt the same way. He allowed Mama Black to have her moment. He let her get things off her chest.

He eventually replied by saying, "Yes. You're right. You're absolutely right."

"I'm just disappointed with how things turned out. But maybe all of this happened for a reason," Mama Black said trying to find some hope out of the situation.

"We will get through this, Lorraine. We will. Well, I will see y'all soon. I'll be there when I get off work," Papa Black said.

"Okay. See you soon," Mama Black replied.

By the time Papa Black got in from work, we were preparing for bed. Mama Black made sure we went to bed earlier than we usually did when we had our own apartment. Mama Black knew how rowdy and lively we could get. Even though Grandpa Joseph Sr. loved having his grandchildren around, Mama Black tried her best to not add any extra stress on the already-packed household. So, Mama Black had us in the bed no later than 7pm.

That evening, Papa Black finally made it in by 6pm. Everyone was having dinner when he arrived. We had hot dogs and French fries for dinner. We drank cherry Kool-Aid that night.

All of us kids would squeeze ourselves at the kitchen table while all the adults would sit on the couch and eat dinner. My siblings and I would always have the same seating arrangement. Gracie and I always sat next to each other; Meaven and Audacious would sit next to each other so they could crack jokes and giggle; Strength and Joy sat next each other.

After dinner was finished, we said our goodnights to everyone and went to bed. Papa and Mama Black stayed in the living room. They sat and talked with Grandpa Joseph Sr., Great-Grandma J and Aunty V all night. As they talked, they brainstormed other options for Papa and Mama Black to find somewhere to live and hopefully find a program that helps with security deposits. Papa and Mama Black needed the extra support because trying to save up for a security deposit would have kept them at Grandpa Joseph Sr.'s house for another six months. Papa and Mama Black didn't want to wait that long to find something else.

After they finished talking, Papa and Mama Black decided to go out for breakfast Saturday morning to talk and look up programs to help them find our next home.

"Thank y'all for helping me and Lorraine. You've been a huge help," Papa Black said after taking a sip of the cherry Kool-Aid.

"You're welcome, son. Don't get discouraged. You'll be back on your feet in no time" Grandpa Joseph Sr. replied.

Papa Black said, "Thanks, Pops. Do you mind if we leave the kids here with y'all? Me and Lorraine won't be out for long. We want to make sure we spend most of our time finding something and not telling the kids to sit down, be quiet and leave each other alone." Everyone chuckled. Grandpa Joseph Sr. could relate since he and Nana Josephine also had six kids.

"Oh, yes. That's fine, son. They're in good hands. You won't have to worry about a thing! Grandpa Joseph Sr. said without hesitation.

Papa Black replied laughing, "Okay, Pops. Make sure me and Lorraine come back here with our kids in one piece!"

"Joe, don't worry. I think you and your siblings came out fine. Y'all turned out pretty decent," Grandpa Joseph Sr. said while laughing.

"Dad, that's debatable!" Papa Black continued to joke.

Aunty V interjected while also laughing, "Joseph, you and Lorraine go head and take care of your business. The kids will be fine. There are three adults here so don't worry about it." Aunty V smiled reassuring Papa and Mama Black that everything would be fine.

"Okay. Okay. Thanks, Aunty V," Papa Black responded.

Papa Black had finished his last sip of Kool-Aid. He and Mama Black said their goodnights and headed to bed.

The next morning, Papa and Mama Black got up early to take care of business. Before they left, they woke up Strength and Meaven to let them know what was going on.

"Strength and Meaven, wake up," Mama Black said while putting her shoes on. Papa Black was in the bathroom getting ready.

"Yes, Mama?" Strength said with her eyes half-way opened. Meaven just opened his eyes to show Mama Black that he was listening. He just laid there, too tired to answer and too tired to sit up.

"Me and your father are going out to find out about some apartments for us. Your grandfather will be watching y'all today. You are in charge so make sure y'all are on y'all best behavior. If I hear that y'all weren't listening and cutting up, y'all are going to get it. Do you hear me, Strength?!" said Mama Black.

All Strength could say was, "Yes, Mama. Okay. I'll make sure they listen."

Papa Black had finally made it out the bathroom and was dressed. He sat on the edge of the bed to put his shoes on. While doing so, he woke up Meaven.

"Meaven, sit up," Papa Black said.

Meaven sat up immediately and said, "Yes, Pops?"

Papa in a stern and serious tone, "Listen, make sure you look out for your sisters. Me and your mother are going to find out about some apartments. Look after your sisters. Do you hear me?"

"Yes, sir," Meaven replied. Then, he laid back down.

"Alright y'all. We will be back soon. Make sure y'all listen to your grandfather. See y'all later," Mama Black said.

Strength and Meaven just waved good-bye to Papa and Mama Black.

They grabbed their jackets and closed the bedroom door behind them. Strength and Meaven laid there for a while before getting up for the day. After an hour or so, they eventually got up. When Gracie, Audacious, Joy and I woke up for the day, Strength told them where Papa and Mama went. Strength made sure to relay the same message to them that Mama Black had given to her and Meaven.

Once we got dressed, we went to the living room and had breakfast together. Grandpa Joseph Sr. made his traditional home fries with peppers and onions. He also made scrambled eggs with cheese. We also had orange juice to drink. We really enjoyed breakfast that day.

Strength complimented Grandpa Joseph Sr. on his cooking that day while eating at the table. After chewing her food, Strength said to Grandpa Joseph Sr., "Thanks for cooking, Grandpa. Your breakfast is always delicious!"

"Well, thank you, granddaughter. I'm glad you like it. Have more if you want," Grandpa Joseph Sr. said.

"Okay. Thank you," Strength said while going up for a second serving.

The rest of us also chimed in saying, "Yes. Thanks for cooking for us, Grandpa."

Grandpa Joseph Sr. was happy his grandchildren enjoyed his cooking. He replied, "You're welcome, grandkids. Eat as much as you want." Once Grandpa Joseph Sr. said that, we all went back up for seconds.

After breakfast, we stayed in the living room with Grandpa Joseph Sr., Great-Grandma J, and Aunty V. We watched cartoons and laughed with and cracked jokes on each other. We listened to Mama Black. We were on our best behavior.

While watching TV, a commercial ad had come on about back to School shopping. School was two weeks away, and Papa and Mama Black were still looking for somewhere to live. Mama Black didn't want to go into a new school year without a place to call home. She wanted her family settled and under a roof of their own. Papa and Mama Black left the house not knowing what would happen, but they trusted that God would work things together for their good.

Papa and Mama Black went to the Hopeville Housing Authority to find out what programs could help them find housing and provide them with a security deposit. When they arrived, they didn't have to wait long. They arrived before the crowd arrived. Papa and Mama Black waited for 15 minutes before seeing a housing counselor.

A middle-aged woman, 4 foot 11 inches, with ebony brown-skin, and short tapered brown hair and bifocals came to the receptionist desk and grabbed the brown wooden clipboard calling out the next family on the list.

"Joseph and Lorraine Black. Is Joseph and Lorraine Black here?" Papa and Mama Black jumped up immediately.

"Good Morning. We are Joseph and Lorraine Black," Papa Black answered as soon as she called their names.

"Hello, Mr. and Mrs. Black. I'm Ms. Vera. You guys can follow me through this door," Ms. Vera said.

Papa Black replied, "Okay, sure."

Papa and Mama Black followed Ms. Vera to her office. Behind the grey door was a large open space with several cubicles with computers, filing cabinets and folders. Ms. Vera had her own office with a door. Mama Black took a quick glance at everything as she walked through the large open space.

Ms. Vera opened her office door and pleasantly said, "Come on in and have a seat, Mr. and Mrs. Black." She closed the door behind them.

Papa and Mama Black responded, "Thank you, Ms. Vera." After a few minutes, Papa and Mama Black had gathered that Ms. Vera wasn't just a housing counselor; she was the Supervisor of the Hopeville Housing Authority. When they sat down, Papa and Mama Black saw her desk name plate that read *Ms. Vera Thomas, Supervisor.*

As Ms. Vera took her seat behind her desk, she gathered her note pad and pen to take notes. "So, what brings you in today, Mr. and Mrs. Black?" Ms. Vera was genuine in her approach and Mama Black took a liking to her demeanor.

Papa Black began to re-tell the story that he and Mama Black had gone through within the past year. Papa Black said, "Well, my wife and I have six children: five daughters and one son. We were living in a one-bedroom apartment for a while and then decided to move into a two-family house. After a month or so, the house caught on fire. We stayed in two hotel rooms for a few months because we didn't have anywhere else to go. The church helped us get a security deposit to move into a three-bedroom apartment. Things were going well. Then, I got injured on the job which impacted my pay. When that happened, we fell behind on our rent. I asked my boss for help and he was able to give us a portion towards the outstanding balance. They evicted us anyway. We ended up staying with three different relatives. We are currently staying with my father, grandmother, and aunt. A few weeks ago, we were finally able to save $1,000 for a deposit. We did find a house that was a great fit, but the landlord took our $1,000 deposit and never showed up to give us our keys to the place. We even signed the lease and confirmed the time for the keys to be picked up. The landlord never showed up or responded to any of my calls. So now we are back at square one with no money. Is there any way we can receive support? Anything? We need it for our family."

Papa Black shared all that he and Mama Black went through in a matter of minutes. Hearing it all over again brought Mama Black to tears again. The tears shamelessly fell down Mama Black's sweet face.

Ms. Vera paused before responding. When she finally opened her mouth, she spoke gently. She replied, "Mr. and Mrs. Black, I am sorry you've been experiencing this with your six children. Life is hard enough and for you both to continue to fight for your family is very telling of the type of people and family you are. I am very compelled by your story. I would love to help you and your family. I am just going to ask you to fill out this packet here. This packet is the Section 8 Housing Program that provides rental assistance for families in need. I'm going to step out the office and give a few minutes to fill it out."

Mama Black replied while wiping the tears from her face, "Thank you, Ms. Vera. We appreciate your help."

"You're most welcome, Mrs. Black," Ms. Vera replied. Then, Ms. Vera left out her office, closing the door behind her.

As Mama Black grabbed the clipboard to complete the paperwork, she said to Papa Black, "I always get teary-eyed when we talk about everything that has happened to us over the years."

Papa Black glumly replied, "Yeah, I know."

Mama Black had completed all the paperwork for the Section 8 Housing Program application. As soon as Papa and Mama Black signed their names on the application, Ms. Vera entered back into her office.

"Alright, Mr. and Mrs. Black, how did you make out with the application? Do you have any questions?" Ms. Vera said.

"For the most part, all the questions were straight forward. My question is how soon does the application take to process and how soon will we know if we've been approved or not?" Mama Black replied.

"Well, Mr. and Mrs. Black. I want to talk to you about that. I'd like to get you approved as soon as possible. I'm going to enter your information into our system to expedite the process and get the ball rolling for your family. Due to you being homeless, we will provide you up to $1,000 in rental assistance. We also have a security deposit program that you qualify for, and we will provide your landlord with a security deposit as well. With that said, if you would like to start looking for houses or apartments in the Hopeville area, you can begin to do so." Ms. Vera spoke so matter-of-factly.

Ms. Vera continued, "Here's my business card, please call me or stop by if there's anything you need but I will be in touch with you. If you find a potential home, please give me a call on my direct line."

Papa and Mama Black couldn't believe what had just happened. It took them a while to process all that was going on in the moment. It was almost as if it was too good to be true. But Papa and Mama Black realized that sometimes all you need is a divine alignment with people through God and things can happen instantly.

Papa Black replied in complete astonishment saying, "Wait a minute. So, we are approved for the application already and can go search for a place to live?!"

Ms. Vera chuckled as she answered, "Yes, Mr. Black. That is correct. You've been approved."

More tears fell from Mama Black's face. This time, it was tears of happiness. They had no idea their day would take this this turn; from being homeless to shopping for a home for their family.

"Wow. Thank you. We are humbly grateful. This will change our lives for the better," Papa Black said. Mama Black was too chocked up to speak. So, she stood up and gave Ms. Vera a big hug. Ms. Vera embraced her. Before they left, Ms. Vera gave them a copy of their application and approval letter.

Papa and Mama Black left out of the Hopeville Housing Authority Office overwhelmed with joy. When they got to the car, Papa and Mama Black hugged. Mama Black wept in Papa Black's chest like she did when they saw their home go up in flames. This time, her weeping was tears of hope.

"Did you want to go grab something to eat? We can go to Harris Diner right down the street," Papa Black asked Mama Black.

"What about your father and the kids? I don't want him to think we are going to be out all day," Mama Black replied.

"We will be fine. We'll call them when we get to the diner," Papa Black said.

"Okay." Mama responded as she wiped her tears away with tissue and cleaned her nose.

Papa and Mama Black pulled into the parking lot of Harris Diner, walked inside, and waited to be seated. Harris Diner was a historical diner that had been in Hopeville for years. It was known for its antique and vintage look. On the outside, the doors were aluminum silver with green piping around the building. The framing outside the diner was like a tin can. Its large windows complemented the vintage look. The *Harris Diner* sign was had red letters that were hard to miss. On the inside, they had vinyl booth seats and green and white ceramic floors. Everyone loved Harris Diner. Towards the back of the diner were the payphones and restrooms.

Once Papa and Mama Black sat down, their waitress came over and took their order. Before they began to talk, Mama Black wanted to check in on us. She said to Papa Black, "Do you have some change? I want to call the kids and check in on them to see how things are going."

Papa Black reached in his pocket and gave Mama Black $.75 cents because he knew she would probably want to speak to all of us, one-by-one.

"Yes, here you go," Papa Black replied.

"Thank you," Mama Black responded.

Mama Black got up and walked towards the back of the diner. She reached the telephone booth, added her change, and began dialing Grandpa Joseph Sr.'s phone number.

It rang twice.

"Hello?" Grandpa Joseph Sr. picked up the phone.

"Hi, Mr. Black. How are you doing?" Mama Black said sweetly.

"I'm doing fine. How are guys making out?" said Grandpa Joseph Sr.

"Well, we've actually made out very well. We went to the Hopeville Housing Authority and spoke with a Section 8 counselor and we were approved for the program on the spot!" Mama said with so much joy in her voice.

Grandpa Joseph Sr. shouted with excitement, "Congratulations daughter-in-law! See, I knew everything would work out fine!"

"Thank you, Mr. Black. Thank you all for your help and support along the way. We couldn't have done this without you, Great-Grandma J, Aunty V, Ms. Josephine and my mother!" Mama Black replied.

"Oh, you're welcome. Hey, we are family. We must stick together," Grandpa Joseph Sr. said firmly.

"Yes, we do. They also told me and Joe that we can begin looking at houses or apartments. Not only that, they are going to help with the security deposit as well," Mama Black continued. As Mama Black talked on the phone, she saw an older woman in her peripheral vision but didn't pay her much attention.

She continued talking to Grandpa Joseph Sr. "We are here at Harris Diner getting something to eat. I hope that's okay. We will be home very soon. How are the kids? Are they behaving?"

Grandpa Joseph Sr. responded very jovially, "Yes! The kids are fine. They all went in the back bedroom to play. I guess they got tired of hanging around us old folks. They have been well behaved and are doing fine. Don't you guys worry about them. Enjoy yourselves."

Mama Black smiled and said, "Okay, Mr. Black. Well, we will see you soon."

Grandpa Joseph Sr. replied, "Okay, signing off." That meant 'talk to you later' in Grandpa Joseph Sr.'s words.

CHAPTER 22
DIVINE ALIGNMENT

Mama Black hung up the phone and walked back to the booth. Before Mama Black reached her seat, the same older lady that she saw while talking to Grandpa Joseph Sr. on the pay phone was now sitting at a booth Mama Black had to walk past.

The older lady's skin tone resembled a brown hickory color – smooth and rich. Although she was an older woman, her skin was smooth and ageless. She had a silver colored Jheri Curl; it was fitting for her. She wore over-sized eyeglasses and had thin lips, a small nose, and wide dark brown eyes. She had above average height for a woman. Her sweet and kind spirit recognized Mama Black's sweet and kind spirit.

Just as Mama Black was getting ready to pass her table, the older woman said, "Hi. I'm Ms. Pearl. I didn't mean to be all in your business while you were on the phone, but are you looking for an apartment or house for your family?"

Mama hesitated before answering. Eventually Mama Black opened her mouth and said, "Yes. My husband and I are looking for somewhere to live for our family."

"Well, I'm actually looking to rent out the second floor of my two-family home if you and your husband are interested," Ms. Pearl said.

"Is that, right? Well, let me bring my husband over to talk to you as well," Mama said. She called Papa Black over.

"Joe. Joe! Can you come over for a second?" Mama said while motioning her hand for Papa Black to come over to where she and Pearl were.

Papa Black got up and walked over with a puzzled expression on this face. When Papa Black arrived, Mama Black did a quick introduction. She said, "Joseph, this is Ms. Pearl. Ms. Pearl this is Joseph, my husband."

They shook hands and said hello.

Ms. Pearl began talking to Papa Black. She said, "Well, I overheard your wife talking on the payphone and she mentioned that you guys are looking for somewhere to live. I was just mentioning to your wife that I am renting out the second floor of my two-story home. I am looking for a tenant."

Papa and Mama Black couldn't believe what they heard. It was hard to believe, but it was something that their family needed.

Papa Black asked, "Wow, Ms. Pearl. Talk about perfect timing. We are looking for housing. Where is the location of the house?"

"It's right on Believer Street. 83 Believer Street," Ms. Pearl said.

"Believer Street?! That's right at this corner," Papa Black shouted with wide eyes. He wasn't expecting that. Mama Black was just as shocked.

"Yes, Mr. Joseph. The house is a few houses from here. It's within walking distance from the diner," Ms. Pearl said with confidence.

"Walking distance?! Papa and Mama Black said at the same time.

"Wow. I can't believe this. My wife and I just left the Hopeville Housing Authority Office and were approved for Section 8's housing rental assistance program. Long story short, we've been homeless for a while – almost a year on and off. Now we are staying with my father and need a place immediately. Do you accept Section 8?" said Papa Black.

"As a matter of fact, I do," said Ms. Pearl.

Mama Black blurted out, "Well, if it's down the street, can we go look at it and see if it's something we can live in?

Ms. Pearl answered without hesitation, "Yes! It would be my pleasure."

Papa and Mama Black ordered their food, but it hadn't come out yet. They told their waitress that they would be right back. The waitress overheard their conversation, so she was accommodating to Papa and Mama Black.

They left the diner and walked down Believer Street. As they walked, Ms. Pearl began to tell Papa and Mama Black a little bit about her story.

"My husband and I purchased this house many years ago and raised our three sons here. My husband died a year ago and my boys are grown now. It was just me living inside all this house and now I want something smaller and more manageable."

"Wow, I'm sorry to hear about your husband. My condolences to you and your family," Papa Black said as he listened intently to Ms. Pearl.

Mama Black was observing the scenery, neighbors, and environment to see if it was a good area to move her family to. So far, she didn't see any red flags.

By the time Papa Black and Ms. Pearl finished their conversation, they were in front of 83 Believer Street. The house sat on a small hill away from the curb. The silver gates were filled with so many branches and leaves that you could barely see the color of the house until you were at the stairs. To the left of the house was an apple tree. The tree was huge with long branches that drooped over the banister. When the apples grew fully, they weighed down the branches. Past the eleven steps, there was a white storm door and mustard yellow door with a mailbox slot.

When they got up the first set of stairs, Ms. Pearl began the tour of the house. She started by saying, "Right here is the closed-in porch with windows. You can come and sit out here whenever you want. To your right, there is a downstairs neighbor. She's been living here for a couple of years. She's a good tenant." Papa and Mama Black continued to listen as Ms. Pearl continued the tour.

Ms. Pearl took out her keys to open the door to enter the second floor of the two-family house. As soon as they entered the house, they went up another set of stairs. Ms. Pearl stopped at the first flight of stairs and said, "This door leads to the basement. In the basement there is a washer and dryer."

Mama Black replied astonished saying, "Did you say there's a washer and dryer?!"

Papa Black and Ms. Pearl chuckled.

Ms. Pearl replied with a smile on her face, "Yes. There is!"

Mama Black didn't say this out loud, but she was already sold! She really liked everything her and Papa Black had seen so far. They continued up the second flight of stairs.

Ms. Pearl continued, "On the first level is the bathroom which is to your immediate left, down the hallway is the kitchen which has a back door that leads to the backyard. On right is the master bedroom and directly across from the flight of stairs is the connecting living room and dining room. You can take a walk around."

Papa and Mama Black went into the bathroom first. It was spacious. Everything was white, the toilet, bathtub & shower, and floor tiles. There was also a storage shelf in the bathroom. This was a highlight for Mama Black since having five girls meant having lots of hair products, combs, brushes, blow dryers, curling irons, skin care products and more. Papa Black and Meaven were simple. They just had a brush, Murray's Hair Dressing, and a wave cap. Nonetheless, they really liked the bathroom.

Next, they toured the kitchen. The kitchen was spacious as well. It had a walk-in pantry to store food and cleaning products. The cabinets were large. The counter space alongside the sink is what Mama Black had always wanted. It also came with a large refrigerator and stove. The distinct feature about the kitchen was its black and white tiled floor and the window that overlooked the backyard. Papa and Mama Black looked out the window during the tour. This was their favorite feature in the house so far.

Next, they toured the dining room. It was another large space with a window. It had crème-colored carpet that also led into the living room. The dining room also had a closet. After viewing the dining room, Papa and Mama Black walked through to the living room. Although it had two separate entrances, the dining and living room were connected; it was a cool short-cut that Papa and Mama Black knew we would like. The living room was large and had a closet. There were three large windows that wrapped around the living room adding extra natural light inside the space. They continued the tour.

Papa and Mama Black went in the master bedroom – that bedroom would be for Papa and Mama Black. The bedroom had three windows.

Taking it all in, Mama Black couldn't help her excitement and hope. She said, "Wow. This is so nice. I love the space for our family."

Papa Black replied, "Yes. It is."

Ms. Pearl saw that Papa and Mama Black really liked what they saw so far. Ms. Pearl said, "Well, you guys have seen everything on the first level. Now, you can go and see the three bedrooms upstairs. I would go with you, but my knees are bad. You'll see all the rooms as soon as you get to the top of the stairs. I'll be right here when you return."

Papa and Mama Black liked Ms. Pearl's demeanor and personality. She was an accomplished and seasoned Black woman that was genuine and willing to help another Black family in need. Her motives seemed pure to Papa and Mama Black.

Before heading up the stairs, Papa and Mama Black said, "Okay. Thank you."

They turned towards the stairs and went up the first two steps. After the two steps, they made a slight turn as the staircase had a slight curve to it. There were eight stairs. The room on the left was the smallest, the room in the middle was the largest with three windows and the room on the right was the second largest with two windows. Each room had carpet.

Papa and Mama Black said to each other, "This house is just perfect for us."

After they finished looking at all three bedrooms, they went back downstairs. Ms. Pearl was standing in the hallway when they returned. She had a smile on her face and said, "So, how did you like it? Do you have any questions?"

Papa and Mama Black couldn't contain their excitement, hope and happiness. They both knew they wanted the house for their family, but they asked a few questions before saying yes. Papa Black started off.

"Ms. Pearl, thank you for the tour. We do have a few questions. Are heat and hot water included or is that separate?" Papa Black asked.

"Heat and hot water are included, Mr. Black," Ms. Pearl replied.

"Oh ok. What about parking? I didn't see a driveway coming in," Papa Black responded.

"There's no parking. I usually park down the street in a lot that I pay for or you can call the city of Hopeville to see if you can purchase an overnight parking pass," Ms. Pearl stated.

"Oh ok. Thank you," Papa Black said.

Mama Black envisioned her and her family in that house. Mama Black asked, "Ms. Pearl, are we allowed to use the washer and dryer?"

Ms. Pearl smiled before responding because she knew exactly why Mama Black had asked that question. Having three boys herself meant constantly washing clothes and trying to find time to do so. She could only imagine what Mama Black's schedule was like washing clothes for eight people.

"Well, you would be allowed to use it, but it would cost a little extra due to the size of your family," Ms. Pearl said.

Mama Black simply replied, "Oh okay. I understand."

After they finished talking, Papa Black asked, "Is there a way to get in touch with you Ms. Pearl? We would like to see if we can talk to our Section 8 counselor to see if your house qualifies."

Ms. Pearl replied enthusiastically, "Sure! Please take down my number and I'll take yours as well. My number is (973) 675-1213."

Mama Black pulled out her pen and a piece of receipt paper from her black purse. That was the only piece of paper she had in her purse at the time. She wrote the number on the back of it.

Ms. Pearl responded, "And what's a number I can contact you guys?"

Papa Black said, "Well, as I mentioned before, we are staying with at father's house now. So, I'll just give you his house number and you can ask to speak to me or Lorraine. The number is (973) 675-0223."

Ms. Pearl replied, "Okay. Thank you."

Ms. Pearl, Papa and Mama Black left the house and walked back to Harris Diner. Papa and Mama Black continued to chat about life and their kids.

Mama Black put her hand out to shake Ms. Pearl's hand. She said, "Ms. Pearl, thank you for speaking to me and allowing us to see the house on such short notice. I am so grateful you did that."

Papa Black echoed what Mama Black had said. He responded, "Yes! Thank you, Ms. Pearl."

Ms. Pearl replied very humbly, "Oh, thank you. Any way I can help a family. We will be in touch."

Ms. Pearl walked back to her booth. Papa and Mama Black walked to their booth. Their food had just come out as they sat down. Eating their meal felt different for Papa and Mama Black. They were so excited and full of hope that they couldn't eat all their food. After taking a few bites, Papa Black paid for their meal and they left. Ms. Pearl was still eating so they waved and made their way back to Grandpa Joseph Sr.'s house.

Papa and Mama arrived back to Grandpa Joseph Sr.'s house after being out for a few of hours handling business. When they arrived, we were still in the room playing. When they entered the apartment, Mama Black went straight to the bedroom to check on us while Papa Black went straight to the living where Grandpa Joseph Sr., Great-Grandma J and Aunty V were.

Mama Black opened the bedroom door with a happy glow. In a playful manner, she said, "What are y'all doing?!" Gracie, Audacious, Joy and I dropped everything we were doing, jumped up and ran to hug Mama Black. We hugged her tightly. She hugged us back just as tight. My siblings and I weren't used to Mama Black being away from us that long unless we were in school or away at camp.

We shouted, "Hi Mama!" Strength and Meaven spoke to Mama Black from the bed.

Mama Black replied to them, "Hey. I hope y'all were on y'all best behavior and listening to your big sister, brother and Grandpa Joseph."

Strength told Mama Black, "Yes. They were good for the most part. We ate, watched television, and played in the bedroom for most of the time."

Mama Black responded, "Okay. Well, me and your father had a good day today. We were able to go to the Section 8 Housing Authority Office and looked at a potential house." Mama Black was always open and honest with us. She felt good about the process, so she wanted us to feel good, too. So, she told us what she and Papa Black did that day.

Meaven, practically yelling, "Y'all saw a house today?! Do I get my own room?!" Poor Meaven. He was cool with having five sisters but wanted his own space and bed again!

Mama Black laughed knowing exactly why he asked that question. She also wanted Meaven to have his own space and bed. Mama Black snickered, "Yes, Meaven. You would get your own room!"

Meaven replied, "Yes! I can't wait. When do we move in?"

"Well, it will take some time. We will sort some things out with the Section 8 office and then speak with Ms. Pearl to see when we can move in. And I know y'all go back to school in two weeks and I go back to work, too. So, if we do move in, we will have to work together as a team."

Strength asked, "Who's Ms. Pearl?"

Mama Black responded, "Ms. Pearl is the woman that would rent the house to us. We met her at Harris Diner."

Audacious interrupted and said, "Y'all went out to eat without us?!"

Mama Black laughed and jokingly said, "Yes. Is that okay with you?"

We all laughed. Hearing the laughter from the living room, Papa Black made his way to the bedroom. He stood behind Mama Black as she continued to talk.

Audacious smiled and replied, "Yes, Mama."

Mama Black continued, "So, me and your father will call the Section 8 office on Monday and let them know we found a house and take it from there."

Gracie uttered, "I'm excited!"

Papa Black replied, "We are too, Gracie. We are too."

Papa and Mama Black went into the living room to finish talking to Grandpa Joseph Sr., Great-Grandma J, and Aunty V. They closed the door behind them. Papa Black told them what happened. When Papa and Mama Black told Grandpa Joseph Sr., Great-Grandma J and Aunty about the news, they congratulated them.

"Congratulations!" Grandpa Joseph Sr. shouted.

Great-Grandma J responded in her sweet, soft voice, "Congratulations. See what happens when you trust God? Proud of you both."

Papa Black replied, "Yes, Grandma J. You did say that everything would work out." Mama Black smiled, and touched and held Great-Grandma J's soft, wrinkled hand.

CHAPTER 23
NEW POSSIBILITIES

It was Sunday night, and my entire family was excited about the possibilities that Monday could bring. This time, Papa and Mama Black were very hopeful about finding something that was spacious enough for eight people and renting from someone who was honest and authentic. Everyone went to bed looking forward to Monday morning!

Morning time came and it was the day! Since summer was over in two weeks and Mama Black was home, she and Papa Black had agreed that Mama Black would call the Hopeville Section Housing Authority to speak to Ms. Vera. Mama Black woke up early with Papa Black to talk things through.

Papa Black whispered while getting ready, "So, I think it's best if you called Ms. Vera to let her know about Ms. Pearl and the house that we found. I'll let my father know you'll use the phone to call them. He won't mind."

Mama Black replied, "Okay. I'll give her a call and let her know. I'll also call Ms. Pearl afterwards to let her know what Section 8 says as well. I don't want her to offer the house to anyone else, so I'll follow-up with her to make sure she knows we are extremely interested."

While tying up his boot laces and listening to Mama Black, Papa Black replied, "Okay, sounds good. I'll call you on my lunch break and hopefully we will have good news by then."

"I hope so, too," Mama Black responded with a hug and a smile. Papa Black hugged her back.

"Okay. I'll see y'all later," Papa Black replied.

"Okay. See you later. Have a good day at work," Mama Black replied.

By the time Papa Black left the house, it was 7am. Before leaving out, he told Grandpa Joseph Sr. that Mama Black would need to call to the Section 8 counselor and would like to use the phone. Grandpa Joseph Sr. happily agreed.

Mama Black laid back down for a few and prayed. She had a few more hours before calling the Hopeville Section 8 Housing Authority office. Mama Black prayed, "Dear God, thank you for keeping us this long. You didn't bring us this far to leave us.

Please work things out so that we can get this house. In Jesus' Name, Amen."

Mama Black wanted to call at 9am sharp to talk to Ms. Vera. After praying, Mama Black was too excited to fall back to sleep, so she got up after a while and went into the bathroom to shower and prepare for the call. She refused to wake us up. If she woke us, that meant we would be up asking her a million and one questions. Plus, there was one more week until school started so she gave us the luxury of sleeping in. Mama Black did what any woman with six kids would do – she let us SLEEP.

It was 8:55am and Mama Black was ready for the call. She grabbed her purse and took out Ms. Vera's business card and Ms. Pearl's phone number on the back of that old receipt. She walked down that short hallway and into the living room. Grandpa Joseph Sr., Great-Grandma J and Aunty V were all up watching the morning news. It was their tradition.

"Good Morning, Family!" Mama said with her beautiful smile, looking and feeling very energetic!

"Good Morning, Lorraine! How are you doing this morning?" Grandpa Joseph Sr. responded.

Great-Grandma J and Aunty V also replied to Mama Black, "Good Morning Lorraine."

Mama Black replied, "I'm doing great. I was wondering if it was okay to use the phone. I need to call the Hopeville Section 8 Housing Authority office this morning to see if the house we saw yesterday would qualify."

Grandpa Joseph Sr. responded immediately, "Lorraine, absolutely! You know where the phone is. I also made breakfast if you and the kids are ready to eat."

Mama Black was appreciative of Grandpa Joseph Sr.'s help and support during their stay. Mama Black responded, "Thanks so much, Mr. Black. I'll have a plate as soon as I'm finished with this phone call. The kids are still sleep. I'll wake them up in a little bit to have breakfast. I want to get these phone calls out the way before I get them up."

Grandpa Joseph Sr. shook his head in agreement, "Lorraine, I understand. Take care of your business and take your time."

Mama Black smiled, sat down, picked up the phone, and began dialing Ms. Vera's number. Mama Black dialed (973) 675-0630 and waited with anticipation. Ms. Vera picked up after the third ring. Ms. Vera's voice was as pleasant over the phone as it was in-person. Mama Black was delighted to hear her voice on the other end.

Ms. Vera picked up the phone with the standard office greeting. "Good Morning.

This is the Hopeville Section 8 Housing Authority office. This is Ms. Vera. How can I help you?"

Mama Black matched her same energy and spirit. She replied, "Good Morning Ms. Vera. This is Mrs. Black. My husband and I were just in your office on Friday for our Section 8 application and we were approved. You met with us in your office."

"Oh, hello, Mrs. Black! How could I forget you guys?! How are you doing this morning? Ms. Vera responded.

Mama Black got straight to the point and said, "I am doing great, actually! I was calling to let you know that as soon as my husband and I left your office we went out for breakfast at Harris Diner. I was on the payphone talking with my father-in-law and there was this woman at the diner that overheard my conversation about looking for somewhere to move. When I hung up with my father-in-law, she asked me if I was looking for an apartment. I told her we were. Well, long story short, she ended up showing us her house. She plans to rent it out. I was calling to see if it would quality."

Ms. Vera responded enthusiastically, "Mrs. Black, what awesome news! You and your husband have a powerful story. I've been praying for you ever since y'all left my office. Look how fast God turns things around."

Mama Black nearly crying, replied, "Thank you so much Ms. Vera. That means so much to me. I know things could be worse, but it has been extremely hard and discouraging for us and our six children. I am just so grateful to God for not forgetting us." The tears began to stream down Mama Black's face when she finished her last sentence.

"Well, Mrs. Black. We will do all that we can to expedite this process for you, your husband and your six beautiful babies. I am sure they are excited as well and are ready to have their own space! But, before I confirm anything, I just have a few questions that I will need to ask you," Ms. Vera said.

Mama Black wiped the tears of joy from her chocolate brown golden face. She felt uplifted. Mama Black responded without hesitation, "Yes, Ms. Vera. Whatever you need to know, I'll let you know."

Ms. Vera asked, "Okay. Where is the house located?"

Mama Black responded, "It is 83 Believer Street, 2nd Floor, Hopeville, New Jersey, 07250."

Ms. Vera asked, "How many rooms are there?"

Mama Black responded, "It is a 2-family house. There are 4 bedrooms, 1 bathroom, 1 dining room, a living room, a kitchen and backyard."

Ms. Vera said, "Great! What is the homeowner's name and phone number?"

Mama Black said, "Her name is Pearl Thomas. Her number is (973) 675-1213."

Ms. Vera was writing everything down as Mama Black gave her the information. Ms. Vera continued.

Ms. Vera then said, "Okay. This is my last question: did she say she accepts Section 8 recipients?

Mama Black joyfully replied, "Yes! She definitely mentioned that on Saturday."

Ms. Vera responded, "Wonderful! Okay, Mrs. Black. This is all the information I need from you right now. What will happen next is I'm going to give Ms. Pearl a call to confirm these details with her. Then I will schedule an inspection of the residence to ensure that it is in livable condition. I'll also have Ms. Pearl complete some paperwork. Once those two items are done and if the space is livable, you and Ms. Pearl can decide on a move-in date and you'll be good to go from there."

Mama Black replied, "Thank you so much for everything. I don't mean to rush you, but how soon do you think you'll be able to call Ms. Pearl and schedule the inspection?"

Ms. Vera said confidently, "I will make it my business to give her a call today to schedule an inspection on Wednesday. If fact, when I give her a call and confirm the details, I'll call you to keep you posted. Is it okay to call you back on this number? I think this is the number on your application."

"Yes! The number I called you from is the same number on the application, so you can call me," Mama Black said.

"Okay, Mrs. Black. I will be sure to give you a call before the week is out. Thank you for calling and God Bless you and your family," Ms. Vera said with kindness in her voice.

Mama Black replied, "Ms. Vera, I cannot thank you enough for your help and support. God Bless you abundantly."

"You're welcome. Okay, I'll talk to you soon," Ms. Vera replied.

"Okay. Bye-bye," Mama Black said.

Grandpa Joseph Sr., Great-Grandma J and Aunty V overheard all that Mama Black had said on the phone, but they waited for her to share first. Mama Black gave them a summary of the conversation. She said, "Ms. Vera will call Ms. Pearl to see if they can set up an inspection by Wednesday. Once they do that and Ms. Pearl gives us a move-in date, we will be good to go!"

Aunty V replied, "Oh, Lorraine. That's wonderful news. Things are coming together."

Mama Black replied, "Thank you, Auntie V. I am so excited."

Once Mama Black finished talking to Auntie V, she called Ms. Pearl. When Ms. Pearl picked up the phone, Mama Black gave her the instructions from Ms. Vera with Section 8.

"Hello. May I speak to Ms. Pearl?" Mama said.

"Hello. This is Ms. Pearl," replied Ms. Pearl.

"Hi Ms. Pearl. This is Lorraine Black. I met you in Harris Diner on Saturday, and my husband and I toured your house," Mama Black explained.

"Oh, yes. How could I forget? Hello Lorraine. How are you doing?" Ms. Pearl responded.

"Well, I'm doing great. I hope you are well, too. I just got off the phone with our Section 8 counselor, Ms. Vera. She will be calling you to ask you a few questions and to schedule an inspection of the house to ensure that it is in livable condition," Mama Black replied.

"Oh okay! That's no problem. They can come and do an inspection of the house. My schedule is pretty open this week, so that is fine," said Ms. Pearl.

Mama Black replied, "Great! They said by this Wednesday they will do the inspection. She also asked about the number of rooms in the house, and if you accept Section 8. They will also have you fill out some paperwork," Mama Black said as she tried to prepare Ms. Pearl as much as possible.

Ms. Pearl replied, "Oh okay. That sounds easy enough."

"Yes. Ms. Vera has been immensely helpful and supportive during this time for us," Mama Black replied.

"That's wonderful. Listen, Lorraine. I have a call coming in. I'll make sure to keep in touch with you and wait on the call from Ms. Vera from the Section 8 office. Take care."

"Okay, Ms. Pearl. Thanks so much. I'll talk to you soon." Mama Black and Ms. Pearl ended their call.

Little did Mama Black know it was Ms. Vera from the Section 8 office calling on the other line to speak to Ms. Pearl. She had called Ms. Pearl almost immediately after her call with Mama Black. Ms. Vera and Ms. Pearl talked and scheduled a tour for Wednesday.

No sooner than Mama Black hung up from speaking with Ms. Pearl, Joy came out the bedroom and into the living room looking for Mama Black. She walked in the living room with her two pigtails standing straight on end. Her stocking cap came off from the night before, so her hair was a little messy. When she saw Mama Black, she crawled into her lap and rested her head on Mama Black's chest. Mama Black embraced her with open arms with her endless Mama love. She began rocking Joy back and forth. Soon after Joy got up, the rest of us got up. We began our normal routine. We took a shower, brushed our teeth, got dressed and made up our beds.

Grandpa Joseph Sr. had already prepared breakfast. He made his usual home fries, but also made scrambled eggs, bacon, sausages, grits, toast that morning. Strength, Meaven, Gracie and Audacious and I got dressed and made our way into the living room.

"Good Morning!" Mama said while still rocking Joy. She had fallen back asleep in Mama Black's arms.

"Good Morning, Mama, Grandpa, Great-Grandma J and Aunty V," we all said in unison.

"Good Morning," Grandpa Joseph Sr., Great-Grandma J and Aunty V replied at the same time.

We sat down and began eating.

While eating, Mama Black got up with Joy in her arms. She carried her back to the room and laid her across the bed. Mama Black returned to the living room and ate with the rest of us. We sat quietly at the table while eating Grandpa Joseph Sr.'s delicious food. Then, Strength broke the silence by asking Mama Black questions about the house.

"Mama, when do you think we will be able to move into our new home?" Strength asked. Meaven, Gracie, Audacious and I listened intently while still chewing our food.

"Well, I spoke to our Section 8 counselor and Ms. Pearl earlier this morning. They will inspect the house and complete some paperwork. After that, they will give us a call and let us know the date we can move in," Mama Black answered.

In the background, you could hear Gracie and I whisper a strong *YES* while giving each other a high-five. The more we talked about it, the more excited we became. We couldn't wait to see the house.

Strength replied with excitement, "That's great. We can't wait to see the house!"

Mama smiled while gazing at her kids. She replied in the gentlest way, "I know you guys can't wait. Me and your father can't wait either. We know this has been a lot on y'all with moving from house to house, but soon we will have a place to call our own. Y'all deserve it."

Gracie replied, "You and Papa deserve it, too, Mama." Mama Black just smiled and affectionately rubbed Gracie's back.

Mama Black had a small portion of Grandpa Joseph Sr.'s cooking that morning. Hearing from Ms. Vera and Ms. Pearl was all she could think about. She was excited and anxious. After she finished eating her food, Mama Black went into the bedroom to check on Joy. She was still asleep. So, Mama Black just laid down with Joy to relax for a bit. The rest of us stayed in the living with Grandpa Joseph Sr., Great-Grandma J and Aunty V. We watched television and chatted with each other.

Around noon, the phone rang, and Grandpa Joseph Sr. answered the phone like he normally did. Grandpa Joseph Sr. would answer the phone with the same level of energy every time.

He picked up and said, "Hello!"

"Hey Pops. How's it going?" Papa Black said. Papa Black called on his lunch break to check on Mama Black and the kids.

"Hello, Son. How's work going?" Grandpa Joseph Sr. responded.

"It's going well, Pops. Just another day. Is Lorraine around?" Papa Black asked.

"Yes, she is. She's in the bedroom. I'll have one of the kids get her. Hold on," Grandpa Joseph Sr. replied.

"Okay," Papa Black said.

Grandpa Joseph Sr. told Meaven to go tell Mama Black that Papa Black wanted to speak to her on the phone. Meaven got up and walked to the bedroom. By this time, Mama Black had fallen asleep.

Meaven quietly opened the door and whispered, "Mama. Mama. Papa is on the phone. He wants to talk to you."

Mama Black was a light sleeper, so she was up as soon as Meaven called her the first time. Sitting up on the bed, Mama replied, "Okay. I'm coming."

Meaven walked back into the living room and Mama Black followed him, gently closing the door so that she wouldn't wake Joy up.

Mama Black picked up the phone receiver and answered, "Hello?"

"Hey, Lorraine. It's me. How's it going? How are the kids?" Papa Black said.

"Hey. Things are going well. The kids are fine. I was in the bedroom with Joy and fell asleep for a bit," Mama Black explained.

"Oh. Okay. So, did you speak to our Section 8 counselor or Ms. Pearl?" Papa Black asked as he could barely wait to get his question out.

Mama excitedly replied, "Yes! I spoke to Ms. Vera first. She explained to me that she was going to call Ms. Pearl today. She asked Ms. Pearl a few questions and scheduled an inspection of the house to make sure it is in livable condition. After they've done that, then Ms. Pearl has to complete paperwork."

"Okay. That's good to hear. I'm glad. I'm glad," Papa Black said.

Mama Black continued, "Once all that is done, Ms. Pearl will let us know the date we can move in. Then we'll officially be able to move in."

Papa Black paused for a moment before answering, "This is good news."

Mama Black responded, "It is good news. But we have to start getting the kids ready for school. They go back in the next week or so. They need at least one new outfit."

Papa Black repeated himself and replied, "Okay. We'll figure it out. We'll figure it out, Lorraine."

"Okay. Well, we will see you when you get here," Mama Black said.

"Alright, I'll talk to y'all later," Papa Black responded.

Papa and Mama Black ended their conversation. As soon as Mama Black hung the phone up, the phone began to ring. Grandpa Joseph Sr. looked at Mama Black and motioned to her that she can pick up the phone since she was standing right by it. Mama Black picked up the phone.

"Hello. This is the Black residence," Mama Black answered professionally.

"Hello. May I speak to Lorraine Black?" replied Ms. Vera.

"This is Lorraine Black. May I ask who's calling?" Mama Black said. She had a feeling it was either Ms. Vera or Ms. Pearl but was not sure.

"Yes. Hi, Mrs. Black. This is Ms. Vera from the Hopeville Section 8 Housing Authority. How are you this afternoon?" Ms. Vera said.

"I'm doing fine, Ms. Vera. I'm glad to hear your voice. I wasn't expecting you to call so soon. Is everything okay?" Mama Black said with uncertainty in her voice.

Ms. Vera replied, "Oh, yes, Mrs. Black. Everything is well. I was calling to let you know that I was able to speak to Ms. Pearl. We were able to get the inspection scheduled for tomorrow, Tuesday morning instead of Wednesday. At the inspection, we will have

Ms. Pearl complete and sign off on the paperwork. After that, you and Ms. Pearl can discuss an exact move-in date. But it has to be within one month of her signing."

Mama Black was quiet for a second. She was finally seeing her prayers for a house for her family manifest.

"Hello? Mrs. Black, are you there?" Ms. Vera asked.

"I'm sorry, Ms. Vera. Yes, I am here. I am just so happy that this is finally happening for me and my family. It's been a long time coming and to see it happening just brings me humble joy. I thank you for all your help. You didn't have to be as nice as you have been. So, I really do thank you."

Mama Black could feel Ms. Vera's smile over the phone. She happily replied, "Mrs. Black, I am just blessed to be a blessing. You never know when I could be on the other side of this phone asking for help. I am just doing God's work. We must support and look out for one another. I am glad I can help."

Mama Black's eyes welled up with tears like usual, but the tears didn't fall. Mama Black replied, "You are right. Thank you and Thank God."

"Well, alright, Mrs. Black. I will be in touch with you after the inspection and continue to keep you posted. If there's anything else you need, please feel free to call me. You take care," Ms. Vera said before hanging up.

"Thank you, Ms. Vera. Take care. Bye-Bye," Mama Black replied.

Mama Black hung up the phone and sat in the chair for a moment before moving. The phone rang again. Grandpa Joseph Sr. motioned to Mama Black again to answer the phone.

"Hello. This is the Black residence," Mama Black answered professionally.

"Hello. May I speak to Lorraine Black?" said Ms. Pearl.

"This is Lorraine Black. May I ask whose calling?" Mama Black said.

"Yes. This is Ms. Pearl from 83 Believer Street," Ms. Pearl answered so eloquently.

"Hello, Ms. Pearl! It's so good to hear from you! How are you?" Mama Black replied.

"I'm doing good, baby. Listen, I just spoke to Ms. Vera from the Section 8 office and she said that they are coming in for the inspection tomorrow, and that I can decide on the date that you and your family can move in. So, I know school starts for the young ones in a week or so. So does the third week in September work for you? I just want to make sure I give my sons enough time to help me move all my stuff out and get the house cleaned and ready. How does that sound?" Ms. Pearl asked.

Mama Black responded as quickly as she could. She replied, "Yes! That sounds perfect. Thank you so much for your help and accommodating me and family sooner than later. God Bless You."

Ms. Pearl replied, "Oh, you're welcome, baby. I'm glad I can help. God is good."

Mama Black replied, "Yes, He is."

Ms. Pearl said, "Okay, baby. I'll talk to you soon. Feel free to call me if you need anything."

Mama Black said, "Thank you, Ms. Pearl. I will. Talk to you soon."

Mama Black hung up the phone and smiled. Grandpa Joseph Sr. had gathered what the conversation was about because of Mama Black's excitement. He smiled back at Mama Black and gave her a thumbs-up. Mama Black smiled and nodded her head.

After receiving both phone calls, Mama Black was overjoyed and wanted to share it with Papa Black but, she decided to wait until Papa Black came home from work. She went back into the bedroom to wake Joy up. She helped Joy get dressed and they made their way into the living room with the rest of us. They watched television, had lunch, and relaxed.

Evening came and Mama Black began preparing dinner for her family. She made hot dogs and French fries. When Mama Black did cook, she tried to cook food that was quick and easy to make since she wasn't in her own kitchen. By the time Mama Black had finished cooking dinner, Papa Black returned home.

Papa Black rang the doorbell and Grandpa Joseph Sr. buzzed him in. Meaven opened the door for Papa Black when he got to the apartment door.

"Hello, y'all," Papa Black said while walking in the door. Everyone said hello back to Papa Black.

Mama Black said, "Hey. I'm just about done with dinner if you want to eat with us."

Papa Black said, "Sure."

Aunty V said to Papa Black, "How was work today, nephew? "

Papa Black replied, "Oh, it was good, Aunty V. Kind of a busy day, but not too bad."

Aunty V replied, "Oh, that's good to hear." Then Aunty V went back to watching television.

Gracie and I were setting the table for dinner. I placed the plates on the table while Gracie organized the napkins, juice, ketchup, mustard, and relish on the table. Once we finished, Mama said to us, "Alright y'all. Go wash your hands and come have a seat at the table. It is time to eat."

Strength, Meaven, Audacious and Joy left the couches to go wash their hands and then they sat down at the table. After washing our hands, Gracie and I joined them. We all began eating. Papa and Mama Black sat down and ate dinner as well.

My siblings and I finished our dinner and automatically said our good-nights and prepared for bed. Mama Black had us committed to our routine. After we left the living room, Mama Black washed the dishes. After she finished, she was so excited to tell Papa Black the news. They sat on the couch while Grandpa Joseph Sr., Great-Grandma J and Aunty V listened.

"Joe, I have more great news!" Mama Black said bubbling with excitement and drying the last dish.

Papa Black replied excitedly but he also hesitated. He replied, "Okayyyyy…what's the news?"

Mama Black said, "Well, I spoke to Ms. Vera and Ms. Pearl again. They are moving the inspection to tomorrow instead of Wednesday. Ms. Pearl will complete the paperwork tomorrow for Section 8. We should be good to go by after that. Ms. Pearl said that since school is about to start for the kids, we can move in the third week of September. Her sons are going to hurry and move her stuff out and clean the house. Once that's done, it will be ready for us to move in!"

All Papa Black could say in that moment was, "WOWWWWWW!!! That is great news!"

Grandpa Joseph Sr., Great-Grandma J and Aunty V were excited as well. Then Great-Grandma J began talking. She said, "This is wonderful news. God is good. He's working everything out." She continued, "Here. Take this money and get the kids some school clothes. This is just to get you started."

Papa Black refused to take it. He said, "Grandma J, no, no, no. I can't take that from you."

Great-Grandma J sweetly replied, "Boy, you better take this money. I don't want to hear it. This is not about your pride, but about your family."

Papa Black took the $200 that Great-Grandma J had given to him and Mama Black. He replied, "Thank you, Grandma J. I appreciate it a lot."

Mama Black also replied while touching Great-Grandma J's soft, wrinkled hand, "Thank you, Grandma J. Thank you."

CHAPTER 24
MOVE-IN DAY

The third week of September was finally here. IT WAS MOVE IN DAY! I was so excited. We were finally moving into a house again. Papa and Mama Black were equally excited. Although the school year had already started, Papa and Mama had decided it would be too much to move in during a school day. So, we stayed at Grandpa Joseph Sr. house during the week and commuted back and forth to work and school from there. Papa and Mama Black planned to still move in the third week of September, but instead they decided to move in on Saturday. This gave us more time to organize and move our things in our new home without having to prepare for school the next day.

Friday night was the last night we stayed at Grandpa Joseph Sr.'s house. After hopping to three different homes, we were finally moving into our own home. Saturday morning, Papa and Mama Black got up early to get us ready for the move. Like tradition would serve, Grandpa Joseph Sr. made home fries with peppers and onions for old time sake.

After we were all dressed and packed, we made our way into the living room to have Grandpa Joseph Sr.'s signature breakfast dish for the last time for a while. Mama Black stayed behind for a few moments to clean up and organize the room to make sure it was exactly how Grandpa Joseph Sr. had arranged it for us. After she finished, Mama Black came and ate breakfast with us.

We sat at the kitchen table while Papa and Mama Black sat on the couch. We all ate our home fries with so much excitement that morning. Papa and Mama Black told us that we were leaving as soon as we finished breakfast. We didn't crack any jokes or tease each other like we normally did. We ate with huge smiles on our faces.

While we ate, Papa and Mama Black continued to thank Grandpa Joseph Sr., Great-Grandma J and Aunty V for letting us stay with them until we got back on their feet. Papa and Mama Black were very appreciative.

While resting his plate on the coffee table, Papa Black turned to Grandpa Joseph Sr., Great-Grandma J and Aunty V and said, "I thank y'all for letting us stay here. I know this wasn't the best of circumstances for y'all. I know it was a sacrifice to have us stay here. I thank y'all. I truly thank y'all."

Mama Black also thanked them. She said, "Yes. Me, Joseph, and the kids wouldn't have gotten to this point without y'all, my Mother and Ms. Josephina. After bouncing from place to place and getting that $1,000 stolen from us, we didn't know how things were going to turn out. But God used y'all to bless us. We thank you."

Grandpa Joseph Sr. replied, "Oh, you're welcome son and daughter-in-law. That's what families do!"

Great-Grandma replied, "You're welcome. Just make sure you come back and visit us."

Aunty V said, "It's all good Joseph and Lorraine. Y'all deserve good out of life."

Mama Black replied, "We will come back and visit, and thank you for your words, Aunty V."

By the time we demolished our food, my siblings and I were all set to go! Strength helped gather the dishes, while Gracie washed them, and I dried them off while putting them away. Audacious and Joy cleaned the table off and put the ketchup back in the refrigerator. Meaven pushed all the chairs in.

Papa and Mama Black were finished talking so they stood up and walked over to give Grandpa Joseph Sr., Great-Grandma J and Aunty V a hug and kiss. The rest of us followed behind Papa and Mama Black giving them a hug and kiss as well. Grandpa Joseph Sr. walked us outside to the car to see us off. As they walked down the living room hallway, we grabbed our bags. That's all we had to take to our new home. Just several bags and very few toys.

We loaded up in the car, Grandpa Joseph Sr. waved good-bye, Papa Black honked the horn three times and we waved back to Grandpa Joseph Sr.

After 20 minutes, we finally pulled up to our new home: 83 Believer Street, Hopeville, NJ. As we pulled up, Ms. Pearl was standing on the porch with the most welcoming smile on her face. Papa Black parked the car and rolled the windows up. Everyone got out the car and walked up the stairs.

Audacious and Joy approached the house in amazement. They couldn't believe how big the house was from the outside. They couldn't wait to see what the inside and backyard looked like.

Walking up the stairs, Ms. Pearl kept smiling and said, "Hello, Family! Welcome to your new home!"

Mama Black gave Ms. Pearl the tightest hug and replied, "Hello Ms. Pearl. Thank you! The kids are so excited to see the house. These are me and Joseph's kids: Strength,

Meaven, Journee, Gracie, Audacious and Joy. Say hello kids."

We replied in unison, "Hi, Ms. Pearl."

Ms. Pearl looked upon us with such warmth and pleasure. She was used to having all boys so seeing five little girls made her so happy.

She replied, "Well, hello! It's nice to meet y'all. You have nice parents. They talk about y'all all the time."

We smiled and replied, "It's nice to meet you, too."

Ms. Pearl saw Papa Black standing on the stairs and she waved at him. He waved back and smiled. Ms. Pearl continued talking to us.

"Are you guys ready for a tour of your new home?!" Ms. Pearl said eager to take us on a tour.

Strength replied, "Yes, I know I am!"

Ms. Pearl laughed and said, "Well, all I need is one yes. So, let's go!"

Mama Black had let us walk in front of her since she and Papa Black had seen the house already.

Ms. Pearl walked up the stairs and we followed. While walking up the stairs, all you could hear us say were, "Wow. This is nice. This is big. I love the backyard. This carpet is soft!"

We really loved our new home! Every room we went into, all Ms. Pearl, Papa and Mama Black could hear was our excitement...until we got to the second floor of the house. Then we started arguing over who was getting which room.

Strength being the oldest and strong in her stance, she walked into the biggest bedroom and said, "I'm taking this room by myself!"

Audacious replied with a straight face, "No you're not."

I interjected and said to Strength, "Go sleep on the fire escape, Strength!"

Everyone including Strength couldn't help but laugh. Papa Black just shook his head, looked up in the air and smiled.

When Mama Black heard us arguing about the rooms, she set us straight. After everyone had finished laughing, Mama Black stated, "You will not be getting your own room, Strength. You and Journee will be sharing the room on the right. Gracie, Audacious and Joy you will be getting this room. And Meaven, you will be getting the room on the left."

When Mama Black spoke, there was nothing else to be said. We all replied, "Okay, Mama."

Once the room arrangement was squared away, everyone headed back downstairs.

Ms. Pearl pulled Papa and Mama Black to the kitchen to continue talking to them. My siblings I went into the living room looked out the window and talked amongst ourselves. We were so happy about our new home.

"Joseph and Lorraine, it's official. This is your new place of residence," Ms. Pearl said as she handed Papa and Mama Black two sets of keys.

Mama Black grabbed the keys from Ms. Pearl, and handed the second pair to Papa Black. They were overcome with peace, gratitude, and joy. Finally! They had a comfortable place to call their own. Mama Black hugged Ms. Pearl as tight as she could, and she began to cry. Her tears were tears to hope, thankfulness, and victory.

Ms. Pearl hugged Mama Black as tight as she could, saying, "It's okay, baby. God's got you and your family. He worked it out." Papa Black stood there quietly understanding Mama Black's tears.

Ms. Pearl continued, "Well, let me get going. I'll let you guys get settled in and enjoy your new home."

Mama Black replied wiping the tears from her eyes, "Thank you again, Ms. Pearl. I appreciate all you have done for me and my family. Thank you."

Ms. Pearl responded, "You're welcome, baby. If there's anything you need, you have my number. Give me a call."

Mama Black replied, "Okay, will do."

Papa and Mama Black walked Ms. Pearl downstairs and watched her until she got in her car and pulled off. They closed the door behind them and went back upstairs.

My siblings and I were still in the living room playing with each other. We were doing our usual, cracking jokes and teasing each other. While walking up the stairs, all Papa and Mama Black could hear were their six children laughing...in our new home.

They walked into the living room with smiles on their faces. Mama replied, "What's so funny? What are y'all laughing at?"

Gracie responded with her innocent eyes and voice, "Oh, nothing, Mama!"

Mama Black replied with a smile on her face, "Mhmm. Yeah right. Y'all do know I wasn't just born! Mamas know EVERYTHING." Papa Black just smiled.

Mama Black continued, "So what do y'all think about our new home?"

Audacious and Joy said the same thing, "We love it, here!"

Meaven replied nonchalantly, "It's cool."

Gracie and I responded, "Yeah, this is nice!"

Strength answered, "It's alright. It would be better if I had my own room. Sike! I'm joking. I like it here, too."

Papa Black responded, "Well, I'm glad y'all like it here. This is a nice house and we want to keep it that way. Me and your mother do not want y'all running up and down these stairs. And when y'all are upstairs don't be horsing around up there. Do y'all understand me?"

We quickly responded, "Yes, Papa."

Mama Black continued on saying, "Since we don't have furniture yet, we will have to sleep on the floor tonight. Grandpa Joseph Sr. gave us some extra blankets. Me and your father will order some pizza for dinner tonight."

We excitedly responded, "Yes!"

After the talk, Papa Black and Meaven went to the car to get everyone's bags and our dolls. We didn't have much just our bags of clothes and dolls, but we were thankful – thankful for a new home of our own. My siblings and I didn't complain about having to sleep on the floor because we had been homeless for the entire summer. Like Mama Black, we were just grateful to have a home.

When Papa Black and Meaven came back in, my sisters and I grabbed our bags and went into our rooms. We stayed upstairs for a bit while Papa and Mama talked and hung out downstairs.

Evening had come and Mama Black ordered pizza from Dominos. She had to ask our downstairs neighbor to use her phone to order the pizza. When the pizza arrived, Mama Black set up a nice makeshift dining area. Mama Black grabbed a bedding sheet and laid it across the dining room floor. Since we didn't have dishes and cups, Mama Black had asked for plastic cups, plates, and utensils when she ordered the pizza.

Mama Black set a place for all of us. Mama Black never failed to transform discomfort to comfort, from ordinary to special. Without furniture, Mama Black had already made 83 Believer Street our special home.

After dinner was finished, Papa and Mama Black allowed us to sleep in our own rooms. It was so much fun for us to finally do that. Once we settled in for bed and laid our blankets on the floor, we kept our doors open so that we could talk to each from our separate rooms.

Being her usual silly self, Audacious started off with jokes. She was always silly when she was with us. Meaven would crack up at her jokes, even if they were corny. When Meaven laughed, he would encourage her even more. And she kept going!

That night, Audacious began with her first joke. She said, "Knock, Knock!"

We all shouted from across our rooms so that we could hear each other. Strength, Meaven, Gracie, Joy and I responded, "Who's there?"

Audacious replied, "Brittney Spears!"

Strength, Meaven, Gracie, Joy and I replied, "Brittney Spears who?

Audacious replied, "Knock, Knock!"

Now, we knew the joke wasn't supposed go like that, but we played along anyway.

Strength, Meaven, Gracie, Joy and I replied frustrated, "Who's there, Audacious?!

Barely containing her laughter, Audacious replied, "Opps, I did it again! Get it? She had a song named *Opps...I did it Again*! I repeated the joke and said *Opps I didn't it Again*!" Then we all let out the biggest chuckle!

It took a moment for us to understand the joke. Once we did, we laughed loud! We laughed so loud that Papa and Mama Black could hear us all the way downstairs. Midway into our laugh, Papa Black rushed to the top of the stairs and said, "If you all don't be quiet, I'm giving all y'all a whooping!"

When Papa Black came to the top of those stairs, we got quiet, IMMEDIATELY. Gracie and Audacious even pulled the covers over their heads trying to hide from Papa Black, as if he couldn't see them. Once Papa Black spoke, we kept our mouths shut. But no sooner than he got downstairs, we started snickering and giggling quietly so that Papa Black couldn't hear us.

We continued telling jokes that night until we all fell asleep. My siblings and I had a special bond that was created through cracking jokes and laughter.

Sunday morning came and Papa and Mama Black allowed us to sleep in. Papa and Mama Black discussed how they would get things set up for our new home. First, they planned on taking us clothes shopping for the school year. We would be going back to school on Monday, so Mama Black wanted us to have some new clothes since we weren't able to have them during that first week of school.

As Mama Black was getting us up and ready for the day, she began thinking about church. She thought to herself, "We really need to go back to church. I am just so grateful. I want to give my God some praise because this right here was nobody but Him!"

Mama Black loved her experiences at Grace and Mercy Baptist Church. She knew she'd be going back and bringing all of us with her.

After Mama Black's deep morning thoughts, she called us downstairs. We were all dressed and ready to go. We asked for breakfast. Fortunately, earlier that morning Papa Black went down the street to grab a box of cereal and milk for breakfast. He also bought Styrofoam bowls and plastic spoons.

Yet again, Mama Black turned our new empty dining room into a space where we would feel cozy while eating our breakfast. We sat in the living room until Mama Black was finished. She called us to come into the dining room to eat breakfast. We did and we enjoyed it.

As we sat there, I read the back of the cereal box trying to solve the riddles and read the stories. I loved doing that while eating my cereal. Papa Black purchased *Kellogg's Honey Smacks*. It wasn't our favorite, but we ate whatever Papa and Mama Black purchased and could afford.

After we finished breakfast, we piled up into the car and drove to downtown Hopeville to C.H. Martin to get some school clothes. Papa and Mama Black had to make $200 stretch for six growing children that needed clothes, underwear, bras, and footwear. Somehow, Papa and Mama Black made it work while making it look easy.

After we finished shopping, we went back home and prepared for school the next day. Our Monday morning going back to school and work looked different for us...in a good way! This time, we would be leaving from our own home; we felt so proud.

CHAPTER 25
A NEW TRADITION!

Monday morning came, and the hustle and bustle in our household was underway. With just one bathroom, every morning you were hearing constant knocks on the bathroom door followed by shouts of, "Hurry up! I need to use the bathroom" or "I have to get in there." You're taking too long!" If this were said, most of the time it was because I would always take long in the bathroom.

Papa Black was always the first one to leave the house, so he didn't have to play referee in the morning with all of us. Mama Black played referee. After she finished playing referee, Mama Black did one thing every morning before rushing everyone out the house. She stopped and prayed over us before we walked to school together. With our heavy book bags and jackets on, Mama Black stopped everything she was doing and spoke a prayer over us.

She prayed, "God, thank you for this day. Thank you for our home. Please protect my children as they walk back and forth to school. In Jesus' name, Amen."

Then Mama Black would hug and kiss each of us and let us be on our way. After her prayer and getting everyone ready for school, Mama Black finished getting dressed and would leave for work. This was a new tradition Mama Black started in our new home.

After everyone left, she would walk around the corner to catch the bus to work. Once she arrived at work, everyone loved seeing and being in Mama Black's presence and it showed. She was well-liked in the school community so much so that they promoted her to a Teacher's Assistant for kindergarten students.

Things were finally coming together for us. After all we had been through, perseverance, resilience and togetherness are what Papa and Mama Black built our family on. Brighter days were finally ahead for us.

Mama Black knew that she wanted to start attending church again. She wanted to attend Christian growth class, and Bible study regularly. Since we've been staying with relatives for a while, it was hard for us to go to church. Once we moved into our new home, Mama Black didn't have a way of getting us to church since Papa Black worked most Sundays. Mama Black didn't drive so we didn't have a consistent way of getting there on time.

So, Mama Black made a phone call to the Bluestone Family. Coincidentally, they lived five minutes away from us. Elder and Deaconess Bluestone supported us before and were willing to support us again.

So, Elder Bluestone had agreed to picking up Mama Black, my siblings and I every Sunday for church. Mama Black was grateful and appreciative for the Bluestone Family. Mama Black knew church and God were important, so she taught us about and exposed us to both.

Knowing all that Papa and Mama Black has gone through, the church helped Papa and Mama Black with getting furniture for their new home. Elder Bluestone had kindly recommended Mama Black to purchase furniture from a company his sister worked for.

Sister Beatrice was her name. She was very endearing and kind, willing to help Mama Black get furniture. Elder Bluestone introduced Mama Black and his sister Beatrice. Sister Beatrice was also a member of Grace and Mercy Baptist Church. Mama Black had seen her before but was never formally introduced to her.

One Saturday, Mama Black took Gracie, Audacious, Joy and I with her to pick out furniture for our new home. Since they were the oldest and didn't want to go, Strength and Meaven stayed home. They were about to graduate high school and go to college, so Papa and Mama Black would often let them stay home by themselves. Those two were always together.

Mama Black, Gracie, Audacious, Joy and I took the bus to the furniture store. The furniture store was a big vintage looking building with four levels and a freight elevator. Every floor had beautiful furniture displays set up as if it was someone's home. As we walked around, Mama Black allowed us to pick out some of the furniture pieces for the house. There was one piece of furniture that Mama Black had decided on herself. She picked out a burgundy couch. Mama Black's favorite color was burgundy.

After they finished furniture shopping, Mama Black and Sister Beatrice talked for a little bit, getting to know one another more. When they finished talking, we hopped on the bus and headed back home. When we got home, Gracie and I told Strength and Meaven about the furniture we picked out.

Two weeks later, the furniture arrived, and we no longer had to sleep or eat dinner on the floor. We were finally able to decorate our rooms. In each of our rooms, we hung posters of our favorite celebrities on our bedroom walls. My siblings would rip posters from *Word Up* and *The Source* magazine. We had our favorite celebrities on the wall like: Aaliyah, Biggie Smalls, Puff Daddy, Faith, Mary J. Blige, Lil Kim, Jagged Edge, 112, Total, Foxy Brown, Mase, The Lox, The Lost Boyz, Maya, Jodeci, Missy Elliot, Ashanti, Ja Rule, Jay Z, Eve, DMX, Nelly, Nas, Tupac, Busta Rhymes, Usher, TLC, SWV, The Refugees & Lauryn Hill, Mariah Carey, Brandy, Monica, Erykah Badu, Case, Carl Thomas, Ciara, X-scape, Ginuwine, Jon B, Immature, Kriss Kross and Dru Hill. Surprisingly, Papa and Mama Black didn't mind because this was our opportunity to personalize our space.

We were also finally able to watch television. Mama Black would watch her talk shows, we would watch music videos and Papa Black would either watch boxing or his new Luther Vandross VHS tape. With the support of Elder & Deaconess Bluestone and Sister Beatrice, we had settled in our new home.

Since the move, every week we attended Grace & Mercy Baptist Church. Mama Black had a special love for that church. Because of her loving and kind spirit, Mama Black connected well with everyone at the church. Her friendship with Elder and Deaconess Bluestone was special.

Mama Black, Gracie, Audacious, Joy and I were incredibly involved in the church. From attending vacation bible school, Sunday school, ushering and singing in the choir, we were involved in different activities. However, Strength and Meaven were about to graduate high school and attend college so they were not as involved as us.

Gracie and I sang soprano in the Youth & Young Adult choir. We always sat next to each during choir rehearsal. Being born in the same year, Gracie and I were inseparable. We had the same friends, wore the same clothes and were even in the same grade since kindergarten. We were each other's first best friends.

We would bring our friends to church, too. Izzie and Ivy would visit church with us. Izzie visited more consistently; Ivy didn't come that often. When she did come, Ivy always cracked jokes to make us laugh. Ivy and I were remarkably close and were best friends as well.

Ivy was tall and thick. Her flawless features reminded you of supermodels on a magazine. She had beautiful ebony-brown skin, alluring eyes, full lips and perfectly defined contoured cheekbones. She had a care-free and fun personality.

We were all best friends that grew up in Hopeville, NJ together. Mama Black didn't mind that they attended church with us. Mama Black knew Ivy's mom very well. Overtime, they had become friends. Mama Black knew of Izzie's family and knew that she came from a good family.

While in church we would all sit together, joke, laugh and talk when we should have been paying attention to Rev. Watkin's sermon. Often, Mama Black would catch us talking. When she did, she gave us that *Mama look* to let us know we needed to stop playing and pay attention in church. When Gracie and I saw that look, we immediately stopped and gave Izzie and Ivy the stop playing look.

One Sunday after church, Mama Black, Gracie, Audacious, Joy, Izzie, Ivy, and I were waiting on Elder Bluestone to take us home. Elder Bluestone had helped with counting the tithes and offering that Sunday, so he took a little longer than usual to take us home.

It was a nice autumn day and Mama Black decided to wait outside to enjoy the fresh air and nice weather. Gracie, Izzie, Ivy, and I were grouped together talking while Audacious and Joy were talking with Mama Black. We had been waiting for a while so Elder Bluestone had sent his son, Khase, to tell Mama Black that he'd be out soon.

Walking out the side entrance of the church, Khase charmingly walked up to Mama Black while greeting her with a hug and kiss, "Hey, Sister Black. How are you doing? My father wanted me to come and tell you that he's still counting the money and should be out to take y'all home soon."

Mama Black replied, "Hey Khase. I'm doing well. Thanks for letting me know. How are you doing?"

Khase responded, "I'm doing well, Sister Black. Just in school trying to finish up this degree and playing football."

Mama Black answered, "That's good to hear. Wow, football?! That's great. What school are you attending?"

Khase replied, "I go to Hopeville University."

Mama Black answered impressed, "Oh, good for you! That's a great school."

Khase charmingly smiled and responded, "Thank you. Thank you."

Mama Black said, "You're welcome."

Shortly after, Elder Bluestone walked out the same side door. He had his black brief case in one hand and his suit jacket in the other.

Being apologetic, Elder Bluestone said to Mama Black, "Sister Black, I'm so sorry to have you and the girls waiting. It took a little longer than I had anticipated. I had Khase come out here and tell you that I would be out soon. Did he mention it to you?"

Khase immediately replied with smile on his face, "Uhhh. Yes, Dad. I did."

Mama Black replied with a smile on her face, "Yes. He did tell me, Elder Bluestone. And it's no problem. I'm thankful for the ride."

Elder Bluestone responded while laughing, "Oh okay. Just checking. I know sometimes he gets sidetracked like me. So, I wanted to make sure."

Mama Black, Elder Bluestone and Khase all laughed. Khase said good-bye to his father, Elder Bluestone, Mama Black, and us. He went to his car while we piled into Elder Bluestone's gold minivan.

Finally pulling up to the house, Mama Black ensured we thanked Elder Bluestone for dropping us off at home. Before we got out the van, Elder Bluestone reminded Mama Black about Youth Choir rehearsal.

Parking the car, Elder Bluestone said, "Oh, Sister Black. I just wanted to remind you that Youth Choir rehearsal is this Friday. My wife will be picking up the kids at 6:30pm. I have a basketball game that I'm coaching that evening, so I won't be able to take you guys."

Mama Black humbly replied, "Elder Bluestone, okay, no problem. I will make sure the kids are ready on Friday. I appreciate you guys making sure me and my family are involved in church. Joseph and I thank you and Deaconess Bluestone for your support."

Elder Bluestone jokingly responded, "You're welcome, Sister Black. That's what my wife and I are here for. We are happy to help in any way that we can. Plus, your dad is a good friend of mine and I don't want him to beat me up for not doing right by his family!"

Mama Black and Elder Bluestone laughed. Mama Black replied, "Well, thank you for that. Have a good night, Elder Bluestone."

Elder Bluestone replied, "You, too, Sister Black." He also said his good-byes to us. He uttered, "Bye girls…I mean young ladies!"

We laughed before responding. We replied in unison saying, "Bye, Elder Bluestone! Thank you!"

Elder Bluestone responded, "Oh, you're welcome!"

We climbed out the gold minivan and went upstairs. When we got in the house, we went straight to the living room to watch television, specifically music videos.

Mama Black went to her room and sat on her bed and relaxed. With a busy week ahead, Sundays were often her chance to prepare for the week. Mama Black took her Sunday naps before cooking. Between working with kids at school, dealing with six kids of her own at home and being a wife, Mama Black wanted to rest as much as she could.

As we got older, Mama Black cooked less. When we told Mama Black that we were hungry, she would say, "Go in there and cook something or make you a sandwich! You know how to cook on your own!"

This was true, but we loved Mama Black's cooking. When Mama Black didn't cook, we would either make a sandwich or go to the corner store and order a ham and cheese or turkey and cheese sandwich. That Sunday Mama Black cooked pork chops with gravy, buttered mash potatoes and corn. Mama Black had begun adding a vegetable to each meal.

CHAPTER 26
CHOIR REHEARSAL

It was a long school and work week for us. Friday evening had finally come, and Mama Black was relieved for the weekend. At 6:00pm, Mama Black received a call on the house phone. They had caller ID so when Mama Black looked at the phone, she knew exactly who was calling. Bluestone popped up on the screen.

"Hello?" Mama Black gently answered the phone.

"Hello Sister Black. This is Deaconess Bluestone. How are you?" Deaconess Bluestone replied.

"Hi, Deaconess Bluestone. I'm doing great. How are you?" Mama Black answered.

"I'm doing fine. Are the girls still going to choir rehearsal this evening?" Deaconess Bluestone asked.

"Oh, they don't have a choice Deaconess. Yes, they will be going!" Mama Black eagerly responded.

Deaconess Bluestone laughed and said, "I know that's right! Well, I'll be there at 6:30pm."

Mama Black also laughed. She responded, "Okay. No problem. I will make sure the girls are outside waiting."

Mama Black didn't like to have people waiting to pick us up. That was her way of showing her appreciation for every ride we received. She couldn't really afford to give gas money, so she showed her gratitude in other ways.

Deaconess Bluestone responded, "Okay. Thank you. Take care."

Mama Black said, "Thank YOU. Have a good rehearsal. Bye-bye."

As soon as Mama Black got off the phone with Deaconess Bluestone, she called us to come downstairs.

Mama Black shouted up the stairs, "Girls! Journee, Gracie, Audacious and Joy! Come down here."

As soon as we heard Mama Black calling for us, we came downstairs immediately.

"Yes, Mama?" We all answered.

"Deaconess Bluestone will be here at 6:30pm to pick y'all up for choir rehearsal. I do not want her waiting so do whatever y'all need to do to get ready. I want y'all outside waiting on the porch at 6:25pm," Mama Black said firmly.

We replied again, "Yes, Mama."

It was 6:10pm by the time Mama Black had finished talking to us. We went back upstairs to grab our pocketbooks and headed back downstairs. We went to the bathroom and grabbed something to drink before waiting on the porch.

6:25pm came and Mama Black made sure we were ready. We went downstairs and waited on the porch. Mama Black waited with us. 6:30pm came and the gold minivan was making its way down Believer Street. The minivan pulled up and Mama Black walked us to the car. As we approached the car, Deaconess Bluestone was driving and Khase was in the front passenger seat.

Approaching the van, Mama Black waved, smiled, and said hello to Deaconess Bluestone and Khase.

Deaconess Bluestone parked the car so we could hop in. Khase got out of the van and greeted Mama Black with a hug and kiss. He then opened the door for all of us to get in. As we climbed in the van, Mama Black and Deaconess Bluestone chatted for a bit while Khase made sure we got into the van safely. Mama Black thanked her again for picking us up and dropping us off. Deaconess Bluestone assured Mama Black that she would have us back by 8:30pm. Mama Black stood outside until we pulled off, waving good-bye to us. Then she made her way back upstairs.

On the ride to choir rehearsal, Gracie and I sat next to each other in the back seat of the van while Joy and Audacious sat next to each other in the middle seat. As usual, Gracie and I talked the entire time about the guys we liked at school and what they said to us that week in school while giggling. We whispered so that no one could hear what we were talking about. Deaconess Bluestone would try to have conversation with us. She took a personal and genuine interest in us. Khase also asked questions on the ride to choir rehearsal.

Khase asked, "So what grade are you girls in now?"

I answered, "Well, me and Gracie are in the same grade. We are freshman in high school." Gracie and I loved telling people we were in the same grade but weren't twins. We got a kick out of sharing our age and seeing how confused people would become.

Khase responded confused, "Wait, so are y'all twins?"

Gracie laughed and replied, "Nope. We were just born in the same year!"

Khase thought they were being sarcastic. He jokingly responded, "Well, duh! All twins are born in the same year!" Everyone busted out laughing.

Journee responded while laughing, "That is true, but we weren't born on the same day. We were born in the same year. I was born in January and Gracie was born in December...of the same year."

Finally understanding what we were saying, Khase said, "Ohhhh... okay. I got you. They call that Irish twins, right?"

Gracie replied, "Yes!"

Deaconess Bluestone finally pulled up to the church and the conversation ended. We got out of the van and walked inside the church.

There were a lot of youth and young adults that attended Grace and Mercy Baptist Church and the choir rehearsal. Deaconess Bluestone played the organ while her daughter, Kimber Bluestone directed the choir. She was younger than Khase.

When Deaconess Bluestone and Kimber did music ministry together, you could hear Heaven rejoicing. Friday night choir rehearsals were more than rehearsals. It turned into Sunday morning service! The youth and young adult choir at the Grace and Mercy Baptist Church sang powerfully. That night, we rehearsed *He Reigns Forever* by The Brooklyn Tabernacle Choir. Deaconess Bluestone and Kimber would always add a special touch to the songs we would sing on Sunday mornings.

Strength and Meaven weren't home that evening. They had picked up part-time jobs to make some money. Strength worked at Checkers and Meaven worked at The Gap, Inc. inside the mall. They were saving money for their senior prom and graduation.

Papa Black wasn't home yet. Friday nights he would often go hang out at his Uncle Floyd's house. Uncle Floyd didn't live too far from us. Papa Black would enjoy a cold one and listen to music. Papa Black loved his uncles.

That Friday night, Mama Black had the house to herself for a few hours. She enjoyed it. Mama Black watched television, read her bible, and spent time praying on her knees. Sometimes we would find Mama Black on her knees only to realize she had fallen asleep while praying. But that evening, Mama Black stayed up until we returned home from choir rehearsal.

Choir rehearsal had come to an end and Khase prayed out rehearsal that evening. We piled back into the van with Deaconess Bluestone and Khase. We all sat in the same

145

seats riding back.

When they pulled up to the house, we got out the car and said good-bye to Deaconess Bluestone and Khase. When we got to the top of the stairs, I rung the doorbell. Mama Black came down to open the door. Deaconess Bluestone and Khase waited to pull off until they saw someone come and open the door for us. Mama Black opened the door to let us in while waving to Deaconess Bluestone and Khase. They honked the horn three times and drove off.

CHAPTER 27
SUNDAY MORNING

Sunday morning came and it was time for the Youth and Young Adult Choir to sing. Rev. Watkins always enjoyed hearing us sing. Service started at 11am and everyone had to line up in the vestibule at 10:45am to march in. That Sunday everyone wore white tops and black bottoms. The ladies wore skirts while the gentleman wore dress pants. Papa and Mama Black were able to get us a white blouse and black skirt over the weekend.

Gracie and I lined up with the sopranos; Audacious lined up with the altos and baby girl Joy was with the tenors. Deaconess Bluestone was at the organ and Kimber was standing in the pulpit where she would direct the choir during service.

The choir stand had two rows and the church had two aisles, so we marched in two lines. The tenors would lead the choir since they were always placed in the middle of the choir stand. The sopranos would march in on the left side while the altos marched in on the right side.

Deaconess Bluestone began playing the organ while the congregants stood for morning worship. Mama Black sat proudly in the pew and Izzie sat right next to her. Izzie began to visit the church more often as her friendship with Gracie and I grew.

Elder Bluestone was the praise and worship leader that morning. The Bluestone family was well represented and involved in the church. Everyone knew and loved the Bluestone Family.

As soon as 11 o'clock hit, Deaconess Bluestone struck the organ keys. The morning hymn for the day was *We've Come This Far by Faith*. When Deaconess Bluestone played, she would play with everything in her. We began marching in. Like most traditional Baptist churches, the Youth and Young Adult Choir marched in with the *church sway* down the aisle while singing the hymn. They made their way into the choir loft and Kimber began directing the choir until Deaconess Bluestone ended the morning hymn.

Elder Bluestone stood in the pulpit at the microphone and opened the morning service up with a powerful prayer. As he prayed, you could hear saints from the congregation shouting, "Yes, Lord! Hallelujah! You're worthy!"

One Mother of the church shouted, "Sure, nuff!!!" when she agreed with something Elder Bluestone said in his prayer. The church pews were filled and there was no doubt that the spirit of the Lord was in Grace and Mercy Baptist Church.

After morning prayer, Elder Bluestone led the call and response for the morning. The call and response was Grace and Mercy's declaration and words of affirmation as a church body and community. As a black church, it was important for Grace & Mercy Baptist Church to recite the declarations because of the history of the African American community and church. Mama Black always recited it with conviction and authority. It was important to her.

After Elder Bluestone had finished the call and response, first church announcements were delivered and then the Youth and Young Adult Choir began singing. Kimber made her way to the corner of the pulpit so that she could direct. She motioned her hands for the choir to stand and rock side to side while Deaconess Bluestone began playing the organ.

The tenors started off singing. You could hear Khase's distinct voice. His deep, masculine voice carried the tenor section while the tenors blended their tone with his. Next, Kimber directed altos to sing, then the sopranos. Each section had a chance to sing the first part by themselves.

Everyone finished their parts and Kimber brought in all three sections to sing in unison. Once we sang it in unison, she directed us to harmonize in the three distinct parts. Kimber was like the female maestro for Baptist choirs. God used her to direct the choir and his spirit manifested through the song that Sunday morning.

Harmonizing in our angelic voices, we sang so powerfully the walls vibrated with "He Reigns Forever. He Reigns Forever. All Hail King Jesus!" The sounds of God's praises echoed beyond the church walls and out into the street. The Youth and Young Adult choir had powerful voices and Mama Black was so proud that she heard our voices that day.

Some of the church members were standing on their feet clapping and singing along. Of course, Mama Black was up on her feet giving God some praise. She couldn't help it. Even Rev. Watkins had stood with joy and conviction knowing that *God Reigns Forever* in his life. First Lady Watkins was on her feet as well.

Kimber continued directing the choir while Deaconess Bluestone played and followed her lead. When she pointed to each section, they followed her. Singing in our harmonized parts, "He reigns, He reigns, He reigns, He reigns, He reigns, He reigns, He reigns, He reigns, He reigns, He reigns, He reigns, He reigns…and ever more!"

We repeated the bridge again and Kimber directed with more power. We sang the next part of the song. The choir delivered joyful, melodic music, "He Reigns Forever! He Reigns Forever! He Reigns Forever!"

As we continued singing, Deaconess Bluestone would switch up the beat and eventually dropped the music while the choir sang acapella. When that happened, the tambourine appeared, saints danced in the aisle, foot stomping shook the floor, and hand clapping and shouts made it to Heaven. God was pleased when we sang that song! The saints couldn't help but forget about their troubles and problems because *He Reigns Forever*!

Eventually, Kimber ended the song as she directed the choir to sing, "All Hail King Jesus!" That's how Deaconess Bluestone knew the song was ending. She motioned for the choir to sit down and we did. The members in the congregation continued praising. Shouting, aisle dancing, and the tambourine continued. Deaconess Bluestone couldn't help but play again. When she laid her hands on the organ, Kimber returned to the pulpit and motioned for us to stand and rock side to side. We sang it a second time. The spirit in Grace and Mercy Baptist Church that Sunday was high!

After we finished singing the second time, Rev. Watkins rose from his seat in the pulpit, kneeled and prayed before taking his place at the podium. His Sunday sermon was entitled, *This Battle is Not Yours.* Rev. Watkins preached from the book of 2 Chronicles 20: 1 -12. He reminded the congregation of the power of Jesus Christ. He boldly professed to the congregation, "Now what to do with fear. It's time for Grace and Mercy Baptist Church to come together. Learn how to seek God. There are times in your life when all you can do is stand. Help me Holy Spirit!"

Rev. Watkins continued proclaiming God's word, "God isn't intimidated by the size of your problems. The battle is not yours. It is the Lord's. He may not come when you want Him, but He's an on-time God. He moves. There's power in praise. When praise goes up, hope, strength, love, joy, help, and peace come down. Put on your garment of praise. The devil can't take your praise. And we don't have the right to judge or condemn anyone. Trust God and don't retaliate."

Always preaching a sermon filled with unapologetic boldness, Rev. Watkins knew how to bring forth God's word for his people. Mama Black always enjoyed Rev. Watkins sermons as she felt they were just for her. Izzie also felt a connection visiting the church. Once Rev. Watkins had finished, he prayed out and the church concluded with singing "Amen."

Before walking out the choir stand, Khase turned to Gracie and I and said, "Y'all sung well today." He reached his hand out giving us a high-five.

Gracie and I returned the high-five. "Thanks," we replied.

As soon as church ended, Gracie, Audacious, Joy and I walked over to where Mama Black and Izzie were sitting. With a huge smile on her face, Izzie excitedly said, "Y'all sang great today! You all sounded good."

I replied, "Thanks! So, when are *you* going to join the choir?"

Izzie hesitated with a puzzled look on her face and responded, "Uhhhh. I don't know about all that. I'm just a pew choir member."

I responded with a smile on my face, "So basically, you will only sing from the pews?"

Izzie replied, "You got it, my friend!"

They both laughed and I just shook my head and smiled.

Shortly after, Khase came over to Mama Black and said to her while greeting her with a hug and kiss, "Hey Sister Black. I just spoke to my dad and he asked me if I could take you guys home because he is going to a football game. He's going to head straight there now, so I'll take you guys home."

Mama Black replied, "Okay. No problem. That's fine with me. Thank you."

Elder and Deaconess Bluestone made their way over to speak to Mama Black after church as well. Mama Black and Deaconess Bluestone greeted each other with a hug and kiss as well.

Mama Black said, "Deaconess Bluestone, your hands are anointed! You blessed me today through that organ."

Deaconess Bluestone replied, "Oh, thank you Sister Black. I appreciate. To God be the glory." She responded humbly.

Elder Bluestone interjected the conversation and said jokingly, "Well, what about me? I can play the organ. My wife isn't the only talented one in the family." Everyone busted out laughing. Elder Bluestone always enjoyed joking and having a good laugh.

Deaconess Bluestone replied laughing and shaking her head, "Yes, Elder. You can play the organ." He really didn't know how to play. Deaconess Bluestone was just going along with the joke.

Elder Bluestone replied, "Sike. Sike. I'm just joking!" Everyone continued to laugh.

He also went on to say, "Sister Black, I have a football game that I'm going to, so I'm heading straight there. Khase will take you all home if that's okay with you. Or if the girls wanted to come with me to the game, they can do that, too. I don't mind."

Mama Black turned to the girls and said, "Did y'all want to go to the football game?"

Almost immediately, we all shouted, "Yes!"

Mama Black responded with a smile, "Yeah, I bet y'all do!" Mama Black knew her girls.

Deaconess Bluestone replied cracking up in laughter, "Wow! That was fast!"

We started laughing too.

Elder Bluestone laughed too. He replied, "Okay, the girls can come with me and Khase to the game and Sister Black, you can ride with my wife."

Deaconess Bluestone, "I'd be happy to take Sister Black home."

Mama Black replied, "I'd be happy as well Deaconess Bluestone. Thank you."

Elder Bluestone replied, "Okay, great. See you guys and be safe. I'll bring the girls back home around 7:30pm."

Mama Black replied, "Okay. No problem. You girls have fun and behave your-selves." Mama Black gave all of us a hug and a kiss, including Izzie.

Mama Black and Deaconess Bluestone walked out the front door of the church to Deaconess Bluestone's car. Elder Bluestone, Khase, Gracie, Audacious, Joy, Izzie and I got in the gold minivan and headed to the football game.

When we arrived at the high school football game, we sat in the bleachers while El-der Bluestone and Khase were on the field. We talked and laughed, went to the concession stand to buy snacks and watched the game. We didn't understand all that was going on but had a good time hanging out and being there. When the game was over, we headed home.

CHAPTER 28
THREE YEARS LATER...

The Black household was now down to six people: Papa and Mama Black, Gracie, Audacious, Joy and me. Strength and Meaven had left the house. During their senior year in high school, they attended the prom, graduated from Hopeville High School and now were in their third year at Medgar Evers University.

Now that Strength was in college, I finally had my own room! Gracie and I would hang out a lot in my room, though. When Izzie and Ivy came over, we would all hang out in my room too. Gracie, Izzie, Ivy, and I were all seniors in high school, so we constantly talked about the prom, college and of course boys! Gracie and I sat on my bed while Izzie and Ivy sat on Strength's bed.

Ivy asked, "So who are y'all taking to the prom? I already know who I'm taking!"

I asked, "Who are you taking, and did he ask you?!?!"

Ivy replied, "Girl, Trevor asked me last week. Of course, I said YES!"

Gracie, Izzie, and I screamed like a bunch of high school girls. Well, we were a bunch of high school girls.

Izzie replied, "Ivy, Trevor is tall, dark, AND handsome! That's a good date to take to the prom."

Ivy responded, "Girl, who you telling?! But I knew he would ask me because he used to check me out when he sat behind me in Mrs. King's English class. He asked me at my locker after class."

I excitedly replied, "Y'all gonna look da bomb at the prom together!"

Then Ivy asked the rest of us, "So, who y'all taking to the prom?! Y'all gonna look popping in y'all prom dresses, too!"

I scratched my head in confusion, "I have no idea. Donovan asked me, but I am not sure if I want to go with him."

Everyone started cracking up laughing.

Gracie replied laughing, "Journee, that boy has been trying to get with you for the past four years of high school and you always turn him down."

I started laughing too, "I know. I know. He has been. But, I don't know. I might say yes. We will see." I continued, "Now Gracie, what about you?! Who are you taking? I know you have the fellas lined up asking you!"

Gracie, Izzie, and Ivy laughed hysterically. Before answering, Gracie jumped up from sitting on the bed and started doing dance moves. Gracie was silly and would randomly do things to make us laugh while she would crack up while doing it.

She responded while dancing, "I'm taking Usher to the prom. He called and asked me last week!"

Izzie, Ivy, and I paused for a second trying to figure out if we heard Gracie right. Once we realized what she said, we started cracking up laughing!

We laughed so loud that Mama Black yelled from the bottom of the stairs, "Y'all better be quiet up there or that's it!"

I softly responded, "Okay. Sorry, Mama."

We all started giggling while covering our mouths. Gracie and I didn't know what Mama meant by "...or that's it," but it didn't sound good. So, we closed the bedroom door and continued talking and laughing at Gracie being silly.

I laughed while being serious, "Gracie, you better stop making us laugh before we really get in trouble." I snickered some more.

Gracie also laughing, replied, "Sike. Sike. Seriously, I don't know who I'm taking either. Jesse asked me too, but I told him I'll let him know by next week."

I responded, "Oh ok. Jesse is a nice guy. He's handsome, too." Izzie and Ivy nodded their heads in agreement.

Ivy then asked Izzie who she was taking to the prom. She had a bright smile on her face and raised eyebrows, Ivy asked Izzie, "So, Izzie. You're quiet over there. Who are YOU taking?!"

It was a suspenseful silence before Izzie answered. She replied with a smirked on her face, "Well...I'm taking Bryson."

Gracie, Ivy, and I looked at each other and replied, "Bryson Harper...THEE BRYSON HARPER!"

We got up from the bed and jumped around in a circle with our arms around each other. We had forgotten for a moment that Mama Black just told us to be quiet. So, I immediately put my finger over my mouth to remind them to be quiet. We sat back down on the bed and started asking Izzie a million questions.

I said while crossing my legs and smiling, "Girl, he is foine! Not fine, but FOINE! Y'all gonna look good together at the prom!" Bryson Harper was one of the most popular athletes at Hopeville High School. He was smart, good looking, and a gentleman. All the ladies wanted Bryson Harper.

Gracie was in the background doing a happy dance while Ivy was snapping her fingers in a circular motion while smiling. Izzie just sat there and laughed.

Ivy replied, "Ohhh. You thought you were just going to sit over there quiet and not say anything, huh?" They all bust out laughing.

Izzie replied, "Nah. Between Gracie dancing and saying she was taking Usher and Mrs. Black about to get us, I was just waiting for the right moment." We all laughed again.

We talked some more before calling it a night. Izzie ended up staying the night with Gracie and I. Ivy went home that evening. The next morning Mama Black, Gracie, Audacious, Joy, Izzie and I went to church. Papa Black continued to work long hours. When he wasn't working, he would hang out with his uncle Floyd.

Mama Black grew closer to Deaconess Bluestone. They talked on the phone occasionally and would talk to each other after church service. Mama Black and Deaconess Bluestone both worked in the education field for the same school district. They had a lot in common.

When they did talk, Mama Black would always talk and brag about us. She and Papa Black were so proud of Strength and Meaven for going to college. It was something Papa and Mama Black didn't have an opportunity to do since they started a family at a young age. My siblings and I were living out our parents' wildest dreams and aspirations.

Me and Gracie's senior prom were three months away and we still hadn't decided who we were taking. We really didn't want to take the guys that had asked us. Gracie and I were ready to be each other's dates if it came down to it. After all, the year before we were each other's junior prom dates, so we were fine being each other's dates again for our senior prom. We were best friends and sisters, after all.

One day after service while waiting in the dining area for Elder Bluestone to finish counting the tithes and offering, Mama Black and Khase were talking to each other while Gracie, Audacious, Joy and I were in the bathroom.

Mama Black said, "Hey Khase. How you doing today?" Mama Black was easy to talk to and genuinely cared for others.

Khase replied, "Heyyyy Sister Black. I'm doing well. How about yourself?" Khase took a seat at the table where Mama Black had been sitting for the last twenty minutes.

Mama Black responded, "I'm doing well. How's school going for you?"

Khase said, "Oh, it's going great. I have a really great opportunity that's coming up that I'm trying to decide on."

Mama Black responded with a curious expression on her face, "Oh? Great opportunity? What kind of opportunity?"

Khase replied, "Well, I was selected to play professional football overseas in Berlin, Germany."

Mama Black was so excited and happy as if he was her son. She replied with so much joy, saying, "Wow! That's great! God Bless you! Sounds like a once in a lifetime opportunity."

Khase smiled humbly, "Thank you. Thank you, Sister Black. Yeah. I'm excited. Yes, it is. I am leaning towards going."

Mama Black responded, "You should be excited! You are a nice, respectable young man that comes from a good family. That is great news. So, when do you leave? And what team are you playing for – they do have teams out there right? I'm not sure how it works overseas."

Khase couldn't help but smile as he was extremely excited about playing football overseas. He replied, "Thank you. Well, I leave at the end of the summer, the third week in August. I'll be playing for the Berlin Rebels."

Mama Black jokingly replied, "That's wonderful. I know you will do great out there. Now don't go over there and forget about us, okay?"

Mama Black and Khase started laughing.

He responded, "I won't. I won't. I'll make sure I give you guys a call and check in to see how y'all are doing. I'll be back for the holidays."

Mama Black replied, "Okay, great to hear."

They continued talking until Elder Bluestone finished counting the tithes and offering.

Khase replied, "So, how are YOU doing Sister Black?"

Mama Black responded, "Oh, I am doing fine. I'm just getting ready for Journee and Gracie's prom. They still haven't found prom dates yet."

Khase replied, "Oh, they haven't? I thought they found dates already."

Mama Black answered, "No. They haven't. They know the dresses they are going to wear, but that's pretty much it. And Mr. Black and I don't want them taking just any guy. We want someone that they can have fun with and will be gentlemen to our girls."

Khase shook his head to show Mama Black he was actively listening. He paused and then immediately said, "Well, if it's okay with you and Mr. Black, I don't mind taking them. Me and my best friend from college can take them to the prom."

Mama Black was surprised by his response as she wasn't expecting it. Mama Black replied, "Oh, you would do that?! That's nice of you." Mama Black had developed a strong trust for the Bluestone Family. Mama Black felt it was a blessing that her father, Grandpa Millie, introduced her and Papa Black to the Bluestone Family. She felt comfortable around them and knew she could trust them with her children.

Khase replied confidently, "Yes. Sure! That's not a problem."

Mama Black replied, "Okay. Can I ask the girls when they come out the bathroom? I just want to see what they say."

Khase responded, "Sure!"

Two minutes later, Gracie, Audacious, Joy and I came out the bathroom after being in the mirror for twenty minutes, talking, and chatting.

We walked over to the table where Mama Black and Khase were sitting. Mama Black had a huge grin on her face, but we couldn't really understand what the smile was about. Soon after, we discovered what it was.

Mama Black said, "Girls, guess what? Well, this is for Journee and Gracie."

Journee and Gracie replied, "Yes, Mama?!"

Mama Black responded as if she had won a million dollars, "I know who's taking you to your PROMMM!" Khase just sat there with a huge smile on his face waiting for Mama Black to break the news.

I responded not having the slightest clue what Mama Black was going to say. All I said was, "Mama, NO!"

Gracie looked as if she was bracing herself for what Mama Black was about to say. She had one raised eyebrow.

Mama Black jokingly put me in check, "Girl, hush! You don't even know what I'm about to say! Shut your mouth and listen." I shut right up like Mama Black said.

Mama Black continued, "Khase said that he and his best friend were willing to take y'all to the prom if y'all wanted to."

I replied relived, "Oh. That that's it." Meanwhile Gracie bust out in a hysterical laugh that made everyone else to laugh.

Gracie said, "Mama, you hyped up that moment just to say that?!" Everyone started laughing again.

Mama Black laughed saying, "Girl, you hush too! So, what do y'all think?"

Gracie and I responded, "Okay, that's fine."

Gracie and I didn't think much of it since we were close to the Bluestone family and we had known them for several years now.

Khase just sat there and watched Mama Black interact with us.

Next thing you know, Elder Bluestone entered the dining hall with his brief case in one hand and suit jacket in the other.

He heard us laughing as he walked down the hallway. He entered the space and said, "Hey guys. Sorry I had you all waiting. But, what's so funny?"

Khase said, "Hey Dad. Sister Black and I were talking, and I told her me and my best friend would take Journee and Gracie to the prom. When the girls came from the bathroom, Sister Black told them that they had prom dates not knowing I had offered to take them. So, they thought Sister Black had asked some random dudes to take them to the prom.

Mama Black sat in the background shaking her head as Gracie, Audacious, Joy and I were laughing.

Elder Bluestone laughed and replied, "Oh. Oh, okay. They thought it was someone they wouldn't want to take to the prom?"

Mama Black jokingly said, "Yes they did. They didn't even give me the benefit of the doubt."

Mama Black turned to Gracie and me with a smile on her face, "I'm your mother. Y'all my girls and I got y'all! I know how to hook y'all up!"

Everyone laughed at Mama Black. Mama Black and Khase got up from their seats and gathered their belongings. Elder Bluestone and Khase locked up the church. Elder Bluestone took us home while Khase took a separate car home.

CHAPTER 29

PROM NIGHT

Prom night had finally come. Khase escorted me while Khase's best friend escorted Gracie to the prom. That evening it had poured raining so badly that the color of my shoes started to run because I had dyed my shoes to match my prom dress. My hard-earned money working at Kentucky Fried Chicken didn't go to waste other than having runny shoes. However, the rain didn't stop us from having a great time!

Gracie and I looked sharp for our prom! I wore a mint green jacket and skirt with a feathered white fedora hat. My designer cut a piece of my mint green material and added it to my fedora. My jacket was custom made with feminine tails and the skirt was long with a split. Khase matched my ensemble. He wore a three-piece all white tuxedo with masculine tails and a white fedora matching hat. It was the perfect match.

Gracie wore a beautiful lavender glitter gown with a split. Khase's best friend that escorted her wore an all-white suite as well. We looked like a million bucks!

After prom was over, we went to a diner in Hopeville. I ordered an omelet, pan-cakes, and home fries while everyone else ordered a burger and fries. Breakfast is my favorite meal, so I order it no matter the time of the day.

After we chatted, laughed, and hung out for a while, Khase and Khase's best friend dropped us off at home. We didn't get home until 2:30am. Papa and Mama Black weren't worried because they trusted Khase and his family.

Mama Black had given me a key to get back in the house that night since she knew we may be hanging out late after prom. Gracie and I tip-toed in the house so that we didn't wake anyone up. As soon Gracie and I got to the top of the stairs, Mama Black stood there with a huge smile on her face.

Mama Black was full of excitement trying to whisper to not wake Papa Black. She asked, "So, how was it? Did y'all have a good time? What did y'all do?" Mama Black was a mama that wanted to know the details, so she asked!

I responded, "Hey Mama. We had a really good time. Gracie and I didn't win prom queen, though. But we still had fun!"

Gracie replied, "Yup, Mama. We had a great time. We just came back from Hopeville Diner. You can have some of my leftovers if you want some."

Mama Black replied, "Oh. That's okay, Gracie. You enjoy it. I am so happy y'all had such a great time. Did y'all dance?"

I replied while laughing bashfully, "Yes, Mama. We danced!"

Then Mama Black asked, "Did y'all slow dance?"

Gracie and I bust out laughing. When we did that, Mama Black laughed quietly while putting her finger over her mouth. Papa Black was in the next room and she didn't want to disturb his sleep.

I responded with a chuckle, "No, Mama. We didn't slow dance. They just played fast songs."

Mama Black replied, "Oh. Okay. I just thought I'd ask. Geesh."

Gracie and I continued to snicker at Mama's questions.

She ended the conversation with us saying, "Well, I am glad you girls had a good time. That's what matters to me and your father…for y'all to experience things we didn't and for y'all to have fun doing so. I love y'all dearly!"

I walked closer toward Mama Black and gave her a hug. I replied, "Aww. Thank you, Mama. Love you, too."

Gracie hugged Mama Black too. She replied, "Thanks, Mama. We love you, too."

Mama Black said, "Okay, y'all go to bed and get some rest. Good night."

Gracie and I replied, "Good night, Mama."

Mama Black went back into the bedroom and finally went to sleep. Gracie and I went into the kitchen to put our leftover food in the refrigerator. Then, we went upstairs to get ready for bed. Gracie didn't sleep in her room with Audacious and Joy that night. She slept in my room on Strength's bed since Strength was away at school. We talked for a bit about the prom before falling fast asleep and laughed about how much fun we had.

Gracie and I slept in that morning since we got in late from the prom. We chilled and watched television with each other for most of the day before Izzie came over. When Izzie got there, we continued to talk about the prom and how much fun we had. Izzie and Ivy ended up going home right after the prom was over.

Izzie asked, "So, what did y'all do after the prom?"

Gracie replied, "Oh, we went to Hopeville Diner afterwards and just hung out and chilled. It was cool."

Izzie replied, "Oh ok. That's cool!"

I asked Izzie, "What did you and Bryson do afterwards?"

Izzie responded, "He dropped me off right after prom was over. My father wasn't having it. He told Bryson before we left for the prom to bring me straight home or else, he wouldn't make it home. So, my father pretty much scared him."

We couldn't help but laugh. Izzie's father was overprotective of her like Papa Black was with me and my sisters.

We hung out and talked about our upcoming high school graduation and attending college in the fall. All of us were accepted into a college and were so happy about our next chapter.

Our parents were excited for us too. Mama Black was especially excited and proud. Two more of her kids were preparing to gradate high school and go to college. Getting an education was extremely important to Mama Black and she emphasized it to us every chance that she could.

That Sunday after church service had ended, Mama Black and Khase talked again. Khase would always greet Mama Black with a hug and kiss.

Khase said to Mama Black, "Heyyy Sister Black. How are you doing?"

Mama Black replied, "Hey Khase. I'm fine. How are you?"

Khase replied smiling, "I'm well. Can't complain. Me and the girls had a good time at the prom the other day. Well, at least I hope they did."

Mama Black responded with a big smile on her face, "Yes. They had a good time. I was up when they got home. They told me that y'all had fun at the prom and then went out to eat afterwards. That was nice."

Khase chuckled before responding, "Yes. We had a good time. We took them to me and my best friend's favorite Diner in Hopeville. It was cool."

Mama Black replied, "Well, I thank you and your best friend again for taking the girls. I appreciate it."

Khase responded, "No problem, Sister Black. Anyway, I can help, I don't mind. By the way, I know their graduation is coming up and I wanted to surprise them by coming. When is their graduation?

Mama Black said, "Oh, that's nice of you. It's June 22nd at 11am. It'll be at the Al-thea Gibson Stadium."

Khase said, "Oh, dang. I'm not sure if I can make it. I'm working at an overnight summer camp that week and won't be in town that day. I will see if I can leave for the day and try to make it."

Mama Black responded, "Oh, don't worry about it. You're going to be away. We understand if you can't make it."

Khase replied, "Okay. I'll let you know if anything changes."

Mama Black responded, "Okay. Sounds good."

Gracie, Audacious, Joy and I came upstairs from the bathroom and made our way back into the sanctuary where Mama Black and Khase were.

As we walked over, Khase said, "What's up y'all?" He gave each of us a hug.

I replied, "Hey. What's up?"

Gracie responded, "Hey."

Audacious and Joy responded, "Hey, Khase."

Khase being the silly and charming young man that he was, he began showing Mama Black how Gracie and I were dancing at the prom.

"Sister Black, this is how your daughters were dancing at the prom the other night," Khase unexpectedly blurted out. He then began doing the butterfly dance while holding onto the arm of the pew in the middle of the aisle in the sanctuary.

Mama Black, Audacious and Joy started laughing hysterically. Gracie laughed too while I tried to contain my laughter knowing he wasn't telling the truth and just poking fun.

Laughing at Khase trying to imitate our dance moves, I responded, "Nah, that's how you were dancing. You didn't see me doing no butterfly!"

Gracie just laughed.

Whether it was the butterfly or not, Mama Black knew her daughters and knew they weren't just a fly on the wall at the prom. Mama Black enjoyed dancing herself, so she knew her daughters were on the dance floor at the prom.

After laughing and doing the butterfly, Khase finally came clean and said, "Sister Black, I'm just playing. The girls weren't doing the butterfly. I'm just messing with them."

Mama Black continued to laugh. Khase knew how to make anyone laugh no matter the joke or story. He had a gift for making people laugh.

After they had finished laughing and joking, Khase took them home after service that day. Elder Bluestone was still counting the tithes and offering. So, Khase had asked his father to switch cars with him so that he could take us home. Elder Bluestone gave him the keys to the gold minivan while Khase gave him the keys to their other car.

On the ride home, Mama Black sat in the front and we sat in the back as Khase drove. Mama Black had grown to like and appreciate Khase as well as his parents.

CHAPTER 30
GRADUATION DAY!

It was graduation day for Gracie and me. It was a scorching hot summer day in June, but we didn't mind because we were so excited to graduate high school together. I was at the house waiting for Gracie and Izzy to return home so that we could get to our high school early and prepare to walk to the stadium for graduation. They made it back home just in time.

Papa and Mama Black were proud to be there for another pair of their children graduating. Even Grandpa Millie was able to attend our graduation. Strength, Meaven, Audacious and Joy were there too.

After they announced me and Gracie's name, we heard our family shouting and rooting for us from the bleachers. Mama Black spared no feelings as she yelled our names to show how proud of us, she was. Gracie and I hugged as soon as we got our diplomas. We did it...and we did it together as sisters.

A few days after our graduation, Gracie and I found out that Khase did try to make but couldn't because traffic was too congested for him to get to us on time. Instead, he had to turn back around and go back to his summer camp job.

Graduation was over and that summer Gracie, Izzie and I continued to hang out with each other almost every day until we went to college. Ivy went into the military, so we didn't get a chance to hang out with her at all that summer. There were also days that Khase would hang out with us too.

When Khase would hang out with us at our house, Mama Black would say in passing to Khase, "You know, you and Journee sure would make a handsome couple." Mama Black would have a sweet smirk on her face after saying it.

Khase replied as cool as he was, "You think so?!" He would also have a smile on his face.

When I heard this, all I could think to myself was, "Mama, NO!"

Somehow, I didn't utter any words. I just stayed quiet.

That summer, it was a full house. Strength and Meaven were home from college. Izzie and Khase would stop by often. Sometimes Khase's friend would hang out with us as well. It was so fun for us. Papa and Mama Black were used to having a house full of people. It was typical for them to have a lot of people at 83 Believer Street at any point of the day.

The summer days went by fast. Gracie and Izzie were a part of an EOF program at their college, so they stayed on campus for four weeks in August. Even though Gracie and Izzie attended different colleges, they both had the opportunity to experience living on-campus before the semester began.

I wasn't a part of an EOF program. I was enrolled to attend the Hopeville Community College in the Fall of 2002. When I wasn't visiting Gracie and Izzie, I was working at Kentucky Fried Chicken or hanging out at home. Some nights Khase would pick me up so I didn't have to take the bus home at night.

When I visited Gracie at her school, Khase would take me. He would even bring his best friend to visit sometimes. Other times, Khase also visited Gracie by himself. When all of us did hang, it was a guaranteed good time like the prom.

In between hanging out with me and Gracie, Khase also began training and preparing to go to Berlin, Germany to play football. Before leaving for Germany that summer, Elder and Deaconess Bluestone surprised Khase with a going-away party. Strength, msyelf, Gracie, Audacious and Joy attended. Papa and Mama Black stayed home and Meaven had to work that day. Khase was excited for the next chapter in his life. His family and friends were just as excited for him.

Since Mama Black couldn't make it, Khase stopped by the house a few days after the party. He wanted to see Mama Black before leaving for a few months.

When he got to the house, Mama Black and Khase only talked for a little bit because he had to rush back home to finish packing.

As soon as she saw Khase, Mama said, "Hey Khase. How was your going away party?"

Khase replied, "Hey Sister Black. Oh, it was nice; I had a good time! I was surprised and didn't have a clue. It was a nice turn-out too."

Mama Black replied, "Oh, how nice! I am glad to hear that. So how long is your flight?"

Khase replied, "It's 15 hours, including the layover."

Mama Black was astonished, "Wow! 15 hours?! That's a long flight. Take some books with you to read so you can have something to do on the flight. It'll make the time go by quicker."

Khase laughed and responded, "Yes. It's a long flight. I do plan to bring some books with me to keep me occupied. I think I'm going to stay up the night before so that I can just rest on the flight."

Mama Black replied, "Oh, that's smart. Well make sure you keep in touch and let us know when you get there. Be safe and God bless!"

Khase responded, "Thank you, Sister Black. Appreciate that."

Mama Black and Khase talked a little longer before Khase eventually left. Everyone said their good-byes after they finished talking.

CHAPTER 31

STRENGTH'S 22ND BIRTHDAY

Summer ended; September meant back to school. Strength and Meaven returned to college, Gracie and I were in our first year of college, and Audacious and Joy were still in high school. Mama Black went back to work as well, teaching kindergarten students. Papa Black worked all year round, so he didn't get summers off like us.

I was thrilled to begin my first day of college at Hopeville Community College. I got up early that morning so that I could find my classes and be on time. Attending Hopeville Community College was a new endeavor for me, but I didn't shy away from change. Not only was attending college a new and different endeavor for me, but it was the very first time Gracie and I didn't attend school together. We had gone from spending all our time together to seeing each other only on the weekends. That's when Gracie would come home.

Things seemed to be going well for my family and I. Papa and Mama Black's four oldest children were in college. Audacious and Joy were attending Hopeville High School and doing well. Mama Black supported us while developing her own personal relationship with God. She also continued to strengthen her relationships with her church family from Great and Mercy Baptist Church. As always, Papa Black continued working hard and long hours.

One day, things changed suddenly. It was like any other Friday morning. The sun was shining, the sky was clear and blue, and the weather was warm. It seemed to be a good day. We got the most devastating and crushing news of our lives. On September 27th, Strength's 22nd birthday, we received a phone call that our dear Mama Black died.

Shocked and saddened, we did not know how to take the unexpected loss of Mama Black. She was the one that held our family together. Mama Black was the matriarch of the Black family and she was no longer around to hold my family together. Shocked and hurt was an understatement.

When everyone got the news, my siblings and I were heartbroken. Papa Black was devastated, too. Crying and wailing filled 83 Believer Street that day. No one could make sense of it. Not even Strength. As Mama Black's first-born child, Strength was especially impacted. Strength's birthday would never be the same.

Later that afternoon, Khase called to wish Strength a happy birthday. He had finally made it to Berlin, Germany and had been there for two weeks. He was still settling into his new apartment and had met with his football coach and agent earlier that day. His first game wasn't until a month after he moved there, so he had time to really get settled in.

When Khase called, he didn't have a clue as to what was going on with Mama Black. He greeted Strength with his usual silly, upbeat demeanor.

He greeted Strength and said, "Hey, girl. What's up?! I just a called to wish you a happy birthday. So, Happy Birthday! What you got going on today?"

Strength couldn't hide the sadness in her voice over the phone. She responded in a solemn tone, "Thank you. I'm not doing anything anymore."

Khase responded, "What you mean you're not doing anything for your birthday?!?"

Strength responded, "Khase, I have to tell you something." She paused before saying anything else further.

Khase nervously said, "What? What happened?!"

Strength took a deep breath while tears began to flow down her face. She said sadly, "My mother passed away this morning."

Khase was not expecting to receive that news from Strength. After hearing the news about Mama Black, Khase sat quietly on the other end of the phone. Strength did, too. Neither of them knew what else to say to the other. Everyone was still in shock and denial.

Khase finally responded, "I don't even know what to say. I just spoke to and saw your mom not too long ago. How is this even possible?! I just don't get it."

Strength didn't have any words to say, so she just sat on the phone quietly.

Khase continued, "Did my mother and father stop by there?"

Strength replied, "Yeah. They stopped by and left not too long ago. Your mom went grocery shopping for us. She took Journee with her when she went."

Khase replied, "Oh okay. I'm glad they stopped by. What are the rest of your siblings up to?"

Trying to hold it together, she replied, "They are in the living room with my father and they are just watching television."

Khase responded, "Oh okay. Did anyone else from the church stop by?

Strength said, "Yeah. Rev. and First Lady Watkins stopped by earlier."

Khase replied, "Okay. Well, I'll give y'all call tomorrow. Keep me posted on the services because I'm going to come back home so that I can be there for y'all. I'm praying for y'all."

Strength responded, "Okay. Thanks for calling. Talk to you later. Bye-bye."

Khase replied, "Alright. No problem. Bye."

After Strength had gotten off the phone, she came back into the living where the rest of us were.

Growing up we had a lot of cousins. A lot of them stopped by during the day and some of them stayed the night as well. Our big cousin, Big Nat, was close to Meaven. Big Nat and Meaven grew up like brothers. Since Meaven was the only boy, Papa Black made sure he hung around Big Nat. They spent most of their time playing video games and making up songs.

The night that Mama Black had died, Big Nat, Cousin O and Izzie stayed the night. We all slept in Gracie, Audacious and Joy's room. Some of us slept on the floor while others piled in the bed with each other. We just wanted to be together. When Meaven and Big Nat were together, I knew something funny would go down. It was always comedy central when those two were together.

After everyone had fallen asleep, there was sudden beat boxing going on that woke everyone up. Big Nat had dropped a beat while banging his knuckles and fist on the metal frame of the bunk bed. He and Meaven were at it again! Big Nat had started his beat. Then he began rapping, "Stop stepping on my foot…stop stepping on my foot…stop stepping on my foot…."

It was catchy and they didn't stop there. Meaven interjected his part. Adding to the song, he rapped, "…these Prada, witch…these Prada, witch…these Prada, witch!" Meaven also added to the club mix singing, "OUCH…OUCH…OUCH!" They kept the song going for at least five minutes.

When everyone heard Big Nat and Meaven's new club mix, we all just bust out laughing! They kept the song going while Audacious and Gracie jumped out their beds and started dancing to the song. They laughed even harder. It was a miracle that Papa Black didn't even come upstairs to tell us to be quiet. Papa Black didn't even have the energy or strength to say anything that night. He just let us be.

My siblings and I always knew how to laugh even when it was hard for us. That night, we needed laughter. That night, we needed a relief. That night, we needed each other. That night, we needed that song to get us through the start of what would be a long road ahead. After their club mix had ended, we were able to fall asleep again.

Preparing for and attending Mama Black's funeral was one of the hardest days our family had to face. As Papa Black, Strength, Meaven, Gracie, Audacious, Joy and I entered Grace and Mercy Baptist Church to lay her to rest, life as we knew it would never be the same. Literally. Life. Changed.

Mama Black was very well-known at her job and in the community. So many people came out to pay respect to Mama Black and to support us. Everyone knew how much Mama Black loved her family, including us. Mama Black read us bedtime stories, gave us surprise birthday gifts and cards, braided all five of her daughters' hair every two weeks, prepared home-cooked meals, and helped us with homework. She attended every school event and parent night, fashion show, band event, and prayed over us before leaving school. She randomly danced, supported every prom and graduation, and instilled wisdom in her children during teachable moments. Mama Black was the ultimate example of following Christ. In addition, she was a great wife to Papa Black and phenomenal mother to all six of her children. Her actions showed that she loved us. Mama Black was truly special. Her family and the community knew it.

Two days before the funeral, Khase flew back home to attend Mama Black's service. Khase and his family were there that day to support. The entire Grace and Mercy Baptist Church was there to support. Izzie was able to be there as well.

After a long and emotionally draining day, we went back home. Walking back to 83 Believer Street later that afternoon, I couldn't help but feel that things were not the same without Mama Black around. She was the reason we got the house in the first place.

The house felt empty, awkward, and different. I knew I had Papa Black, my siblings and Izzie, but I couldn't shake those feelings on the inside.

Even with a support system, I just still couldn't understand how a woman, who was a good person, wife, mother who genuinely loved God could pass away at the tender age of 41 – a week before her 42nd birthday.

I couldn't help but think to myself, "How do I continue to go through college and life without my mother…" I didn't get my answer that night. At 18 years old, I felt that life didn't seem so promising anymore. Life for me would never be or feel the same.

After the repass, it was a packed house again. Mama Black's mother – Grandma Eve stopped by. Mama Black absolutely adored her mother. Seeing Grandma Eve and

Mama Black interact with each other taught me how to treat other women.

Mama Black's brothers, sisters, nieces, and nephews stopped by as well to sit with us. Auntie CeeCee was closest to Mama Black when she had died. She was there too. Izzie, Khase and Khase's best friends also hung out with us that night.

Around midnight, everyone had left except Khase and Khase's best friend. They stayed behind to hang out with us a little longer. Khase especially wanted to be there to support since he had a close relationship with Mama Black and had established a friendship with us.

Later, when everyone had left for the evening, Khase pursued his interest in me. Although I was surprised, I liked him and enjoyed being around him, especially since he had taken me to my senior prom. Plus, Mama Black had always mentioned how we would make a handsome couple.

The very next day, weeks and months ahead, things became confusing for me. I began to see a subtle change in Khase's behavior towards me. He started treating me different and as if his interests weren't made explicitly known to me. Things would continue to go downhill from there.

A few days later, Khase returned to Germany to continue playing football overseas. He would often call to see how everyone was doing. When he did call, he spoke to me sometimes but then began spending most of his time talking to Gracie. One day while they were talking, Gracie revealed a secret to Khase. Whatever the secret was, it was obvious that it had bothered him. Neither Gracie nor Khase told anyone what was going on. I didn't know what was going on; I had the slightest clue.

Keeping things amongst each other was a bond that Gracie and Khase had developed that no one else knew about. A few months earlier, Gracie, Izzie, and I were hanging out one summer afternoon. There were some speculations that Khase and Gracie has been talking, but Izzie and I weren't sure.

Until one summer afternoon, Izzie and I had asked Gracie what was going on with her and Khase. Gracie turned into a U.S. Navy Seal that day! She didn't want to say but she had shared with me and Izzie that something went on between her and Khase. She laughed it off. From there I decided to get Khase out of my head. That was until he pursued me after Mama Black's funeral.

CHAPTER 32
SECRETS & CONFUSION

After I had found out that Gracie had shared a secret with Khase that day over the phone, I couldn't figure out what it could be. Izzie and I talked about it, but we didn't have a clue as to what it could be.

Although Mama Black was no longer with us, we continued with our routines: school and work. Our normal routines were no longer normal anymore. When I returned to school, I spoke to my English professor explaining why I had missed a few classes. After the professor instructed the class to start our writing assignment, I raised my hand to speak to the professor.

When I finally got my professor's attention, I said, "May I speak with you, professor?"

The professor replied, "Sure. Come on up."

I walked up to her professor's desk and sat in the blue plastic chair that was near his desk.

I responded, "Professor, I wasn't in class these past few days because my mother passed away last week."

Looking surprised, astonished and speechless, the professor exclaimed, "And you're here in school?!?! My goodness. I'm sorry to hear that!" His big blue eyes pierced my soft brown sad eyes when he looked at me. My English professor wasn't expecting me to say that.

I really didn't have much of a response other than, "Yes. I'm here. Is there any way I can make up the worked I missed? I don't want to get a zero for it."

The professor replied, "Of course. You can submit your work next week. That will be fine. If you need more time, please let me know."

I replied, "Okay. Thank you."

Walking back to my desk, all I could think about was Mama Black's words and Papa Black's example. Mama Black would often say, "Make sure you get your education."

Little did that white professor know, I had a Mama that had already instilled grit, resilience, and power in me. Papa Black showed me what it meant to fight and not give

171

up. I didn't realize why I would need that from Papa and Mama Black. I carried it with me since childhood.

CHAPTER 33
WHEN IT RAINED, IT POURED!

When it rained, it poured! A month after Mama Black's death, foreclosure notices were being mailed to the house. The bank was coming after Ms. Pearl's house if payments were not made by the end of the month. Ms. Pearl couldn't make the payments on the house, so we had to find somewhere else to move. Again!

As if burying Mama Black wasn't enough, we had another loss we would experience in a short time frame. We had to move. We had to be out of 83 Believer Street by the end of November or else the doors would be padlocked. The water had been cut off. Since the water had been cut off, there was no heat and the cold season was about to begin. Loss after loss…we just couldn't catch a break.

We had to establish a different routine to survive and make it to the next day all while being in college and high school. Papa Black would wash at his Uncle Floyd's house. My sisters and I went to Elder and Deaconess Bluestone's house since they lived around the corner, and Meaven went to Big Nat's house. Our new routine lasted until December, when we finally found an apartment.

With the help of a church member from the Grace and Mercy Baptist Church, we were able to get a decent apartment that was still in the area. The apartment was in Hopeville and close to Audacious and Joy's high school. When we moved in, we had to figure out how to adjust without Mama Black. Waking up for school to get there on time, doing homework, cooking dinner, buying groceries, cleaning the house, paying bills were all routines we had to take on without Mama Black. Papa Black had to adjust without Mama Black as he continued to work long hours at his job.

Since Audacious and Joy were still in high school, Strength stepped in to help them get through the rest of their high school years. Between their proms, graduation and life after high school, Strength made sure she was there for her little sisters. She tried to be there for all of us while dealing with her own grief of Mama Black passing on her birthday.

I continued going to Hopeville County Community College. I had an interest in nursing and decided to pursue that as a major. I wanted to help and serve people. So, every day I took the bus to school and back home. Every night, I would pull up a chair to my dresser as if it were a desk so that she could do my homework comfortably. Gracie continued going to Hopeville University but was no longer staying on campus. She commuted back and forth to school.

Khase continued playing football in Germany. When he would call, Khase's conversations with me had become shorter while his conversations with Gracie got longer. I didn't really understand what was going, but I continued to live my life the best I knew how.

During the holidays that year and his off-season, Khase returned home and would visit us when he was in town. When he did visit, he and Gracie hung out while he treated me has if nothing had ever happened. Confused as to what went wrong, I would talk to Izzie about it, but we couldn't make sense of the situation.

It had been four months since Mama Black died and we had received some more unexpected news. Gracie was having a baby. When Gracie hesitantly shared the news, my family and I were shocked and happy at the same time. Although Mama Black was no longer here, we were excited about the joy of having a niece and nephew. Papa Black was excited to become a grandfather.

Although it was new news for me, it wasn't for Khase. This was the same news that she had shared with Khase a few months prior, and the same news that made him upset with her.

The day had finally come, and Gracie gave birth to baby Glorie. She was the most beautiful little girl we had ever laid eyes on. Even though Mama Black didn't get a chance to meet her first granddaughter, we were happy about Gracie's new bundle of joy. Baby Glorie had brought so much happiness into the family, and it was needed.

After the birth of Baby Glorie, Khase decided that he was no longer pursuing his football career overseas in Berlin, Germany. He returned home for good and quit playing football. When he decided to do that, Khase, Gracie and Baby Glorie really became a family.

While I was happy and excited to have a new niece in my life, I couldn't make sense of the situation nor did I have the right answers on what to do, how to feel, and how to handle the situation. Not only did Khase, Gracie and Baby Glorie operate like a family, they portrayed a "family" image to the outside world and to our Grace and Mercy Baptist Church family. The outside world or the church didn't really know the be-hind-the-scenes story about Khase and me, but they had their suspicions. I just continued going to college and hanging out with Izzie.

CHAPTER 34

RAYCE

One afternoon while on the bus going home from a long day of school, I met this really fineeeeeee brother. He resembled the famous actor Khalil Khan. His name was Rayce. Not only was Rayce fine, but he had a great sense of humor, was down to earth and very smart. His personality matched his fine looks. Rayce stood 6'2 in height and was very muscular. His sandy-brown skin tone and exotic hazel-brown eyes were his most admirable features. With pearly white, straight teeth and full lips, Rayce could captivate anyone with his smile, let alone his eyes. Rayce always wore fresh waves with a nice shape-up and sideburns. Rayce had a deep, masculine voice. He was fine and masculine in every sense of the word. Rayce was also from Hopeville.

We locked eyes on the bus while sitting several seats from each other. Rayce spoke to me. He said in his deep voice while smiling, "How you doing?"

I smiled and replied, "I'm doing good. How are you?"

With a sensual smirk, Rayce responded, "I'm doing good. Are you from around here?"

I replied, "Yes. I am. How about you?"

Rayce responded, "I'm from around here, too." He continued and said, "So where are you coming from or on your way to?"

I answered, "I'm coming from school."

Rayce said, "If you don't mind, can I come closer to you? I really can't hear you. This bus is kind of loud."

I moved my book bag off the seat that was next to me and put it on my lap so that Rayce could sit next to me on the bus. I replied, "Sure."

Seeing that I had moved my book bag, Rayce got up while the bus was still moving and made his way to sit next to me. We continued talking to each other on the bus ride home.

I asked, "How about you? Where are you coming from or going to?"

Rayce responded, "I'm actually coming from my mechanic. I had to put my car in the shop, and it won't be ready until tonight. So, I just took the bus back home."

I responded, "Oh, okay. Cool."

Rayce continued talking, "So what are you in school for?"

I proudly replied, "My major is nursing. I want to become a nurse."

Rayce said, "Oh! That's what's up. Nursing is a great field, and they make a lot of money."

I smiled and answered, "Yeah, they do. But I'm not doing it for the money. I want to do it to help and serve people."

Rayce stared and paused before responding, "That's what's up. I can respect that."

I replied, "Thanks. So, what do you do?"

Rayce replied, "I'm a Branch Manager for J&P Bank."

I responded, "Oh, you're fancy!" We both began laughing.

Rayce's stop was coming up so he was getting off the bus at the next stop. He replied, "So is there any way I can keep in touch with you?"

I replied, "Sure. You can have my cell phone number." Rayce gave me his number as well.

Rayce replied, "Aight. I'll hit you up later to see what's up. Nice meeting you, sweetheart."

I kept my cool and replied, "Nice meeting you too."

Rayce walked off the bus but gave me one last look and smiled. I smiled back at him.

I finally made it home from a long day of school. I entered in the house and went into me and Gracie's bedroom. Gracie wasn't home so I had the bedroom to myself that day. I took off my clothes, got in the shower, made a sandwich, and started doing my homework.

Like usual, I pulled up a chair to my dresser and started doing my homework. Although I was excited about meeting Rayce, my heart was still heavy. I didn't even know how to begin to process the emotions from the loss of my mother and the empty feeling I had constantly felt after Khase had treated me as if I was a 'nobody.' I had never felt so thrown to the side, hurt, betrayed, and unprotected.

I could barely pray for myself. Somehow, by the grace of God, I found an outlet. In between my homework breaks, I began writing in my journal. My first journal entry said:

"Today was a good day. It's already been one year since my mother died. I miss and love her dearly. There is no other like my mother."

I didn't have much to say that day. The pen and hurt in my heart couldn't get pass those four sentences. So, I went back to doing my homework. After a few hours, my phone rang. Unexpectedly, it was Rayce. I was happy to hear from him, so I picked up with a smile on my face.

"Hello?" I answered with a smile on my face.

"Hello. May I speak to Journee?" Rayce said politely with his masculine baritone voice.

"This is Journee. May I ask whose calling?" I responded. I knew exactly who it was by that deep voice, but I asked him anyway.

"It's Rayce. We met on the bus earlier today," replied Rayce.

"Oh, yes. I remember you! What's up?" I replied.

"How you doing? What are you up to?" Rayce said.

"I'm good. I was just taking a break from doing some homework. How are you doing? How did you make out with your car?" I responded.

"I'm doing good. Everything worked out with my car. I was able to get it back a couple hours ago. I'm good to go now," Rayce responded.

"Good to hear. Glad it worked out for you," I answered.

Then Rayce asked, "So what's up? Can I come through and see you?"

I wasn't expecting that. Rayce was truly a man that went after what he wanted. I jokingly replied, "Come through and see me?! I don't know you like that. You could be crazy!" I started laughing and so did Rayce.

Chuckling as he answered, "I'm not crazy. I'm as friendly as they come."

I smiled and responded, "Mhmm. Sure, you are."

Rayce replied, "So, may I? Is that cool with you?"

I waited before responding. Then I replied, "Okay. That's cool. I would love to, but I can't hang for long. I have to get back to my schoolwork."

I could hear the smile on Rayce's face. He responded with his deep voice, "I won't take up too much of your time. I just would like to hang out and chill with you for a bit."

I replied, "Okay, cool. That would be nice. What time are you coming?"

Rayce answered, "Is 8pm okay? And what's your address?"

I responded, "Sure. That's fine. It's 75 Prosperous Lane."

Rayce replied, "Okay, cool. I'll call you when I'm downstairs."

I said, "Okay. See you soon."

We hung up the phone and I immediately began getting ready. I went in my walk-in closet and threw on some light blue jeans, a white tank top and some flip flops. I grabbed a light jacket just in case it was cold. Then I went into the bathroom, removed my bobby pins, and combed down my doobie. I loveddddd wearing doobies! After I had finished combing down my hair, I placed a white headband on to push my hair back out of my face.

Just as I was applying my lip gloss, Rayce called to let me know he was downstairs waiting. After I had finished getting ready, I grabbed my cell phone and keys and took the elevator downstairs.

When I walked out the front door, Rayce was standing outside his 2003 Black 4-door Acura TL with his hands in his pockets. As soon as Rayce saw me, he smiled and greeted me with a hug. While leaning in for a hug, he said, "Hey. How are you doing? You look nice."

I hugged him back and couldn't help but notice is cologne. He smelled good. I replied, "Hey. I'm well. How are you? You smell nice."

Rayce replied, "I'm good. And thanks."

I replied, "I see you officially got your car back. I know you're happy about that."

Rayce responded while gently rubbing his car, "Yeah. I got my baby back." We both laughed.

I replied while smiling, "Oh your baby? Does your baby have a name? Every car should have a name."

Rayce jokingly responded, "Yeah. Her name is Blackie!"

I chuckled before responding, "Oh, ok. Blackie. Nice. Hey, whatever works for you."

Rayce continued while laughing, "Sike. Nah. Her name is Power."

I immediately stopped laughing and responded to him in a serious tone. While nodding my head in agreement, I said, "I like that. Power. Nice name."

Rayce replied, "Thanks. So, how did the rest of your studying go? Did you get a lot of homework done?"

As soon as I started to respond to Rayce, I saw Khase, Gracie and Baby Glorie pull up. Khase parked the car and they all got out. To get into the building, they had to walk past Rayce and I. I instantly stopped talking. As they walked by, Khase and Gracie said hello to Rayce and I. Rayce and I said hello back.

When they walked into the building, Rayce immediately asked, "Who was that?"

I replied, "Oh that was my sister, niece, and a guy from my church."

Seeing my energy change, Rayce replied, "Are you okay?"

I replied, "Yes. I am fine. Thanks for asking."

Rayce not fully convinced, he asked a second time, "Are you sure?"

I insisted that I was fine. I replied, "Oh. Yes. I'm fine. I'm sorry. I just got a little distracted. But you were asking me about my homework. To answer your question, YES! I was able to get a lot done."

Rayce responded, "That's what's up. I know you are a good student. You seem like it. So, who do you live here with?"

I responded, "My family."

Rayce began laughing and said, "Okay...your family like...who?"

I laughed and replied, "Oppps. Well, everyone but my mom. She died last year."

Rayce paused for a moment before responding, "Wow. I'm so sorry to hear that. My condolences to you and your family. I know she was a beautiful woman because you're beautiful. And I know she's proud of you for continuing with school. I know it's a lot. I've also experienced losses in my family, so I understand."

Hearing those words from Rayce made me feel good amid what I had going on. Rayce didn't even know about the situation between me, Gracie and Khase, but hearing those words meant a lot to me in that moment.

I replied, "Aww. Thanks, Rayce. That means a lot. I appreciate you saying that. It's been rough but we've been trying to make my mother proud and keep going."

Rayce replied, "Well, I know every situation is different, but I'm here for you if you need me."

I looked in Rayce's eyes and replied, "Wow. So, you AREN'T crazy, huh?!"

We both looked at each other and laughed! Rayce wasn't expecting me to say that.

Rayce responded, "Ha. Ha. Very funny. And no, I'm not crazy. Well I'm not going to hold you up from doing the rest of your homework, so I'll let you go."

I replied, "Okay. Well, thanks for stopping by and for the encouragement."

Rayce said, "No problem. That's what I'm here for. Is it okay if I hit you up over the weekend and maybe stop by again?"

I thought to myself, "Of course you can! I would love that!" But I ended up saying, "Yeah. That's cool. If I'm not doing homework, then sure."

Rayce replied, "Aight, bet. Good seeing you."

I replied, "Good seeing you, too."

Rayce leaned in to give me a hug. When we hugged, I got a second whiff of his good smelling cologne again. Then, I walked to the front door and waved good-bye. Rayce waved back until he could no longer see me. He pulled off when I was no longer in sight.

Rayce and I had an instant connection and undeniable chemistry. I needed that positivity in my life at the time.

When I got on the elevator, I pressed the button for the 9th floor. All I could think about on the elevator ride up was how uncomfortable I would feel and what the energy would be like when I walked in.

I opened the door and Khase was standing in the kitchen by himself. It was obvious that he had been looking out the window watching me as I was hung out with Rayce.

Khase stared at me as I walked in and said, "Who was that?"

Not even making eye contact with him, I replied, "Somebody I know," and kept walking.

I could feel Khase's energy as I walked by him, but I went straight to my room. Although Gracie and I shared rooms, Gracie wasn't in the room, so I just closed the door, charged my phone, changed my clothes, and got in the bed.

CHAPTER 35
A CHANGE FOR JOURNEE

Rayce and I continued to hang out and developed a good friendship. We enjoyed each other's company and found out that we had a lot in common. Rayce's sense of humor kept me laughing and giggling when he was around. When we hung out, we drove around and ate delicious food from the local spots in Hopeville.

We continued to keep in touch and hang out until I completed my two years of schooling at Hopeville Community College. I was accepted to Robinson University in Cairo, NJ where I would attend school for the next three years. I was so excited to confirm my acceptance to the school. It was two hours away and required that I stay on campus. So, I would be moving two hours from my family. When I had informed my family that I would be transferring and going to another school, somehow Khase found out as well.

One afternoon, Joy and I attended a football game with Elder Bluestone since he had invited us to attend. Joy and I didn't mind and had nothing else to do, so we went. To my surprise, Khase was at the game as well. We barely talked while at the game.

When the game had finally ended, Joy and I were standing around waiting for Elder Bluestone to come from the locker room. Just the two of us. While waiting, Joy got stung by a bee unexpectedly. Khase just so happened to walk by when it happened. He asked Joy and I if we were okay.

Trying to help my baby sister, I replied frantically, "No. Joy just got stung by a bee! Is there an ice pack in there? I don't want to go in the boy's locker room and ask for one."

Khase replied, "Oh, shoot. I'll go in and grab one for her."

Joy was a good sport and did everything to keep her composure. I could tell she was in pain from the tears that formed in her eyes.

Khase came back out and passed Joy the ice pack. Joy replied, "Thank you!" She couldn't have placed that icepack on her lip any quicker if she wanted to. After she placed it on her lip, the pain subsided, and she felt better.

There was an awkward silence between Khase and I until Elder Bluestone came out the locker room after the game. His team won and he was happy about it. As we walked to the car to go home, Khase turned to me and whispered that he would call me later so we could talk. Caught off guard, I shook my head in agreement.

Later that evening, Khase called me and we spoke for a short time.

Khase immediately began the conversation, "Hey. I know things have been awkward lately. Things aren't what they look like. I'm just trying to help. I wasn't trying to hurt your feelings or do wrong by you. I respect your mom too much."

At first, I couldn't make sense of what exactly Khase was saying to me about the situation, but my heart believed him.

I replied, "I don't think what you did to me was right. You started treated me like I did something wrong and I didn't."

Khase answered, "I know you're right. I can't talk much right now, but maybe we can talk in-person later."

Thrown off again and surprised he was even speaking to me again, I replied, "Uhhhhh. Okay."

I wasn't sure what more he had to say or why he even wanted to see me since he had treated me as if I had done something wrong. But I was curious about what he wanted to say to me.

A few hours later, he called to let me know he was downstairs. I made my way downstairs and got into the car with Khase. He immediately began talking. This was nothing new. Khase had the gift of gab.

"What's up?" Khase said as soon as I got into the car.

"Hey. What's up?" I replied.

"How you doing?" Khase continued the conversation.

"I'm good," I hesitantly replied. I wasn't sure how the conversation would go, so I kept my defense up.

"I know I said a lot earlier. But I just wanted to speak with you face to face. Like I said before, I know things have been awkward lately. Things aren't what they look like. I'm just trying to help. I wasn't trying to hurt your feelings or do wrong by you. I respect your mom too much," Khase said.

"What you did was very f-ed up. How is dealing with two sisters respecting my mother?" I asked with hurt in my voice, really wanting to know.

"I understand what you are saying. Your feelings are valid. And you're right; it's not respecting your mother. You know, I really loved and cared for your mom. She always showed me love when she was here. She's the reason why I'm helping. I do everything for your mom. Your mom wouldn't want us going through this. She even said we made a handsome couple," Khase said as tears fell down his face.

Somehow everything Khase had said, in that moment, made sense to me. After all, Mama Black always said we did make a handsome couple. I didn't hate him. I just didn't like what he did to me. Somehow my hurt turned into guilt. I began feeling guilty and bad for Khase.

"Our families were close. His parents were good people. He was in the church. That made him a good person, right? Grandpa Millie brought our families together so that meant he came from a good family, right? He couldn't possibly do anything intentionally to tear two sisters apart…right?" I thought to myself when I saw the tears falling from his face. Somewhere inside of me I still cared about him.

We continued driving around for a little while longer. After he stopped crying, Khase asked me, "So, when do you leave for school? You're transferring to Robinson University, right?"

"Yes. I leave at the end of the semester," I said.

"How are you moving and getting your stuff down there?" Khase asked.

I paused before answering because I hadn't even thought that far. I just confirmed my acceptance not too long ago and was ready to just leave. I was excited to finally have the chance to live on-campus. I commuted every day to Hopeville Community College, so I looked forward to the days of rolling out the bed and walking to my college class that was only 5 minutes away.

Eventually I answered Khase's question. I replied, "Um, I am not sure. Everyone's schedule is crazy and none of us have a car big enough to fit all my things in. I have to figure it out, I guess."

Khase responded, "I can take you. I'll ask my mom and dad to use the mini-van that way you will have enough room to bring all your stuff in one shot. That shouldn't be a problem."

I hesitated to say yes, but she didn't have any other option, so I thought. I replied, "Okay."

By the time we finished talking, Khase pulled up in front of the house to drop me off.

"Alright, I'll talk to you later. Thanks again for the talk," said Khase.

I opened the car door, looked at Khase and replied, "You're welcome," and shut the door behind me.

The semester ended for me and in a month, I would be leaving Hopeville to finish my degree in nursing at Robinson University. I didn't know anyone at Robinson University, but I was confident in making new friends. Traveling to new places by myself was something I wasn't afraid of. I also wanted to get away from the drama.

CHAPTER 36

"MAKE SURE YOU GET YOUR EDUCATION" – MAMA BLACK

The day had finally come. I was leaving for college and moving 2 hours away from home. The week leading up to leaving, I spent time preparing for the move. I went shopping for things I would need for my dorm room, washed, and packed my clothes and brought pictures that would make my dorm room feel at home. I even took pictures of Mama Black.

I was so excited for the next chapter in my life. While making the decision to leave my family and all the craziness behind, Mama Black's words continued to resonate in my soul: "Make sure you get your education. Make sure you get an education. Make sure you get an education." This was the motivation I used to leave and keep pressing ahead.

I finally finished packing all my things. The main items I packed were her clothes, shoes, sneakers, boots, a coat, toiletries, a pillow, bedding, a book bag, and my cell phone. Oh, and my journal. I couldn't forget my journal. Khase helped load up my stuff in the van while everyone went downstairs to see me off. Strength, Meaven, Gracie, Audacious and Joy hugged me before I got into the van. Khase and I got into the car, pulled off and started the two-hour drive.

When we finally reached Robinson University Campus, the first building we went to was the Office of Residence Life. Since it was January 2005 of the Spring semester, moving in was a piece of cake! Khase and I walked to the residence life security desk to get more information on where to go.

I excitedly said to the security guard on-duty, "Hi. I'm new here and will be moving in. Do you know where I pick up my dorm room key?"

The security guard replied, "Hi. Welcome, young lady. You see that door behind you? Go into that office right there and they will help you out."

Khase and I turned our heads in the direction the security guard pointed. There was a big sign that read, *Robinson University Office of Residence Life.*

I replied, "Oh. It was right there. Thank you, sir."

Khase also responded, "Thank you, sir."

Khase and I walked inside the office and the first face I saw was another college student sitting at the desk. Her name tag said Treasure. Treasure's eyes were not only captivating but friendly. She had beautiful, round, and endearing hazel-brown eyes. Her dewy, flawless light skinned complexion made her eye color more vibrant. Her smile and welcoming spirit are what made me feel like she was in the right place.

When we entered the office, Treasure greeted us saying, "Hi! Welcome to Robinson Office of Residence Life. May I help you?"

I smiled back and said, "Hi. I'm a new student. I am supposed to move in today and just needed my room number and key."

Treasure responded, "Oh, okay. What's your name?"

I responded, "Journee Black."

As she looked up my name on the computer, Treasure responded, "Oh, that's a powerful name!"

I smiled proudly and said, "Thank you!"

Khase had taken a seat while Treasure and I talked.

Treasure replied, "You're welcome. Okay. Give me one second. I have to let the Director of Residence Life know you are here."

I replied, "Okay. No problem. Thanks for your help."

When Treasure got up from her desk, I admired her sense of style. For a college student, Treasure was a fly dresser! She had on a black blazer with the cuffed sleeves, a gold butterfly broch pinned to her blazer, a white V-neck cotton shirt, a leopard-print scarf that hung softly from her neck, black jeans and black suede booties. Her hair was styled in big soft curls and her make-up looked natural and feminine.

Treasure went into the office and came back with the Director of Residence Life. He was tall, had smooth brown-skinned, dreads and a lean frame. He was a handsome man. He was also welcoming to me as a new student on campus.

Extending his hand to shake mine, Director Trevor said, "Welcome, Journee! Glad to have you here at the Robinson Office of Residence Life."

I shook his hand and replied, "Hi. Thank you. I am glad to be here." Khase immediately got up from his seat, extended his hand to the Director. Aggressively, he interjected himself in the conversation. He said, "Hi. I'm Khase."

Director Trevor extended his hand and professionally responded, "Hi. Nice to meet you."

Trevor immediately returned his attention back to me. He replied, "Journee, so we are going to get you set up with your room and keys. Before we do, there's some paperwork that Treasure is going to have you complete. It's relevant information about your keys, lock-out policy & fee, quiet hours, drinking and smoking policy, supplies and materials you're allowed to have in your dorm room, your ID, etc. As you go through the paperwork, ask me, or Treasure any questions that you may have. Treasure is going to get you the paperwork while I get your room keys. You'll be in room 603."

I am so excited! I replied with the biggest smile on my face, "Thank you!"

Treasure handed me a clipboard, pen, and all the necessary paperwork while Director Trevor went to a separate office to grab my dorm keys.

I sat down next to Khase and completed my paperwork. Once I completed it, Director Trevor explained the room set up to me.

"Journee, here is your room key. You are on the Tower side in Room 603A. You've been placed in a suite. There are three rooms but lucky for you no one has been placed in your room. So, you will have a room all to yourself," Director Trevor said.

My eyes widened. I exclaimed, "Really?! So, I basically have my own room?" That made me even more excited about attending Robinson University.

Director Trevor chuckled at my reaction. He replied, "Yes. That means you have your own room."

I couldn't have smiled wider.

Director Trevor continued, "Here is your key. You only get one for the semester. If you lose it, there will be a $75 fine. I also want to mention the amenities we have in this building. On the first floor, there's the laundry room. You will need quarters to wash your clothes. The laundry room is open 24/7 so you can wash your clothes at your leisure. Also, on the first floor is the Student Lounge. There's a pool table, couches, and a television in there and you can go there anytime as well. Lastly, there are two computer labs on the Tower side. One is on the third floor and the other is on the 5th floor."

I asked, "Tower side? What's that?"

Director Trevor said, "The Tower side has more dorms room and is designated for under classmen. On the other side is the apartment side for upper classmen."

I responded, "Ohhhhh. Okay. I understand."

Director Trevor told one last thing I needed to know about being on campus. He said, "Before you go to your dorm, you have to get your Student ID from the Student Campus Center. They are still open. You can head over there now to get your ID and come back. You will need your Student ID for your meals, gaining access to this building, making copies at the library, and borrowing the move-in carts. The student ID's are just $5."

I replied, "Okay. I'll go and do that now. Can you direct me to the building?"

Director Trevor said, "Sure! If you go back out the way you came in, cross the street. You will pass the campus quad, and the building will be on your right-hand side. When you enter the building, you will see a red and black colored booth. Let them know you are a new student on-campus and you need your Student ID. They will only need to see your personal ID."

I replied, "Okay. Thanks! I'll be right back."

Khase and I walked over the building. I grew more and more excited that I was finally on a college campus. The world had just become my oyster. I took my ID picture, and we walked back over to the Residence Life Office.

We entered the building. Treasure had my dorm room key ready. I grabbed the key and we headed to my new dorm room.

It was a typical dorm room. There were cheap carpeted floors, two sinks, one bathroom, a living room with couches, two end tables, two lamps, and a coffee table. The thing that I loved the most about the suite was the large windows that provided a nice view of the school. I also had two large windows in my room.

When we finally walked into my room, Khase helped me wipe down everything before I would unpack my clothes. Khase helped me unpack as well. Inside my room was an extra-long twin bed, a dresser, desk, two closets and a mirror that hung on the door. I had a room all to myself.

After we finished unpacking, we walked to the cafeteria and grabbed something to eat. We went back to the dorm room to eat and hang out.

Khase said, "This is a really nice set-up. Big room, too."

I responded so excited, "Yes. It is. I had no idea I would get my own room!"

Khase chuckled and replied, "Yeah that is kind of cool for this to be your first year here."

Khase continued, "I know you didn't have a television to bring down here with you. So, when I come back the next time, I'll just give you my television I used when I was in college. It's small but it should be fine."

I replied, "Oh, thanks! I appreciate that. I don't know what I was going to do without one."

Khase said, "No problem. I'll bring it in the next few weeks, so you'll have it sooner than later."

I replied, "Okay. Thanks."

It was started to get late and Khase decided that he would head out. As we finished up our food, Khase said, "Alright. I'm going to head out now. Congratulations on your new endeavor. I know you will do great here."

I smiled and said, "Thank you. And thank you driving me here and helping move in. I really do appreciate it."

Khase replied, "You're welcome. Not a problem."

I walked Khase down to his car. We hugged and Khase made his way back home.

It was a week before the semester would start and there were a few things I needed to get squared away before class started. I went to the bursar office to make sure I had money for books and that my tuition was paid. When I went, everything was already set.

Since I didn't hang out with my suitemates, I just walked around campus, by myself, to become familiar with the campus and community.

When I visited the computer lab or just walked the campus grounds, I would run into the same four young ladies that were always together. When the semester started, I had a class with them: Psychology of Marriage & Family and Anatomy & Physiology. Naveah, Symphony, Divine and Destiny had all met each other during their time in the EOF program. They were also roommates. When I would pass by them, I smiled at them and they would smile back at me. I also met other students on-campus. I eventually met Blessing, Reign, and Noble. I also had become friends with all of them including Treasure.

Neveah was the group's Ms. Congeniality. Her kind and friendly spirit was how I became a part of their sister circle. Neveah was beautiful on the inside and outside. She had a rich caramel skin tone, long silky hair, a friendly smile, and small mocha-colored eyes. Most people said Neveah looked like a young Angela Bassett. She also had a twin that didn't attend Robinson University, but she was an honorary student at Robinson University because she was always there and hung out with her. She was as beautiful as Neveah. They called her Twin.

Now, Symphony was the feisty one in the group; she was awesome at debating. She was super attractive and had a strong personality. Symphony had carob-brown flawless skin, deep-brown eyes, full lips, a nice smile, and gorgeous legs. She often wore her hair in her natural silky, full coils. Symphony also had a beautiful mole on her neck that added to her already attractive features.

Blessing lived up to her name. It was obvious that Blessing's skin tone has been kissed by God's sun. Her hazelnut skin tone never needed a tan. She had the perfect complexion. Her small eyes, infectious smile, high cheekbones, and pleasant personality were all the reasons why her parents named her Blessing. She was the President of the Living Branch Ministries on-campus ministry.

Divine was beautiful as well. She was very smart & witty, enjoyed laughing, making jokes, and having a good time. Divine was the one in the group that kept everyone on their toes. Everyone enjoyed being in her presence. Divine had a witty smile that complimented her tawny skin complexion, innocent brown eyes, full lips, and straight sandy-brown hair.

Destiny's quiet and observant personality made you almost forget that she was there. When she was there, she also was fun to be around. Destiny had a ginger-tone complexion with a wide Kool-Aid smile, long light brown hair, and almond shaped eyes. Destiny was extremely smart and down to earth.

Reign was the most festive of the group. She loved telling jokes, even if they were corny. When she laughed, you couldn't help but laugh with her. Reign's bold features matched her personality. She was ambitious and fearless. She had bronze-olive skin adorned with a mole on her strong, bold cheek bones. Her eyes were dark brown and sincere.

And then there was Noble. Noble was the funniest, boldest, and most ambitious one in the group. Originally from Africa, Noble had fierce features and a strong presence. Noble had mahogany-brown flawless skin, piercing dark brown eyes, high cheekbones, and beautiful course hair. She was the comedian and prankster in the group. One day, while the group on a mission trip, she played a joke on the Living Branch Ministries Campus Minister. While at Golden Corral, she told the waiters that it was the Campus Minister's birthday so they would sing the Golden Corral birthday theme song to him. He had to sit through the whole song smiling awkwardly while his students laughed hysterically at him. There was no limit to Noble's pranking.

Although we all had different features, personalities, temperaments and life circumstances, there was one thing we ALL had in common: we believed in God and had a true desire to walk with Jesus Christ as college students. When I transferred to Robinson University, I didn't know that God had pre-ordained friendships for me that would get me through some of the darkest times of my life. Even during the hell that I experienced; God was up to something in my life. I didn't know it, but God did. I just continued to live my life.

CHAPTER 37
LIVING BRANCH MINISTRIES
JOHN 15: 1 – 17

The girls and I had established such a good friendship early on that Neveah, Symphony and Divine invited me to an on-campus ministry - Living Branch Ministries. LBM was a student-led Christian-based on-campus ministry. Bible study was every Monday at 9pm. When they asked me to attend, I happily agreed.

The first bible study I attended there was a man that was passionately teaching bible study that evening. His name was Rev. Paul Williams. He was brown-skinned, tall, lean, and strong. Rev. Paul was unique and had a true calling for building young Disciples of Christ. He desired to see college students walking in their true calling, identity, and purpose in life. Rev. Paul was an intellectually brilliant man that empowered his students educationally, socially, mentally, professionally, and spiritually. He was also a Howard alumnus and would constantly remind us that he attended, "Howard University – The Mecca of Higher Education!"

After bible study, Rev. Paul introduced himself to me.

Rev. Paul said, "Hi. How are you doing? I'm Rev. Paul."

I replied, "Hi. I'm good. I'm Journee."

Rev. Paul responded, "Nice to meet you, Journee. So where are you from?"

I replied enthusiastically and chuckled, "North Jersey!"

Symphony, Treasure, and I were the only ones from North Jersey. When I did say North Jersey, I guess I said it with a "North Jersey twang" because Rev. Paul immediately bust out into laughter. He wasn't from North Jersey, so he got a kick out of how I said where I was from. From then on, Rev. Paul didn't call me Journee, but North Jersey.

He jokingly replied, "Okay, North. Jer-seyyy!"

I laughed as well.

Rev. Paul continued, "Well, it is nice meeting you. Who brought you to tonight's bible study?"

I responded, "Neveah, Symphony and Divine invited me here tonight."

Rev. Paul said, "Oh, that's so awesome. That's great to hear. Please be sure to sign in. We want to stay connected."

I replied, "Oh, I think I've signed it already."

Symphony confirmed, "Yes. She already signed it, Rev. Paul."

Rev. Paul replied, "Great. Well, we hope to see you next week, North Jer-sey."

I smiled and replied, "I will be back next week. Great lesson by the way."

Rev. Paul replied, "Thank you."

I responded, "You're welcome. Okay. Have a good night and see you next week."

Neveah, Symphony and Divine had waited for me until I finished speaking with Rev. Paul. I usually hung out with Neveah, Symphony, Divine and Blessing after bible study before calling it a night and going back to my room. We would chill in Neveah, Symphony, Divine and Destiny's dorm room, eating snacks, cracking jokes, telling stories, and laughing.

I loved hanging with my new friends especially since I didn't know anyone when I first moved on campus.

CHAPTER 38
TRIALS AND TRIUMPHS

That following weekend, Khase visited me again. When he did come, he brought the television for me. I finally had something to do when I wasn't doing homework. Khase came to visit me on-campus several times. While there, he also met my new friends. Journee's friends took a liking to his charismatic, comical, and friendly personality. He also met Rev. Paul, too.

The semester ended, I had to move all my stuff and return to school by the end of August. Khase was able to borrow his parent's minivan again to help me move back home.

I was going to miss my friends for the summer, even though I would see them in a few months. I had developed a personal relationship with each of them. They were not only my friends, but they had become my sister-friend-support-system I needed now. I didn't know I would need them in the future too.

That summer we kept in touch. Some days we would talk on the three-way with each other. Just like living on-campus, we cracked jokes, laughed, and complained about the Robinson dorm rooms and the school-wide systemic issues.

When I wasn't talking to my friends, I was either with Khase, at home or church. During the summer months, Grace and Mercy Baptist Church kept the congregation engaged. Khase organized several Youth & Young Adult outings and services to keep the youth involved and active. That was something he enjoyed doing.

He also felt that he had been called into ministry. That same summer, Khase had been appointed to lead the Youth & Young Adult Ministry. He was also a Minister-in-Training studying to become a licensed minister.

Although we were still dating, I continued to struggle with my relationship with Khase. On the outside, he acted as if I was just a "sister" to him. Privately, between us and certain groups of people, he would treat me as his "girlfriend." He never asked me to be his "girlfriend" but sure reaped the benefits of having me as one.

That made me even more confused, lost, and uncertain about our relationship. In the moments I spent time to myself, I often wondered to myself, "Journee, how did you get into this place? Why did you even go back? Why are you still putting up with this?"

I would also answer myself and say, "Well, there really isn't anyone else for you. You can't get out of the situation, so you might as well just stay. What he did to you wasn't that bad. It'll get better one of these days. Maybe if we get married, he will change. Well, Journee, it is your fault. We all make mistakes so just learn forgive him and hang in there."

I continued to have those internal thoughts and battles about Khase. I was constantly overcome with so many different emotions at any given moment. Ashamed. Betrayed. Guilty. Defensive. Stuck. Confused. I had become more acquainted with those feelings than any positive emotion, feeling or thought. Life as I knew it was hard and I guess I needed to get used to it.

I experienced yet another tragedy right before I returned to school. Two weeks before I had to go back to school, my father got more devastating news. Meaven, our only brother, died. Another unexpected death for the Black Family.

Devastated, heart-broken and numb were the only feelings Papa Black, Strength, myself, Gracie, Audacious and Joy could feel. Still experiencing the residual pain and trauma from Mama Black's death, my family and I had to bury another one of our loved ones. We all had the wind knocked out of us for the second time.

Meaven's funeral was on a rainy and stormy August Saturday afternoon. Papa Black made sure that his only son was celebrated. Somehow, I managed to celebrate my brother by doing a praise dance at his service. Although I had never done a praise dance before, God had placed this song on my heart while at school, but I didn't understand why.

I was overwhelmingly nervous, so the night before I practiced in front of my sisters, Strength, Gracie, Audacious and Joy. Izzie was there as well. I ministered to More Than I Can Bear by Kirk Franklin. Those lyrics were exactly how I felt about things in my life. I felt each word:

> *"I've gone through the fire. And I've been through the flood.*
> *I've been broken into pieces*
> *Seen lightnin' flashin' from above. But through it all,*
> *I remember that He loves me*
> *And He cares. And He'll never, put more on me, than I can bear.*
> *I said, never put more on me*

No, no, never put more on me
Never put more on me
Never. His word said He won't
I believe it. I receive it. I claim it. It's mine
No he'll never, put more on me
Than I can bear. Can bear…."

I couldn't believe I was able to get through that. I did it for my only big brother, Meaven Black.

We laid our brother to rest on a Saturday. I went back to school that Monday. Somehow, I just kept going. God gave me supernatural strength. I knew my strength was coming from God, but I also felt too numb to process the trauma and pain. I. Just. Kept. Going.

When I returned to school, I told all my friends that my brother died. They were surprisingly shocked that I was even back in school, but they supported me.

Symphony replied, "Wow, Journee! I am so sorry to hear that. I will be praying for you."

Destiny said, "Wow, and your back at school?! Girl, you are strong. I'm praying."

Divine compassionately replied, "I'm so sorry to hear that. You're in my prayers."

Blessing genuinely responded, "Wow. I'll lift you up in prayer. I know it's not easy."

Treasure uttered with tears in her eyes, "Awww, Journ!! You've been through so much. I am sorry to hear that. You have my prayers and condolences to you and your family."

Neveah responded after everyone and said, "I know it's hard, but your brother would be so proud of you for coming back to school. God got you. I am praying for you. If you need anything or need to talk, I'm here for you. WE are here for you."

Holding back the tears and trying to save face, I simply replied, "Thank you."

From then on, those girls continued to be there for me in so many ways. They were one of the many reasons why I was able to keep going. They supported me tremendously.

Khase and I had gotten even closer since the passing of Meaven. Surprisingly, he was there for me even more, reminding me that he loved me and would always be there for me. I believed him. We continued to talk on the phone, email, and visit each other consistently.

We especially became close when I went on a mission trip to Africa while in college. While there, we emailed one another almost every day. I even wrote journal entries to Khase sharing my experiences with him.

I never intended to travel to Africa until one day after bible study Rev. Paul had extended an invitation to the Living Branch Ministry student group to go on a mission trip to evangelize to Muslims. Although apprehensive about going, I decided that I would go. Neveah and Reign went as well.

We stayed in Accra, Ghana for three weeks and had the opportunity to experience the life and culture of Africa. The second day being there, Neveah, Reign and I got our hair braided for 10 American dollars! I had box-braids; Neveah had Senegalese Twists; Reign had cornrows going back. Not only that, but we also had two custom African garments custom made to complete our African Nubian Queen look.

The following day, our host family drove Rev. Paul, Neveah, Reign, and I to Wa, Ghana. Wa was where spent the bulk of our time evangelizing. While in town, I learned that Rev. Paul was the only one that could speak to the men. Due to religion and culture, Neveah, Reign, or I weren't allowed to evangelize to the men.

After we finished the mission part of the trip, Rev. Paul and the host family took Neveah, Reign, and I to Cape Coast Castle. We really got to experience Africa. The Cape Coast Castle was the very castle that was used to transport and imprison millions of African slaves. When visiting the dungeons, listening to the tour guide, and seeing the *Door of No Return,* I couldn't help but realize how blessed I was. My very feet touched the grounds that my mother and brother would never touch. I thought to myself, "This is for you Mama and Meaven. Thank you for watching over me." A few days later we also experienced the Canopy Walk in Kakum National Park.

Thanks to Rev. Paul, Neveah, Reign, and I learned and experienced so much on the mission trip. My life would never be the same after my experiences in Africa. I had become even prouder of my black skin, culture, and history.

CHAPTER 39
THE LETTER

When I returned from home from my trip, Khase and I seemed to be in a "drama-free" and good place until I visited home one weekend.

One Friday evening, Khase organized a Youth & Young Adult ministry event for Youth Weekend. It was hosted at the Grace and Mercy Baptist Church. Whenever I visited, I would always sense weird vibes from the other young ladies that attended the church. Hmph. I gave off my own vibes too.

I wasn't home often, so I did not have all the details about what was going on or who Khase was dealing with or even entertaining. But I certainly had my suspicions. Unfortunately, Izzie and I had stopped talking due to my relationship with Khase. I was really in the dark about what was going on back home.

At the end of the ministry event, Khase decided that he would walk another young lady to her car that evening. This was the same young that he had previous interactions with while dealing with me at the same time. As I waited for him to return to the car, I was tired, angry. and could no longer take it in anymore.

With a straight face and attitude, I asked, "So, you just gonna walk her to her car?"

Khase responded with a confused face, "What are you talking about?!" He knew exactly what I was talking about but tried to act as if he didn't.

I replied, "So you're gonna act like you don't know what I'm talking about. I'm talking about you walking HER to HER car knowing she likes you. Why do you keep entertaining her if you don't like her?"

Khase replied throwing his hands up in the car, "What??? I just walked her to her car. It's dark out and I was trying to be nice by walking her to her car!!"

I asked, "So, if a guy liked me and walked me to my car, would you see that as him just being *nice*?"

Khase responded, "First of all, you don't have a car. Second, ain't no guy walking you anywhere. Third, you are bugging!"

I grew extremely frustrated at that point. I didn't respond and immediately shut down. That was my way of coping and dealing with all the emotions I felt when Khase would do things and minimize my feelings. I remained quiet and shut down.

Khase continued, "Hello?! I just said something to you. So, are you going to answer or what?"

I remained silent. I remained silent because I knew it would make Khase upset and because I really didn't have the words to say anything. After I didn't answer he put the car in drive and pulled off. I kept quiet the entire ride home.

When he pulled up in front of the house, I got out the car, closed the door and didn't say anything to Khase. No good-bye. No kiss. Nothing. I was still frustrated and disappointed. When I closed the car door, Khase sped off so fast that he made a loud noise with his tires. I turned around to see if he would hit someone with the car because of how fast he pulled off. He just sped down the street and vanished.

When I got upstairs, I went into the bathroom and cried. I didn't want my family to see me crying or admit that I needed help or was hurting. I cried. Alone. I grabbed some tissue and silently wiped my tears. After my tears stopped flowing, I began writing. This time it was a letter to Khase about how he made me feel that night. Writing became a safe space me. I let my pen do the talking since I didn't have the voice in that moment. I wrote:

"Why did you engage my heart only to hurt it twice? Why do I still love you and want to be with you forever? Why do I see you as my future husband and father of my children? Why is it that I love you, but you've caused so much pain in my heart? How am I supposed to recuperate and heal from the pain that still hurts and exists to this day? Did I do anything to you? Can you tell me why this is happening if we are "called" to be together? I could never understand how two people that love and pursue each other but don't understand each other. I try hard not to think about all the hurt or allow my negative thoughts to overtake our positive moments. My heart still hurts. Am I not good enough for you? I allowed you back into my heart and body. I don't understand how you say you love me but hurt me so badly. How do I move on and forgive as God forgave? How can I be with you and other people think you are with someone else? Why would you walk her to her car if we are supposed to be together? Why would you come and totally dismiss me like nothing ever happened between us? I can't be with you knowing that other people think you are with her. I can't do it anymore. I don't think you're a bad person, nor do I love you any less. I need more details and I think I deserve it after all these years. It's important to address this now so that if God is "calling" us to be together these questions are answered. I am sorry if I came on too strong or said something that hurt you. I am asking that you forgive me! This was to express to you how I feel and not to get on you. Please don't take this as me hating you. I just need to get this off my chest."

After I finished writing my letter, I gave it to Khase the next day before heading back to school. Khase didn't drop me off at school that weekend. I took the train back to school instead. It was a 2-hour commute and I was in my thoughts the entire train ride. It was the longest train ride that day.

When I finally got back to my dorm room, I unpacked, ate, and took a nap. I was tired.

Later that evening, Khase called me. We talked about the letter.

In a captivating and convincing way, Khase responded, "Wow. I had no idea you had all these feelings. I am glad that you've shared them with me, but I was just doing ministry that night. It was nothing more than that. Walking her to her car meant nothing to me. In fact, she asked me to walk her to her car. I really didn't want to do it, but it was late, and I would have felt bad if something would have happened to her. That's why I walked her, but I understand what you are saying. Thank you for sharing your feelings and thoughts with me. I appreciate that."

I was caught off guard by Khase's response. Not even sure how to respond, I just said, "Yes. That's how I feel and it's not a good feeling."

I continued, "Well, I'm going to get ready for class tomorrow. I'll talk to you later. Good night."

Khase responded, "Okay. Thanks again for the letter! Have a good night. Love you."

I replied, "Love you, too."

I hung up still feeling the same way. Uncertain. Unresolved. Defeated. Stuck.

CHAPTER 40
THE PHONE CALL

In two months, I would officially be a college graduate from Robinson University. I felt so excited and proud. I was so close to the finish line of earning my Bachelor's degree. Although I had to switch my major to psychology and was no longer on the track to becoming a nurse, I was still excited about the idea of graduating college. This was major for me because through everything, I was graduating college. All I could hear during my last semester in college was Mama Black's voice echoing in my heart and ear, "Make sure you get your education." And I was doing just that!

I was graduating with five of my sister-friends: Symphony, Treasure, Divine, Destiny and Reign. That made it extra special for me.

I couldn't have been happier. My last year in college, I shared a dorm suite with Symphony, Divine and Destiny. We all had our own rooms. I was a Resident Assistant and soon to be college grad, so things were looking up for me. So, I thought. The drama in my relationship with Khase continued.

A month before my graduation, I walked into my dorm room from class and experienced one of the most heart-wrenching moments with Khase. I called him to share my good news about graduation with him. I was so excited to tell him the news.

I walked into my room, placed my book bag on her chair and hung my jacket up in the closet. I sat on my bed and called Khase. No answer. 10 minutes later he called me back.

Khase replied, "Hello?"

I happily replied, "Hey what's up?! What are you doing? I have some good news!"

Khase paused before responding. It was an awkward silence but some obvious background noise going on that sounded like he had been out.

Finally, Khase boldly replied, "I'm leaving from Mother Beulah's 60th birthday party and I'm dropping Eva off at home."

I paused before responding to his statement. I just couldn't believe Khase's audacity to share that he was dropping off the same lady he had walked to the car that night. The same lady I was fussing with him about because he was "entertaining" her knowing she liked him. Yet, he claimed he didn't "like" her. I wouldn't have known about it had I not called him. Khase never mentioned the party or dropping off Eva to me in our previous conversations.

After processing everything Khase had said in the moment, I angrily responded, "WHY ARE YOU DROPPING HER OFF KNOWING THAT SHE LIKES YOU?!?"

Responding in a cynical yet calm tone, Khase replied, "I am just dropping her off at home. She needs a ride."

I immediately hung up the phone on him. I couldn't stomach his excuses anymore in that moment. I could not believe it. I threw myself on my dorm room bed, yet again, and I laid there crying. Thankfully none of my friends knocked on my door because that was the last thing I wanted, for people to see me cry and vulnerable, and explain how my "boyfriend" was dropping off another woman at home.

I didn't even get a chance to tell him the good news that I was calling him for in the first place. He never even called back to try and explain himself. He just…left me hanging. Two hours away from home, I felt betrayed, hurt, and helpless.

I cried the entire night. I went from being extremely happy and excited about my future to sad and hopeless. As I laid there and cried, I couldn't quiet all the negative thoughts I was having in my mind about him and myself. One thought came across my mind loud, clear, subtle, and calm. It said, "Just jump out the window. You won't feel the pain anymore. Just jump." In the dorm room…with those big dorm windows… while having those negative thoughts. I laid there a little longer and the thought came back again, "JUMP."

I didn't move. I didn't even have the strength to get up from my bed. I cried until my eyes were red and puffy. Eventually, I fell asleep.

The next morning, I heard my phone ringing. Of course, it was Khase. I ignored it because I was running late for class. I hopped up out of that college dorm extra-long twin bed and made my way to class. I wasn't my normal self. I was somber the entire day when I should have been excited about graduating and making Mama Black, Meaven and my family proud. Instead, I wasn't. I was emotionally, mentally, relationally, and spiritually exhausted and drained.

After class was over, I went into the dining hall to get breakfast. While grabbing an orange juice from the refrigerator, Neveah walked over to me. Neveah was so excited that I was graduating. Every time she saw me, she had a new dance that she would do to show her excitement. This time, Neveah did The Wop. Seeing Neveah out the corner of my eye, she was doing The Wop and walking towards me.

After she finished her dance move, Neveah excitedly replied, "What's up, Journee!? Ms. Soon-to-be RU Graduate!!!"

I tried my best to hide my mood, but Neveah picked up that something was going on with me. Neveah had a special gift for picking up if something was wrong with one of her friends.

Neveah replied concerned, "Journee, is everything okay? Something seems off."

I just replied, "I can't talk about it right now or else I'll break down in tears. Can we go to my room and talk?"

Neveah looked extremely worried. She said, "Yes. Of course! My next class isn't until this afternoon, so I have some time."

I responded, "Okay. Thanks. I appreciate."

I finished swiping my meal card, bagged my food and we walked through the quad and finally made it to my room.

As soon as I closed my dorm room door, Neveah said, "So what's going on? Is everything okay?"

Tears filled my face. I couldn't hold them back. Barely able to put my words together, I replied, "Yesterday I called Khase to tell him some good news about the graduation. He had the audacity to tell me that he was dropping off the same lady he had walked to the car that night. The same lady I was fussing with him about because he was "entertaining" her knowing she liked him. Yet, he claimed he didn't "like" her. I wouldn't have known about it had I not called him. He never mentioned anything about the party or dropping her off in any of our previous conversations."

Neveah responded, "I remember you told me about him walking her to the car. Is this the same lady that goes to y'all church?"

I replied with frustration in my voice, "Yes! The nerve of him! I'm so upset."

Neveah shook her head and replied, "Wow. That's so wrong. I'm sorry you had to experience that. You don't deserve that, Journee. Did he explain why he had to drop her off? Did you speak to him today?"

I said, "Thanks. He didn't explain because he was with her when I called. They both were at the party together. And he called me today, but I didn't answer. I didn't feel like being bothered."

Neveah paused before she responded. Then, she gently said, "Oh, okay. That's understandable. You needed a moment to breath and collect your thoughts. I get it."

I cried and replied with a shaky voice, "Yeah. I did need a moment."

Neveah responded, "Well, look. Here's what you can do. How many classes do you have left for the day?"

I replied, "Just one more class."

Neveah said, "Okay. Honestly, you aren't in the right mind set to go to class and I don't want people all in your face asking you what's wrong because it looks like you've been crying. Those big, beautiful eyes of yours are red."

I laughed because I knew Neveah was right.

Neveah continued, "Email your professor and let them know that you can't make it to class because you aren't feeling well but you will submit your assignment by the end of the week. Take a moment to gather yourself and just breathe. Now as far as Khase, that's a tough one. I would call him back and tell him how you feel. At the end of the day, you must ask God how to handle that situation. You also have to ask yourself if you want to keep feeling this way."

I listened to everything Neveah was saying. It was all right and made sense. Neveah always gave her friends sound advice.

I replied, "Thanks, Neveah. I really do appreciate you taking the time to help me. It means a lot. Thank you."

Neveah responded, "You're welcome, darling! I know you would do the same for me!" Neveah called everyone *darling*. And she was right. I would do the same for her.

Neveah continued, "Okay. I'm going to get ready for my next class. I'll come back to check-in on you later to see how you're doing. I'll call you. Let me know if you need anything while I'm out. Love ya!"

I responded, "Okay. Thank you! I feel better. Love you too!"

Neveah and I hugged before she left. After she left, I had a little bit more strength. I emailed my professor, ate my food, watched TV, and relaxed in my bed.

Later that evening, I called Khase back. As usual Khase talked his way out of what really happened. I didn't have the energy to go back and forth with him. I had to finish writing papers, work on a group project, research, and finalize my senior thesis. I had to stay focused and graduate. I wanted to finish college career strong.

I knew I would further upset myself by asking too many questions about that night. Instead, I ended the conversation by saying, "I don't know what's going on between y'all, but it doesn't look right to me that you keep entertaining her if nothing is going on between y'all. There are a lot of guys on campus that like me, but I don't entertain them out of respect for you. I could have plenty of guys come to my room, buy me meals, take me to run errands, but I don't. I don't because I respect and care about you. Apparently, you have no idea what care or respect is."

Khase responded, "Oh, so you dealing with some other guys on-campus?"

I replied, "You missed the whole point. You didn't hear anything I said. I'm tired and I have to finish my paper. I'll talk to you later. Bye."

Khase replied, "Bye."

CHAPTER 41
JOURNEE GRADUATES!

Graduation day was finally here! I was so excited and happy. I limited my conversation with Khase that entire day so that he didn't kill my vibe. Instead, Treasure, Symphony, Neveah, Blessing, Divine, Destiny, Noble, Reign and I had breakfast together that morning. Although only Treasure, Symphony, Divine, Destiny, Reign and I that were graduating, Neveah, Blessing and Noble celebrated with us as if it were their graduation.

We had so much fun. I was finally graduating. I wasn't the only one with a story. All of us had our own story of struggle, trauma, and hardship. Although the struggles looked different, we all carried our struggles and triumphs together. God allowed our paths to cross and we supported each other unconditionally.

It was graduation time. I put my robe on while looking in the mirror. As I put my cap on, I said to myself, "Journee, you did it. All the hell you went through to get here was worth it. God kept you and He cleared the path for you. Mama Black and Meaven, WE are graduating today."

I grabbed my dorm key, cell phone and lip gloss. I got on the elevator and there was Treasure, Symphony, Neveah, Blessing, Divine, Destiny, Noble and Reign standing in the lobby of the dorm.

Symphony shouted, "Girl!! It took you long enough! What were you up there doing? Getting ready for the runway!"

Everyone busted out laughing. I didn't even have a response because I did take a long time getting ready. After we finished laughing, we all walked over to the stadium together – it was a five-minute walk from the school's dorm.

It was time to walk across the stage and my family came out and supported me. Papa Black, Strength, Gracie, Audacious, Joy, Baby Glorie, Grandma Josephine and Grandpa Joseph Sr. were there. Khase and Izzie made it to my graduation as well.

Rev. Paul attended the graduation as well and was proud of all his spiritual daughters.

When I walked across the stage, all I heard from Strength, Audacious, Joy and Izzie were their loud audible voices saying, "Yeahhh, Journee!! Gooooo Journee!" I just smiled and walked proudly across the stage in honor of Mama Black and Meaven.

After graduation was over, I was surprised with a red 4-door Pontiac car. Papa Black had rented it for me for three days as a graduation gift. I was sooo excited to walk off the stage to a red car! It even matched my graduation dress and shoes.

Later that evening, we decided to go to a soul food restaurant called Della's. After dinner was over, me and the girls headed back to school. Gracie and Khase rode back home together while Izzie drove separately.

Two days later, move-out day was finally here. Treasure, Symphony, Divine, Destiny, Reign and I had to move out from a place we called home for a while. The days of us hanging out every day, doing homework together, making brownies at 1 o'clock in the morning, attending on-campus bible study, listening to the brilliant teachings of Rev. Paul, cracking jokes and listening to each other's stories was soon coming to an end. We hung out one last time in the Student Lounge before moving off campus. Symphony cooked brownies and Neveah brought sparkling cider. We reminisced on our college life and mission trip stories, professors, group projects and papers, and the fun we had.

At the end of their celebration, I raised my cup of cider and said, "I would not have gotten to this place without God and each of you. You all hold a special place in my heart, and I am going to miss you all."

Symphony replied, "Awww, you too, Journee! We feel the same way about you, but this ISN'T good-bye."

Treasure replied, "We love you, boo!"

Blessing said, "We feel the same way about you, Bishop! I couldn't have gotten here without you either." Blessing and I always had a running joke of calling each other Bishop. It was our inside joke and sisterhood banter.

After we all made our comments, we promised to keep in touch with each other after college no matter what.

After our sister gathering, I went to my dorm room and packed up the rest of my items. I loaded the car Papa Black had rented for me for graduation. Leaving the Robinson University campus made me feel so proud of myself and there was nothing that could take away from my happiness until I moved back home....

CHAPTER 42
LOVE'S CONFESSION

By the time I moved back home, Khase had offered I move in with him until I found a job and an apartment since I didn't have anywhere else to go. Khase had agreed that he would just stay the night at his parents' house and come by during the day. Not having a much of a choice, I agreed.

When I moved back home, me and Khase's relationship seemed to be on decent terms. There had not been any drama. Khase brought me a beautiful gift basket with smell good products to welcome me home. And as a grand graduation gift, he bought me loads of dresses, pants, and blouses so that I had a great wardrobe as a working woman. He treated me like a queen, giving me all his time and attention. Things seemed good between us.

I unpacked my things and got settled in. Day in and day out, I spent majority of my time looking for a job. There were several people that helped and even recommended jobs for me. To no avail, I couldn't find a job as quick as I wanted to. For a while, I had no job, no apartment, no money.

Somehow God still provided for me. One day while going for a walk, I found $5 dollars on the ground. I picked it up and held onto it. That Sunday while in church, I had decided that I would give it to God and trust that He would provide for me. I put it in the offering plate and left it at that. That very next Sunday, one of the Deacons at Grace and Mercy Baptist Church walked up to me at the end of service and handed me an envelope with Journee written on it. When he handed me the envelope, the Deacon said, "This is for you. God placed it on my heart to give this to you."

I was so surprised and knew that it was nobody but God that had done that for me.

I replied, "Awwww. Wow. Thank you so much." I gave him a hug and a kiss.

I didn't open the envelope in that moment, but I knew that it was God winking at me. Afterwards, I went into the bathroom, opened the envelope, and saw that it was $100. While the Deacon didn't know how much I needed, God did. He gave me more than what I had given Him. In that moment, I was fully convinced that God did not leave me by myself. God continued to provide for me to make money until I landed a job. I continued to update my resume and look for a job.

Shortly after I moved back home, Izzie and I rekindled our friendship. We talked about our concerns and were able to move on. We began to talk, hang out again and even sat next to each in the choir stand when we sang on Sunday morning.

In 2009, on Easter Sunday, things would become real for me while sitting in church. Izzie was sitting next to me when it all happened. During worship service, Khase made comments after the weekly church announcements.

That Sunday, there were over 200 worshippers, people filled the seats, and the choir stand was packed. Grace and Mercy Baptist Church was packed on that Easter Sunday! Everyone had on their beautiful pastel Easter colors, fancy dresses, over-sized hats, and their best Sunday suit. Khase had on a gray three-piece suit, white-collared shirt, and a purple and white polka-dot tie, and matching handkerchief.

After we had sung our first song, it was obvious the Spirit had manifested in service that morning. Grace and Mercy Baptist Church gave their weekly announcements and then Khase got up and delivered his personal monologue.

He walked in the pulpit, adjusted the microphone, and looked in my direction. I sat in the second row on the left side of the choir stand. Izzie sat to right next to me. Gracie and Eva were in the choir stand as well. Before he spoke, he took a deep breath and began to talk.

Khase uttered, "Good Morning. Happy Easter, everyone. I felt this on my spirit, so I must obey what God is telling me. Please pray with me as it's a little rough for me to get through this. Ever since I was a little boy, I've always felt the need to protect the women in my life. My mother can even confirm this. She would go to the supermarket and if she didn't come back within a certain time, I would call her to ask if she was okay. I just felt obligated to be a protector. I even suffered a cut on my left hand some years ago fighting off this robber that was trying to hurt my ex-fiancé. I'm over-protective of the women that are around me, not just my family. Any female! So, for those of you that have been saying things about me…I am not a PIMP! I am not a WOMANIZER! Because of this, I've closed off my heart for years until recently…"

I couldn't believe what he was saying. Trying to keep my composure, my facial expression said it all. My straight face and right eyebrow raised meant I was yet again confused, annoyed, and frustrated. Khase had never mentioned anything to her about this before but decided to get on his soapbox to tell his story. I couldn't believe it.

Khase continued his monologue. While looking back at me and smiling, he continued, "...but I've found love again. God has blessed me with me a love.... a special love and I'm happy. She's the best thing that happened to me and I am thankful. Y'all keep me in prayer as God continues to bless me and my love."

I had no words. I wasn't even impressed by his speech or him for that matter. I was just...tired. Tired of the games; tired of his grand gestures of "love and affection" that were never followed by actions but instead with empty promises; tired of being told lies; tired of living a lie; tired of enabling his lies. I. Was. Tired.

Church service was awkward for the rest of the day and I wasn't sure what to think or do. Nothing about that day sat right with me. It took me a long time to recognize that, but when I did, there was no turning back for me.

Khase continued to profess his love for me after his monologue in church that day. He never admitted all the things he had done and all the women he dealt with while I was away at school. But little did Khase know I did my own investigation to get to the bottom of the lies he told me. I couldn't believe all that I found out, but I wasn't surprised. The information I received confirmed my intuition.

When I approached him about the information, he claimed we weren't together because I was away at school. Yet, he professed his love for me and his desire to be with me.

A few days later, Khase and I had talked about our relationship and had decided to go to couples counseling with Rev. Paul. We scheduled the session but had to reschedule because Rev. Paul could not find Khase's apartment.

CHAPTER 43
SKATE NIGHT

The next day on Wednesday, May 13, 2009, it was a beautiful spring afternoon that day. Clear and sunny skies, birds chirping, and a touch of fresh warm wind filled the New Jersey air. I woke up that day excited to hang out with my home girl Izzie, especially after what happened the Sunday before.

It's was a year since I graduated college from Robinson University with a Bachelor of Arts Degree in Psychology. Finally, a college degree of my own with my name on it: Journee Black. I was so happy to have my degree, but I hadn't secured a job in my major yet let alone any job. It had been a rough year since I graduated college, so doing something fun helped me get my mind off my romantic uncertainty, being jobless, having no money, a home, or a car - ugh! Being back in my hood, hanging with family and close friends, and having a good time was the perfect thing for me to do to cope with the reality of my life.

My home girl Izzie and I talked that morning and planned to hang out. That's what home girls do; they hang. That's exactly what Izzie and I did when I returned home from college. We decided to go skating that night. Boy did Izzie love skating. That was her thing, and she was good at it.

With her cocoa brown-skin, thick shoulder length hair, piercing hazel brown eyes and a shape that resembled the original Foxy Brown, Izzy commanded the skating rink with her beauty and skills. Izzie's beauty and skating skills were effortless.

I, on the other hand, was not a natural-born skater. I enjoyed skating but could not quite get it. I am an excellent dancer but just couldn't get that skating thing down pat. My attempt at skating didn't stop the fellas from teaching me. If anything, it attracted them even more.

I was a magnetic lady, magnetic in my personality, beauty, intelligence, energy, and aura. At 5 foot 7 inches, it was evident that God created something special about me. I had butterscotch skin with curly jet-black hair, big almond-shaped pecan-brown eyes that would light up under the sun, long black luxurious natural eye lashes, thick eyebrows, an infectious and wide smile and nose, with a dimple in my chin. My long butter-scotch-brown legs and slim-thick frame always got me the unrealized attention from the guys teaching me how to skate. Quite honestly, I didn't even realize my untapped potential from within, beauty and personality.

While standing in the bathroom detangling my jet-black coils, I received a phone call from Izzie. I knew I had to start getting ready early; I knew that starting my typical 2-hour routine too late would make Izzie and I late for skate night at Skate 84.

I was excited to finally have something fun to do. I picked up the phone and said, "Hey, what's up, Izzie?" My typical laid-back and chill personality complimented Izzie's outgoing, funny and extrovert personality.

Izzie responded, "What's up? What's up? What's uppppp? Ready to hit up Skate 84 tonight? I have some new moves I wanna try. I've been at work thinking about it all day like bam, bam, bam!" as she snapped her fingers and moved her feet under her desk.

I couldn't see Izzie moving, but I sure could hear her moving over the phone. I replied, "Yup! I am ready, but don't have any new moves. I'm just focusing on not falling!" Izzie and I bust out laughing.

"Okay, so I'm going home to change my clothes. I will pick you up at 8:30pm. We are going have fun!" Izzie always assured I had a good time with her.

I replied, "Okay cool. I'll make sure I'm ready!"

Izzie jokingly says, "Yeah start getting ready now, because you know how you are with your two-hour routines!!"

I snapped back with my infectious smile and saying, "Girl, hush. It's only 11 in the morning. You are picking me up 8:30pm. I got time!"

Izzie busts out laughing saying, "Now you KNOWWWW!!!...."

I interrupt her and say, "Alright. Alright. I'll make sure I'm ready. Now get back to work."

Izzie responds, "Okay. Talk to you later. Love you."

While laughing on the other end, I replied, "Okay. Love you too. Bye."

I continued detangling my coils while standing in front of the bathroom mirror. Thinking about my life and next move, I became over-whelmed and anxious about my future. I just graduated college only to still be homeless, jobless, and carless and in an uncertain relationship. I did not go to college and graduate, accumulate all this student loan debt, and leave my college friends to be homeless, jobless, and carless. I wanted to make my family proud, but I felt stuck. Stuck in my life circumstances, relationship and stuck while looking past myself in the mirror. I asked myself, "How did I even get here to begin with?"

Just as my thought began to spiral down a negative path, I heard the water running in the bathroom. I had forgotten that I had turned on the shower to start my 2-hour routine so that I could get ready for skate night at Skate 84. I snapped out of it and began getting ready so that I could be ready and not hear Izzie's mouth about being late. So, I showered, ate, watched some television, and continued looking for jobs.

8:30pm came along and Izzie was sure enough outside honking her horn and calling me on the phone. Seeing Izzie calling, I picked up on the first ring and shouted, "Ha! I'm ready. I'll be right down."

Izzie replied, "Well, well. You've proved me wrong! I'll be downstairs waiting."

I grabbed my purse, lip gloss and jacket and began heading downstairs. I immediately felt the cool wind graze my butterscotch skin as the sun was just about to set. I walked down a flight of 15 steep stairs and there was Izzie, blasting Single Ladies (Put a Ring on It) by Beyonce to get us hyped for the skating rink. There was always a pre-party before the actual party. I opened Izzie's 2010 two-door apple red Acura coupe. Fully loaded with a sunroof, Izzie always had her music blasting letting everyone know she was coming down the street.

I bust out with a quick two-step, open the passenger car door and slide in the front seat.

"What's up???" I excitedly shouted as I slid in the front seat of Izzie's car.

Izzie was in her own world practicing her skate moves in the driver seat. She screams over the music, "Hey Journ!!!" Izzie was always good for giving her home girls nicknames. "Are you ready to get your skate on? I've been waiting for this all day. And you know it's gonna be some cuties there!"

I chuckled and replied, "I don't know about all that, but like I said, I'm just trying not to fall!" "So how was work today?" I said while turning down Izzie's radio.

"It was good. I had to review and underwrite some mortgage applications for several clients. It's always busy in that office, as usual," Izzie replied. Izzie was an underwriter for B&G Mortgage Company.

Izzie asked hesitantly knowing that work was a sensitive topic for me, "How about you? Have you found anything yet? I know you been looking for a while."

I gave a big sigh before answering, "Besides babysitting the little girl down the street, nothing yet. I'm still looking though. I hope to find something soon because I have to get out of here. I can't keep living like this."

Feeling the energy going south, Izzie changed the subject and said, "Look, everything will work out. You will eventually find the right job."

Izzie and I finally pulled into Skate 84's parking lot. As always, it was jumping with cuties, nice cars, and good music, no matter the day of the week. The fresh crisp spring air made you excited about the summer and the longer days. Izzie and I got out of the car ready to have a good time and skate. Besides, this was exactly what I needed to get my mind off things for a little while.

Izzie made her way to the trunk to grab her Impala Black Professional Skates. Meanwhile, I had to rent the Peanut Butter skates from the rental booth inside the skating rink. Clearly, I was an amateur at the whole skating thing.

As we approached the doorway to the skating rink, we passed through a crowd of chocolatey fine men posted up against the wall. They were fine like Morris Chestnut, Mekhi Phifer and Larenz Tate. You could always count on seeing fine men at Skate 84.

Izzie was not shy speaking her mind. With excitement in her voice, she shouted, "How y'all fine men doing tonight?!"

They all replied in unison, "We are fine!"

Izzie whispered under her breath just so I could hear her, "Yes. Y'all. Are!"

The Larenz Tate-looking guy said, while fiercely gazing at me from head to toe and biting his chocolate brown bottom lip, "How you doing, beautiful?"

Coyishly, I responded, "I'm doing fine," and rushed my way past the guys.

We finally made our way inside the rink. Izzie grabbed herself a locker to put her stuff inside of while I went to the Skate Rental Booth to rent some Peanut Butter skates. By the time I grabbed my skates and sat down to put them on, home girl Izzie was in the rink skating to Buddy by Musiq Soulchild. Backwards skating, twists and turns, Izzie had it down pat! She was the skating queen, and she knew it.

I joined Izzie in the rink and skated a few times around. Izzie helped me get more comfortable by skating with her. That lasted a short while because Izzie was so excited to try the new tricks she had been doing while at her work desk. Izzie began skating by herself. Everyone was admiring her skills too.

Eventually, I stood off to the side while watching everyone skate. Izzie noticed something was off with me.

Izzie, with her cocoa brown-skin and body frame like the original Foxy Brown, glided over to me. "Girl, what are you over here thinking about? All these cuties up in here checking you out, anddddddd the music is rocking! You should be showing off that bad body of yours on them skates!" Izzie jokingly said trying to catch her breath.

"Something isn't right. I feel Khase is up to something," I responded.

Taking a second to register what I was referring to, Izzie replied, "So what do you want to do? I'm down for whatever."

"I just need proof. I'm tired of his lies and him finessing his way out of his lies. Something is off with my relationship with Khase," still standing in skates, I was staring into space and had totally blocked out the music and where I was at in the moment. I knew once and for all I deserved the real answers that I had always felt in my gut. After all, I had nothing to lose at that point It was time for me to get some answers.

Izzie skated a few more times around the rink. She even skated with one of the fine guys that was posted up in the hallway when we entered the rink. My mind was focused on other things, so I mainly spent my time on the side thinking.

I returned my peanut butter rental skates and Izzie gathered her things out of the locker. On our way out, we passed those fine brothers again. This time, the Larenz Tate-looking brother asked for my number. I respectfully declined because he had no idea the drama that he would have found himself in if he and I would have started talking. Plus, I needed answers and he didn't have them.

We got inside the car and talked before driving off. By this time, it was 1:15 Wednesday morning. Izzie reeved up her 2010 2-door apple red Acura coupe and we left Skate 84 for the night.

CHAPTER 44
RIDE OR DIE FRIEND

"Once we get on my street, you can park a few blocks down so your car isn't seen. I'll go upstairs and wait by the door. I'm going to address it very calmly. Honestly, you should probably leave if you want to because I don't want you in the middle of it. Plus, I know you have to go to work in the morning," I said to Izzie.

Izzie, being the ride or die friend in that moment, said "No. I'll just stay behind in case you need me."

At 1:41am, Izzie and I pull up to the house. Izzie parked her car 4 houses down since I didn't want her car to be noticed. Izzie parked her car and turned her car and headlights off. I got out the car and walked up the block and made my way up the back stairs.

The rusty brown and white 3-family house was old but big. The house sat up and away from the street and was long in length. It had 15 very steep stairs. The stairs that led to the back door were old, cracked and cemented. The sky was pitch-black with two streetlights on the block. Darkness overshadowed the entire block. One of the street-lights just so happened to be near the house. It was dead quiet. Literally. On one side of the block were houses and on the other side was a cemetery.

I walked up the steep, old, cracked, and cemented stairs in hopes to get the answer I needed that night and so many other nights leading up to the point. I reached the back door, but it was locked, and the lights were off. Khase wasn't home. Shortly after, I heard a car coming down the street and it eventually pulled up in front of the house. Thankfully, I had on black sneakers, a white t-shirt, and blue jeans that night.

There it was. The moment, in real time, that had me staring in the distance and blocking out the music just a few moments prior at the skating rink. I glided down the stairs not even thinking about looking down to avoid a fall. There they were, in a car like a happy family as if life was all good.

Seconds later, after seeing them, I blacked out. Screaming at the top of my lungs at 2 o'clock in the morning, I shouted, "Are y'all f-ing?! Are y'all f-ing?!"

In the 4-door stone gray 2006 Ford Fusion was Khase, Gracie, and baby Glorie.

I thrusted quickly to the driver side of the door where Khase was. Khase, the self-proclaimed minister, was 6'5 in stature, light complexion, full lips, and charismatic to a fault. He had the gift of gab and could talk himself out of anything. I mean anything. He had a very convincing personality that matched his regal, masculine look. He was a nice-looking brother.

By the time I approached Khase while he was still in the car. I went from being calm to being on 100.

"Are y'all fucking?!" I screamed a third time while standing over Khase while he had his hands on the wheel of the car looking shocked. Khase didn't answer quickly enough, so I landed a right punch on the left side of his chin, knocking off his eyeglasses.

Now Gracie, on the passenger side of Khase's car, was a beautiful woman. She had big round, amber-colored eyes with long reddish-brown eyelashes with curly hair to match. Her smile was perfect. Baby Glorie was a splitting image of Gracie. That was her mama. Gracie stood 5'0 tall and had a brick house frame.

Gracie and I are sisters. And baby Gracie was my niece.

"How. Could. This. Be. Two o'clock in the morning and the man I loved was messing around with my sister!" I had those thoughts swimming around in my mind while my hands were still flying inside the driver side of the car hitting Khase.

Trying to protect Khase from getting swung on again, Gracie got punched in the face in the crossfire. Meanwhile, Baby Glorie was confused with all the commotion that was taking place right before her innocent little eyes.

Khase made his way out of the car, pulling out a stack of papers from his car door. "Journee, Journee, look I have Post-Traumatic Stress Disorder! I took a test on-line and I have PTSD!"

Not even the slightest bit convinced, I could not muster up the words to respond to his fraudulent self-diagnosis. Khase threw the papers back into the car, grabbed me by my wrists to keep me focused on him.

Meanwhile, Gracie jumps out of the car and begins to scream, "Yes, Journee, yes! We are! Are you happy now?! Yes, it's true!"

When Gracie said those words to me, my entire world stopped. No yelling. No reaction. No feelings. Just numbness. This seemed to have been the only time Gracie was honest. Of all moments to have been honest, this was the worst time.

By this time, Izzie had heard all the ghetto drama that was going on. Next thing you know, she was jogging frantically down the street trying to get my attention. She screamed, "Journee! Journee!!"

Immediately, Khase recognized the voice before seeing Izzie's face appear from the darkness. When Izzie was approaching me, Khase turned to Izzie, grabbed her by her shoulders and shook her aggressively while saying, "You made her do this?!?!?"

Typical Khase behavior. He never took responsibility for his own actions and always deflected and placed blame on everyone else.

Izzie pulled back from Khase's grip and firmly said, "No you did this! This is on you! If you ever put your hands on me again, I will get my cousin to whoop your...." I jumped in between them.

Khase focused back on me while still trying to convince me that he had PSTD.

Gracie shouted to me, "This is not Christ-like, Journee! This is not Christ-like!"

I went numb for a second time. No yelling. No reaction. No feelings. Just numbness.

CHAPTER 45

GHETTO-HOT-
ENTANGLEMENT MESS!

There had been so much yelling, commotion and it could have woken the dead. Fortunately, it didn't wake the dead. But it did wake the downstairs neighbors.

She opened her front door and shouted from her doorstep in her Spanish accent, "I called the cops! They are on their way!"

"Great...," I said to myself, "...this was not supposed to go down like this!"

No sooner than the neighbor closing her door after yelling, three cops came on the scene and surrounded the four adults that had been arguing in the middle of the street at two o'clock in the morning. This was some ghetto-hot-entanglement mess!

The officer that approached me was short and stocky, but strong. He was young in the face, but it was obvious that he took his badge serious. He seemed to be very understanding when he saw me.

He approached me in the most professional way asking, "So, what happened?"

Enraged that I had allowed myself to get that angry, I replied, "That's my sister and so-called boyfriend!"

He didn't ask any further questions. He just said, "Okay, have a seat on the curb."

I sat on the curb scared and enraged. The officer walked over to his sergeant and partner.

I was left by myself on the curb while my sister and so-called boyfriend were together concocting a story to make themselves look good while making me out to be the crazy one. This wasn't the first time doing that to me and it wouldn't be their last especially after what had happened.

Two cops and one sergeant surrounded Khase and Gracie getting their version of the story. The sergeant was tall and slim with red hair and blue eyes. He had a no nonsense demeanor. I knew based on his white sergeant collared shirt that he was the one in charge. The other cop was an African American brown-skin handsome man. He was tall, muscular, and strong. His piercing serious brown eyes could put anyone in check.

Izzie was holding Baby Glorie after she was left in the back seat of the car watching her mother and aunt argue over a man. Surely her young innocent mind couldn't possibly understand what was going. Hmph. Kids understand more than what adults give them credit for.

Because Izzie was holding Glorie near the car, Izzie had a better view than I did. Izzie heard what the officers were saying to Khase and Gracie while I sat on the curb.

Khase and Gracie stood side by side in front of the cops. Gracie consoled Khase by rubbing his back as he told his "version" of the story.

Using his gift of gab in yet another moment, he frantically responded to the Sergeant saying, "Officer, I am just here trying to be a big brother to them! They are sisters and I'm trying to help them. Their…"

The Sergeant was not the least bit convinced by his answer. He cut Khase off mid-sentence and sternly saying, "Young man! There is NO way two sisters are out here arguing with each other over you, two o'clock in the morning, over nothing. There is something going on. Clearly, something has to be going on."

The Sergeant never got a clear answer from Khase that night. Gracie didn't say anything either. She continued to rub Khase's back to console him.

The Sergeant moved on and asked, "Whose property is this?"

Khase quickly responded, "It's mine. My name is on the lease!" Khase was finally able to tell the truth that night about something.

The same officer that told me to sit on the curb walked over to me and asked, "Is there anything in the apartment that belongs to you?

"Yes," I replied apprehensively.

The officer continued, "Alright, I'll escort you up there to get your things."

Little did the officers know, I had moved back home from college and had been living with Khase for a year now.

I stood up from sitting on the hard, cold curb. I walked up the old, cracked, and steep stairs with the officer, not even looking at Khase and Gracie. Izzie was still holding baby Glorie. Khase and Gracie stood beside each other watching me get escorted by two officers, one in front and the other behind me.

I got to the third step and Khase snarly shouted to me, "Yeah, and get your stuff out my house!"

I immediately went from 0 to 100…AGAIN. Without even thinking and forgetting I had two officers near me, I turned around to make my way towards Khase – to land another punch. The officer that walked behind me caught me in mid-air, by my arms, as I tried to leap over the officer to get to Khase.

"How could he?! Get my stuff out his house?! The very man whose idea it was for me to move in with him after I moved back home from college. The very man that wanted me in his space. How could she? She couldn't even defend me has her sister or as a woman?" I said to myself as I walked up the stairs with the officers. I couldn't help but have those thoughts while being escorted by two officers to get my stuff.

There were only but so many things I could grab that night. I had nowhere to go; nowhere to put my belongings.

I thought to myself, "Where am I going to put all my things? I can't even grab all my stuff."

The two officers and I made our way inside the house. One of the officers grabbed the keys from Khase before he made his arrogant comment.

I walked through the house grabbing what I could grab as quickly as possible. Still in disbelief with all that went down, I was angry and numb. I had to focus on getting as much as I could, as quick as I could.

I entered me and Khase's bedroom to grab some of my shoes. The same bedroom he created space for me in a year ago.

I entered the room and turned on the light so that I could see where my belongings were. The officer followed me into each room I went in as if I was the bad guy.

A few moments later, I heard Khase through the officer's radio saying, "Tell her to get out of my bedroom!"

Just when matters couldn't get any more humiliating for me, I angrily replied, "Shut-up! I'm getting my stuff!"

I shouted hoping that he could hear me. It didn't make the anger and numbness any less intense for me. Surprisingly, the two officers that escorted me didn't give me a hard time. They felt bad and couldn't even imagine the feeling I felt in my soul. When I yelled back, they didn't say anything to me.

I finally grabbed as much as I could and carried my three bags down the stairs. This would be my last time walking down those stairs. Better yet, it would my last time walking down that same road with Khase. I was done. At least, that's what I thought.

Still standing side by side, Khase and Gracie smirked in victory as they saw me walk down those steep stairs. Baby Glorie was in the car looking out the back-seat window with her big, beautiful eyes. Izzie stood away in a far distance waiting for me.

The Sergeant approached me as I struggled to carry my three heavy bags. Honestly, the weight of those bags didn't even begin to compare to the weight of anger, rage, sadness, hurt, disappointment, and betrayal that I carried.

Releasing his handcuffs from his command belt, the Sergeant began to read me my rights: "You have the right to remain silent. Anything you say, can and will be used against you in a court of law. You have the right to an attorney. If you cannot afford an attorney, one will be provided for you. You can decide at any time to exercise these rights and not answer any questions or make any statements. Do you understand the rights I have just read to you? With these rights in mind, do you wish to speak to me?"

Shocked and confused, I had to release my bags out my hand to be handcuffed. My world started flashing before my very eyes. Enraged all over again, I yelled, "Why am I being taken in?! I did nothing wrong! Sergeant, what am I being arrested for?! This is ridiculous!"

Izzie couldn't believe what was going down. One minute I was having fun, skating, and having a good time. Next minute, I was being taken away in a police car.

Izzie ran back down the street towards me, saying to the cop, "Hold the hell up! Why are you arresting her? You should be arresting their raggedy behinds!! Not Journee!"

The Sergeant replied, "Ma'am your friend is being arrested for simple assault. She's caused all this commotion and punched this young man in his face, causing physical harm."

Izzie couldn't believe it. She responded, "You're freaking kidding me!! You will hear from her lawyer, buddy!" Izzie grabbed my bags and made her way back to her car.

Khase and Gracie stood side by side with a smug look on their faces, saying nothing. Yet again, Khase was able to convince the sergeant that he was physically assaulted, in fear of his life and wanted to press charges against me.

Handcuffed in the back seat of the smelly old police car, looking out the window, I couldn't even muster up the words to speak. I was numb and voiceless. The sergeant pulled off as Khase, Gracie and Baby Glorie walked up those old, steep, and cemented stairs as a family.

The sergeant and I arrived at the local precinct in Hopeville, NJ. He walked over to my side of the door, opened it, and reached his hand inside the car to guide my head so that I didn't hit my head on the door.

He pulled me out the car. As the sergeant and I were walking inside, there was an eerie, dead silence and guilt that filled the air. The sergeant couldn't look me in my eyes for some reason. He avoided talking and making eye contact with me.

They walked inside, and for the first time in my life, I was being booked for a crime because of some dude. They began the booking process.

The booking officer said, "Your full name."

I replied, "Journee."

The booking officer said, "Journee what?"

I answered, "Journee Black."

The booking officer replied, "Alright Ms. Black. We are going to take your mugshot now. You will take three pictures. One facing forward, one of your left side and the last of your right side."

I complied. I didn't have the energy to resist orders or ask questions. The weight of those bags seemed to have gotten heavier, even though I had no bags in my hands.

The officer ordered me to take off my clothes in exchange for an attire that would label me for the rest of her life –an orange jail jumpsuit. After they took my fingerprints and mugshots, I was escorted in handcuffs, to a jail cell with heavy black metal bars and a tiny glass window with dirty white walls. The room was cold, scary, and exposed. Exactly how I felt that night.

I could not believe I allowed myself to get to this place in my life. Just a few hours ago, I was out having a good time skating with my home girl Izzie while trying to get my life together.

Betrayed by my sister. Betrayed by the man I loved. Betrayed by the sergeant who I thought had my back. It seemed so unreal for me, but it wasn't.

A metal bed. Closed-in walls. A grimy and smelly toilet. A small window but I could barely see beyond the black metal bars. Alone. Misunderstood. Hurt. That is how I felt. My tears were the only thing that seemed to be there for me. My ENTIRE life flashed before my eyes.

I laid down on that cold, metal bed and cried myself to sleep…

CHAPTER 46
JOURNEE RELEASED FROM JAIL

Morning came and the sound of a metal rod hitting my jail cell woke me up. The officer yelled, "Black! Black! Journee Black! Someone posted bail for you. You're free to go!"

Half sleep with tear crust in my eyes, I jumped up fast realizing where I was.

I replied to the officer, "Wait! I'm free?! I get to go home?!?" I had my hands gripped so tightly on the bars as if I were going to break it apart since the officer wasn't moving quickly enough.

The officer replied while unlocking my cell, "You are Journee Black, aren't you??"

I replied, "Yes! Yes! That's me! I'm Journee Black!"

The officer unlocked my cell and slid it open, letting me out. He escorted me to the front to gather my clothes. My moisturized coils were disheveled, matted, and dry. My eyes were puffy and red, and my body was sore from sleeping on that hard metal bed. On the walk to getting my things, I wondered who had bailed me out.

I grabbed my items and as soon as the door opened, I ran out like my life depended on it. When I ran out the door, there was Izzie…

SALVATION PRAYER

Dear God, I acknowledge that I am a sinner and confess that you are the King of kings and

Lord of lords. I ask for the forgiveness for my sins and accept you as my Lord and Savior, Jesus Christ. I welcome you into my heart, mind, and spirit. Thank you for dying on the cross for my sins. In Jesus Name, Amen.

John 3:16, "For God so loved the world that he gave his one and only Son, that whoever believes in him shall not perish but have eternal life."

https://www.biblegateway.com/passage/?search=John%203%3A16&version=NIV

JOURNEE'S PLAY LIST

Single Ladies – Beyonce

Level Up – Ciara

Best Thing I never had – Beyonce

Glow Up – Mary J. Blige ft. Quavo, Missy Elliot, DJ Khaled

Cranes in the Sky – Solange

Everything's Gonna Be Alright – PJ Morton

I'm Yours – Casey J

He Reigns Forever – Brooklyn Tabernacle Choir

Man of Your Word – Maverick City feat. Chandler Moore & KJ Scriven

Genesis – Dennis Byrd & Taledo Angelic Choir (1974)

Same Grace – William Murphy

We Wait For You – William Murphy

Tiff Joy – The Promise

Made a Way – Travis Greene

We've Come This Far by Faith – Donnie McClurkin

Praise Him – Anita Wilson

Just Want To Praise You – Maurette Brown Clark

More than Anything – Anita Wilson

Total Praise – Anita Wilson

Worth It – Lacrae ft. Kierra Sheard

ENDORSEMENTS

"Debut novelist, Nicole N. Sweeney arrives on the scene with a compelling page-turner that will have you yearning for more! A super fun read with tons of twists and turns, you'll finish it in no time because you won't be able to put it down!"

-Kim Brooks, National Bestselling Author of,
She That Findeth and *He's FIne...But is He Saved?*

"Nicole Sweeney provides readers an action packed, drama filled story in her book, Life after Hurt: A Sister's Tale. The first 3 chapters kept me eagerly awaiting to read the next sentence to see what the main character, Journee Black's next move would be as she journeyed through the entanglement of hurt, loss, and desperation. I cannot imagine what the next chapters will reveal as Journee learns to navigate life as a woman who has overcome hurt and betrayal."

-Kyla T. Slaughter

"Nicole Sweeney has written an important book for women coming out of a troubled relationship. Although fictional, Life after Hurt infuses her own experiences of how she was able to extricate herself from her own pain. Nicole wrote this book as a solution for women looking to bounce back, move on and flourish. I am excited about the prospects for this book and I'm confident that many women will benefit from Nicole's story immensely."

-Baruti K. Kafele, Educator, Author

"You will be gripped by this story. It will pull you in and invite you to walk alongside, dare I say even share the shoes of a sister as she experiences, endures, and ultimately explore LIFE after HURT. Its frank, first person-savvy exploration of a "Sister's Story" will not only give you a front row seat into each stage on which this "Sister" attempts to be real, find healing, and press forward. It will also give you insight into the very sacred inner workings of the soul and will of a beautiful young lady who insists on BEING, BECAUSE of who she is and whose she is. This debut project of Ms. Nicole 'North Jerscy' Sweeney is a rich narrative possessing at once both raw expressions of joy, hope, rage, shame, and faith as well as reverent reflections of contemplation, self-examination and gut-wrenching honesty with SELF."

Her perspicuous vision and gracefully suave craftsmanship in telling a 'Sister's Tale' will have you celebrating, weeping, cheering and ultimately wiser and wholly resolved to LIVE regardless of whoever, whenever, whatever and 'why ever' you were hurt. Read this book and be strengthened by the formidable imagination of Ms. North Jersey's favorite sister Journee."

-Rev. Stanley D. Williams, Baptist Campus
Minister University of Pennsylvania

ABOUT THE AUTHOR

East Orange, New Jersey native, Nicole N. Sweeney has claimed her rightful space in the creative writing world as a new, up and coming author. As a debut novelist, Nicole hopes to encourage and inspire women by sharing her own personal experiences with life, family, hurt and relationships. Nicole believes that through sharing your story, no matter how traumatic and embarrassing it may be, there will always be someone that can relate. According to Nicole, standing shamelessly in your truth brings godly healing to yourself and others.

Nicole is a two-time graduate of Rutgers University. She enjoys mentoring, teaching, dancing, watching movies, listening to music, baking brownies, reading, writing and spending time with her family and friends.

Words of Affirmation:

1. I am not my hurt.
2. I have the ability to heal and forgive.
3. I have the right resources, networks and relationships around me to heal me well.
4. It is okay to acknowledge my hurt without feeling something is wrong with me.
5. I recognize that healing takes time, and it is not a rushed process.
6. I will be intentional about my healing process.
7. I will give myself grace on days where healing is harder than others.
8. I will say NO to anyone and anything that is counterproductive to my healing.
9. God loves me as I am, but wants me healed, free and whole.
10. Forgiveness looks good on me.
11. Self-love looks good on me.
12. Freedom looks good one me.
13. Joy looks good on me.
14. My healing is not just for me. It is for my future generations.
15. I will trust that God will show me how to heal in a healthy and positive way.
16. I will forgive and free myself of things I wished I knew before I was hurt.
17. I deserve to be healed, whole, and enjoying life.
18. I deserve to be surrounded by positive and healthy-minded people.
19. I will not compare my healing process to anyone else.
20. My healing process is my own personal journey with God.
21. No matter how deep the hurt, I have all that I need within me to live a FREE and ABUNDANT life.
22. I deserve healthy love that promotes and encourages my continued healing.

Notes:

Made in United States
North Haven, CT
14 December 2022

28716019R00134